COCKY VISCOUNT

ANNABELLE ANDERS

ANNABELLE
ANDERS

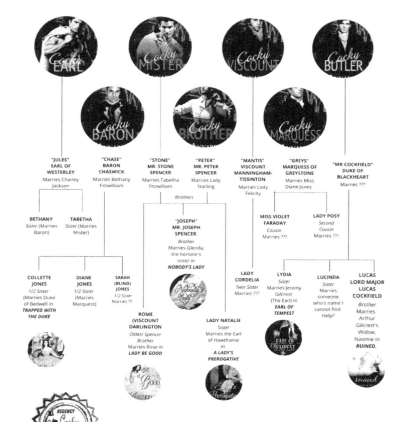

"JULES"
EARL OF
WESTERLEY

Marries Charley
Jackson

"CHASE"
BARON
CHASWICK

Marries Bethany
Fitzwilliam

"STONE"
MR. STONE
SPENCER

Marries Tabetha
Fitzwilliam

"PETER"
MR. PETER
SPENCER

Marries Lady
Starling

"MANTIS"
VISCOUNT
MANNINGHAM-
TISSINTON

Marries Lady
Felicity

"GREYS"
MARQUESS OF
GREYSTONE

Marries Miss
Diane Jones

"MR COCKFIELD"
DUKE OF
BLACKHEART

Marries ???

Brothers

BETHANY
Sister (Marries Baron)

TABETHA
Sister (Marries Mister)

"JOSEPH"
MR. JOSEPH
SPENCER

Brother
Marries Glenda,
the heroine's
sister in
NOBODY'S LADY

MISS VIOLET
FARADAY
Cousin
Marries ???

LADY POSY
Second
Cousin
Marries ???

COLLETTE
JONES
1/2 Sister
(Marries Duke
of Bedwell in
***TRAPPED WITH**
THE DUKE*

DIANE
JONES
1/2 Sister
(Marries
Marquess)

SARAH
(BLIND)
JONES
1/2 Sister
Marries ??

ROME
(VISCOUNT
DARLINGTON
Oldest Spencer
Brother
Marries Rose in
LADY BE GOOD

LADY
CORDELIA
Twin Sister
Marries ???

LYDIA
Sister
Marries Jeremy
Gilcrest
(The Earl) in
***EARL OF**
TEMPEST*

LUCINDA
Sister
Marries
someone
who's name I
cannot find.
Help?

LUCAS
LORD MAJOR
LUCAS
COCKFIELD
Brother
Marries
Arthur
Gilcrest's
Widow,
Naomie in
RUINED.

LADY NATALIE
Sister
Marries the Earl
of Hawthorne
in
***A LADY'S**
PREROGATIVE*

COCKY VISCOUNT

REJECTED

"...*B*ecause I cannot imagine living my life without you in it every single day, will you do me the honor of marrying me?" Jules, the Earl of Westerley, was on one knee, clasping her hands and gazing into her eyes. "And because I love you."

Huddled against the wall, Lady Felicity Brightley watched the man she'd been in love with for as long as she could remember, make a most heartfelt and romantic proposal.

To another woman.

She hadn't meant to eavesdrop. In fact, she wished herself anywhere else in the world. Up until that night, some small part of her heart had hoped Westerley would come to his senses. He would realize, of course, that he loved her.

That it had all been a horrible mistake.

Only it seemed that she was the one mistaken.

"Yes!" The beaming, red-haired beauty answered.

"No..." Felicity couldn't stop the gasp of pain as the couple embraced, her own world falling apart as she watched the man to whom she'd been promised for most of her life gaze into another woman's eyes.

Westerley was going to marry, of all things, an American!

Felicity's fists clenched so tight that the sharp edges of her nails bit through the silk of her gloves. Drat it all, she didn't *hate* Miss Charley Jackson, even though she wished she could. Hating her might have made this easier somehow.

Even if Felicity had become an unintended casualty.

For as long as she could remember, she'd expected to one day be Felicity Fitzwilliam, the Countess of Westerley; Jules' wife! How had this happened?

She was the woman he was supposed to have singled out! Tonight ought to have been *her* shining moment! She'd waited so patiently!

She wanted to rant and rave about the injustice of his betrayal. But, of course, she did not. Because that would not be proper. It would not be polite.

A lady accepted all things with dignity and poise, even when she felt like weeping inside.

If she'd been going to make a fuss, she'd had her chance to do that in private. He'd met with her in his study a few days before and informed her that he would not be holding up his end of their betrothal.

Although the meeting had not, in fact, been in private. Westerley had asked Bethany, his sister, to be present.

And as Felicity sat listening to his carefully worded explanation, she had bit her tongue and smiled. Just as she was doing now and would do for the remainder of the ball.

Even if her mouth shattered into a thousand pieces while doing so.

She couldn't tarnish the evening that Lady Westerley had

so painstakingly thrown as a culmination to her late winter house party.

Tabetha, Westerley's other sister, met her gaze across the room with questioning and concerned eyes.

Felicity nodded to reassure the younger girl.

"I'm fine," she mouthed. "Isn't it wonderful?"

Tabetha sent back a relieved smile.

Her fiancé's sisters, no, her *former* fiancé's sisters, were two of Felicity's dearest friends. Was she going to lose them as well?

Felicity rubbed the spot over her heart.

This pain felt all too real—a piercing of her soul, initially, and now a subtle aching torture. Jules was leading Miss Jackson around the room, accepting the congratulations of Lord Chaswick, Lord Greystone, both Mr. Spencers, and good God, even her father.

Felicity pushed herself off the wall. "Pardon me." She maneuvered her way out of the card room, nodding as the countess of Sheffield complimented her gown. "Thank you, my lady." She flashed a bright smile, knowing people would be watching to see her reaction.

But of course, more than one pair of curious eyes followed her hasty exit. She would apologize later. For now, she only knew she needed away.

She needed to breathe.

She needed—she pushed open a terrace door at the same time a sob tore through her.

She needed Jules.

He was never going to be hers. Felicity would never be his countess, nor would his sisters be hers in truth.

Lord Westerley had thrown her entire future away in

order to marry someone he hadn't known for even a fortnight.

Cold air hit her face as she stumbled across the patio and headed toward a dark and narrow path—away from the pitying stares, away from Jules and Miss Jackson, away from her father.

It was quieter here. Felicity could summon her poise and calm her racing heart, or what was left of it, anyhow.

Clawing branches dangled in her path and she pushed them away, barely noticing the thorns catching at her face and arms. One of them tore along her cheek, but instead of slowing her progress, she hurried along with even greater desperation.

Who was she running from? Herself? She kicked at a branch in her path and would have kept right on going, but...

As though the universe wished to add insult to injury, she tripped over an overgrown root, her momentum throwing her forward onto the ground. Now, along with her heart, her palms and knees were stinging as well.

Pushing herself up, she cursed when something prevented her from doing so—she was caught. Thorns on the offending branch had thoroughly embedded themselves in the delicate material of her gown.

"Blasted little buggers! Release me at once!" It was stupid to think the plant would listen to her request, but that did nothing to keep her from pleading with the unsympathetic shrub. "Let go!" She turned and then twisted, but the more she fought the clawing stems, the greater they took hold of her beautiful gown. *"Please?"*

Wandering outside without a chaperone had been a mistake. In fact, it had been most improper of her. Felicity needed to return to the ballroom before anyone noticed her absence.

The bush had seized her hair now, too, tugging at her coiffure. She moved to brush an errant curl out of her face but instead paused to stare at her hand.

It was shaking.

She deserved this for fleeing, for breaking the rules. She should have known better than to run away so she could give in to a bout of self-pity. "*Nothing good ever comes from losing one's dignity,*" her former governess' voice silently taunted her.

"My lady?" A gentleman's voice called out softly. "Felicity, is that you?"

She held her breath. *No one must see me looking like this!* She'd rather spend all night removing each thorn one by one than be discovered looking so untidy.

And rumpled.

And frazzled.

Heavy footsteps sounded closer. "Felicity?" With nowhere to hide, she flicked a few leaves off her bodice, patted her hair, and twisted her face into a perfect smile.

"Hello," she addressed the very large shadow of a man approaching her.

"Oh, hell." He crouched down. "What are you doing out here?" Illuminated by the moonlight, Felicity made out the scarred face of Lord Manningham-Tissinton—or Mantis, as many called him—as he stared at her with pity in his coffee-brown eyes.

"Please, go away." She straightened her back, ignoring the desire to cover her face to avoid his searching gaze. But of course, she would be discovered by one of Westerley's best friends.

"Needed some air, did you?" His eyes weren't strictly

brown, not really. The moonlight revealed green and blue and even a few specks of gold.

She lifted her chin but then flinched when one of the thorns pricked her scalp. "Yes. The card room, it was... over-crowded—too many..." She forced her voice not to tremble. "What with all the excitement of Westerley's announcement."

"And you were so caught up in the beauty of the night that you entangled yourself in one of Lady Westerley's prized rosebushes?" He wasn't laughing at her. At least she didn't think he was.

"Yes. I was—er—studying the constellations."

"True." He tipped his head back. "Cold nights are often the best ones for stargazing. Almost wish I had my telescope."

"Indeed." Ensnared as she was, she'd all but forgotten the cold until he'd mentioned it. She hugged her arms in front of her. "You study the night sky?"

"Doesn't everyone?" But then he moved closer. "Let me see..." Sizable hands landed in her hair and she stiffened. In all the years she'd been acquainted with the viscount, he'd never gone out of his way to be overly friendly or flirt with her. Nor had any of Westerley's other equals.

No doubt this was mostly due to the fact that she'd been intended for one of their closest friends.

The viscount stood tallest amongst the group of cocky gentlemen; his shoulders broader, his neck thicker. With his face only inches from hers, he seemed even more enormous.

"Ouch!" She jerked away, catching herself on another branch.

"Hold still." His breath warmed her cheek when he issued his command.

"I am." She wasn't going anywhere. "Thank you."

"I don't want them digging deeper into your skin than they already have," he explained.

He wasn't annoyed *at* her; he was annoyed *for* her.

His soothing words, his gentle touch—was the very last thing she needed. She was already on the verge of tears again. He must find her quite pitiful, indeed. "I'm fine, you know."

"Of course, you are," he agreed. "Can you tip your head forward?"

At least he would free her.

"Yes," she barely managed to whisper. Westerley's betrayal, and now—this—had her feeling heavy and... broken. Her arms ached, her throat hurt, and her legs were cramped beneath her.

Allowing herself a moment of weakness, she dropped her forehead onto the warm wool of his jacket.

It was a large shoulder, and she would only rest for a moment while he worked at the brambles in her hair. She doubted he even noticed.

"I saw you leave. After Westerley ..." He extracted a pesky twig. "*How are you?*"

"I'm not upset," she sniffed, squeezing her eyes shut.

"You're going to be all right, Felicity."

"I know. I'm happy for them."

"Of course you are."

"I *am*," she insisted.

Like every other guest who'd attended the ball that evening, Lord Manningham, no doubt, had either witnessed first-hand or been told that Westerley had chosen another woman to become his wife. Hundreds of friends and acquaintances had been spectators to the most humiliating and painful moment of her life. Felicity had no choice but to accept it with grace and dignity.

"I must return inside," she whispered.

"Not with your dress torn like this."

"I'll go first to the retiring room."

"I don't think..." He began, but then seemed to swallow whatever it was he'd meant to say.

"If I don't return soon, people will think I'm hysterical—or some other nonsense." Losing control was unthinkable, despite the tears threatening to overflow. "I—"

"No one expects you to be unaffected."

"But—"

"Let's get you free of this rosebush first, shall we?"

Felicity sniffed, her face all but buried in his sizeable chest. "Yes." She couldn't very well return to the ball while trapped outside, now, could she?

"This is quite a tangle." He wasn't arguing with her, just commenting as his fingers worked in her hair.

She gulped, his scent catching in her throat and nostrils. It wasn't as spicy as Jules'. It was more subtle, straightforward, and clean.

Jules! Her heart cracked.

Westerley had kissed her nine times in all. The first time had been at her coming out when she was just seven and ten, once each year after that, and then twice last spring. Eight years—wasted!

With the understanding that they would marry, she had waited out the best years of her life believing that her future was settled!

She'd trusted him. She'd trusted her father and mother. She'd trusted his parents.

And now, at five and twenty, none of that mattered because *she* apparently didn't matter.

"What am I going to do? What will people think?"

"Hush." He loosened a thorn from her hair and moved on to another one.

"My father gambled away my betrothal! I'm not even sure I still have a dowry." All of it was mortifying. "I'm ruined."

"You're nothing of the sort." He'd freed most of her hair and diverted his attention to the fabric of her skirts. "I'm afraid this gown is, though."

His soft chuckle nearly set her off into a bout of either tears or laughter. She wasn't sure which.

Both his arms wrapped around her now. If anyone were to discover the two of them outside, alone... Did it even matter? All she felt was the pain and emptiness of a future without Jules. "I loved him, Manningham. He was my world!" She hadn't meant to confess this to anyone, let alone one of Westerley's friends. "How could he do this to me?"

The sound of fabric ripping and then, "Forgive me. The thorn worked right through it. Lean forward and try sitting up. I think you are free now."

The sizable viscount walked backward on his knees, taking his shoulder with him until she, too, could sit upright.

You are free now.

Horrible words. Felicity didn't want to be free. A shiver ran through her and she wondered if she would ever feel warm again.

But Manningham wasn't done with her yet. Handkerchief in hand, he reached into his jacket, pulled out a flask and uncorked it.

"You think drinking spirits is the answer?"

"Not what I had in mind, but feel free if you think it will help," he chortled even as he poured some of the liquid onto the handkerchief and then handed her the flask. "I want to clean these deeper cuts."

But how does one clean a broken heart?

Felicity stared at the container, catching a whiff of the liquor and scowling as though it might be poison. "Is it *her* whiskey?" Whiskey was what had brought Miss Jackson into Westerley's life. Her father, known as the American Whiskey King, had traveled with his daughter to England to meet with Scottish distillery owners.

Manningham jerked his chin, encouraging her to take a drink. "Westerley's grandfather's Scotch."

So not *hers.*

Stinging from the first dab of the handkerchief, Felicity tipped back the flask and took a long—

"Oh!" She coughed, sputtered, then coughed again. At least she had a good reason for the tears streaking her face now. And it burned.

In her throat, her chest, and then it settled like a ball of fire in her belly.

The flavor left her mouth spicy and dry.

"It's horrible."

"An acquired taste." His touch on her skin was surprisingly gentle for such a large man. "You should have sipped it."

Just another mistake of many. "I shouldn't have taken such a large drink. I shouldn't have come outside alone. I shouldn't have come to this house party. I shouldn't have waited for him. I shouldn't have turned down Binkerton's proposal—or Lord Harrington's." Or Mr. Williams. Or Sir Riley's... As she spoke, she heard herself sounding more shrill with each word.

She'd wasted so many opportunities!

"Nonsense. You'll feel differently about all of it in the morning."

Oh, but he was wrong. "He didn't want me."

A hard swallow flexed his throat again. Rather than

comment on her miserable moan, Manningham met her gaze sympathetically and dabbed the linen along the curve of her left cheek. "This shouldn't scar."

His ironic words drew her stare to the jagged white line marring the right side of his face. It all but mirrored the cut on her own.

A scar on a man was a sign of his strength, evidence that he'd been tested; on a woman, it was a significant flaw. "Are you sure?"

He paused in his ministrations. "My cut was deep. And it wasn't properly cleaned. Yours is little more than a scratch."

Enough moonlight shone so she had a good look at him, allowing her to study that which she'd always averted her gaze from in the past. "Does it pain you?"

"No." His answer came out clipped.

The viscount was quite handsome, if not a little unrefined. "Did it happen in a duel?"

"I was sparring with my Fath—my teacher. I lunged when I ought to have stepped sideways. Stupid of me. I deserved it."

"No one deserves that." She shivered again. His father. He'd nearly said *his father*. What kind of man spars with actual blades rather than foils and then slashes his own son?

Lord Manningham-Tissinton pocketed the flask and took her arm. "You're shivering. Let's get you out of the cold." He glanced around. "Not the ballroom."

"But Bethany and Tabetha will be wondering where I've gone off to, and my father. Already I may have missed a dance—"

"Not the ballroom," he repeated, pulling her to her feet and removing his jacket. "Take this. I'll escort you to the orangery. You can wait for your maid there." He dropped the coat around her shoulders.

"You don't need to..." But he was right, of course. The orangery would be empty. And after Susan repaired her gown, Felicity could return to the ball with no one being the wiser.

"This way." He dragged her along effortlessly, not allowing her a chance to argue. Nor, it seemed, was he willing to leave her to her own devices. She'd have Susan bring out her lilac silk. If anyone asked why she'd changed, she would say she'd spilled her wine.

Felicity flicked a glance to the forgotten dance card dangling from her wrist. She didn't need light to comprehend the name signed beside the first dance.

Westerley had led her in the opening set and claimed the last waltz of the evening. She wanted him to beg her forgiveness at the same time she never wanted to see him again.

She would fulfill her commitment and perform the dance with him. Everyone would comment if she did not.

Manningham grasped her arm when her knees nearly gave out beneath her. More than once, he kept her from falling as they navigated the perimeter of the manor. Her emotions alternated between anxiety and apathy. The latter, although hardly recognizable, beckoned like a soft glow.

Fragrant, warm air fanned her cheeks when Manningham held the door for her to enter the glass building.

Any other time and she might have found the setting to be romantic and fanciful—but romance was only an illusion.

As had been her entire betrothal.

What else was an illusion? Society? Friendship?

Manningham escorted her to a chaise placed beneath one of the exotic trees Lady Westerley had cultivated. Felicity felt nothing as she welcomed the apathy. It dulled all of these unfamiliar emotions: the hopelessness, rejection. She could be pathetic, and she didn't even care.

"Wait here while I send for…?"

"Susan—my maid. Her name is Susan."

The Viscount supported Felicity as though she was an invalid, assisting her onto the chaise. And once she was seated, he moved away.

Leaving her alone and disconnected. A giant void spread from her heart to her limbs and then threatened to swallow her completely.

"Don't leave me!" Her last shred of composure broke, and she reached out to him like a drowning person. "You can't leave me!"

ONE KISS

antis froze. Comforting distraught women was not something with which he had any experience.

"Please?" Her eyes, which were almost the color of the Mediterranean, implored him.

She was fragile and beautiful and she needed...

"Hold me?" Tears rolled down her perfect complexion, one of them catching on the scratch carved out by the branch of thorns.

How could he deny such a request? Damn it, none of this was her fault.

He would sit with her, allow her a good cry, and then search out her maid.

He moved toward the chaise, and as he lowered himself, tiny hands locked onto his with a surprisingly vice-like grip.

"I'll stay." Even knowing her and Westerley's fathers had all but trapped the earl into the betrothal, Westerley ought to have treated Lady Felicity with more care for her feelings.

"Closer," her voice choked on a sob.

Mantis folded her into his arms. Carefully.

"Shall I send for Lady Bethany?" Indeed, she'd want to confide in a woman—one of her friends.

"Don't leave me." Her knuckles were white from clutching the lapels on his waistcoat.

"Shhh... I won't."

"I need..." She tilted her head back, her arms sliding around his neck. "Don't leave me alone."

Her sweet breath teased his senses. It had just a hint of scotch, but it was mostly feminine and delicate and...

Her.

To distract himself from her mouth, he rubbed one hand comfortingly down her back.

He'd seen the misery in her eyes while Westerley proposed to Miss Jackson. Lady Felicity's lips had tilted upward in what she'd no doubt intended to be a smile, but he'd not been fooled.

Westerley's public declaration had shattered her.

Couldn't the blighter have waited to pledge himself to another woman in private? Over the years, in all their carousing, Mantis—as well as Blackheart, Greys, Chase, and the Spencer brothers—had watched their friend's casual disregard for his betrothal to Lady Felicity Brightley. Westerley had acted as if it didn't exist.

They ought to have seen it coming.

For all his own father's animosity, at least Crestwood hadn't promised Mantis to a woman who wasn't of his own choosing.

Mantis focused on these and other practical matters to distract him from the lovely curves pressing against him.

He'd known Lady Felicity for nearly as long as he'd known Westerley. She had grown up right alongside the earl's sisters.

Which likely had been the problem with Westerley's betrothal to her all along.

But in all that time, Lady Felicity never once lost her composure. He had never seen her cry, lose her temper, or act in any way that might be considered undignified.

What was a man supposed to do in this situation? Another tremor rolled through her slender frame, followed by more silent sobs.

"What can I do?" He smoothed his hands down her back and then tucked his jacket around her more securely. "More scotch?" He cringed at his bumbling attempt to console her.

Curling tendrils of golden hair tickled his neck. Lavender and... citrus. He couldn't be sure if the heady scents were from the flowers growing in the orangery or her perfume. Either way, they summoned a few ill-timed carnal urges.

"Just hhhold mme." He was already holding her, so he simply tightened his arms, carefully, because... she was *Lady Felicity*.

She burrowed into him and ended up sitting across his lap. Her mouth hovered inches from his, the heat of her breath brushing along his jaw, mingling with his.

She was shivering, and she just seemed...

So damned lost.

He brushed her lips with his. One kiss. For comfort.

"Manningham?" Need laced her voice.

"My lady..." He would sooth her pride. A kiss, perhaps two. His mouth brushed hers again, this time capturing it.

To admit he hadn't been attracted to this woman since the first time he'd gotten a glimpse of her would have been an outright lie. But one did not set one's sights on one's friend's betrothed.

Her lips parted beneath his and Mantis tilted his head,

determined to enjoy this unexpected taste of forbidden honey. Any minute she would push at his chest. Perhaps even slap his face.

Because Lady Felicity Brightley was always dignified and proper. He waited for her to pull away, even bracing himself for a well-earned slap.

"More?" Her plea, damn it, sent blood flowing most inconveniently south.

Because she was on his lap!

And demanding more from this kiss.

Oh, hell. Mantis drew back. In a move that was as inexperienced as it was desperate, her mouth clumsily sought his. Her hands dug into his hair as she held onto him. *Don't leave me.*

Mantis shifted. It was only another kiss. If this was what she required to put Westerley's rejection behind her, then he was happy to accommodate.

More than happy.

Emboldened, she trailed her tongue along the flesh behind his lips, and his cock jumped.

"Manningham." Her writhing hacked away at his control. Add to that the throaty little sounds she made when she said his name and...

He reigned in his lust.

"Felicity." He gripped her arms. She couldn't possibly know what she was doing. She was mad with grief. He'd realized that when she had insisted she return to the ballroom with her hair falling around her shoulders and her dress torn.

She couldn't possibly return looking so disheveled.

He studied her eyes, forlorn and swimming with unshed tears, looking more green then blue as she gazed up at him.

Longingly.

"Show me." Her fingers trailed down the lapels of his

waistcoat. "Show me what it feels like. What does love feel like, Manningham?"

"Mantis."

She stilled just long enough to meet his gaze with a questioning one of her own.

"Or you can call me Axel." Hell and damnation, what was he doing? This wasn't an assignation, and there was no reason to tell her his given name. "You were calling me Manningham." His parents called him that. "I don't like it."

"Axel." She spoke his name as though tasting it. "Kiss me again, Axel."

By now, he'd all but given up on denying her much of anything—or himself.

This time, when his mouth sought hers, she fell back onto the cushioned chaise, tugging him so he had no choice but to follow.

This was now a kiss that also involved holding his body inches over hers.

"Don't you want me, Axel?"

He shouldn't answer that. "Of course, I do." Because he did.

He had for a very long time. Being with her like this shouldn't feel right. But... damn it, he'd never known anything better.

This woman kissing him, Lady Felicity, was no longer betrothed to one of his oldest friends.

"Show me, then." Her gown had become twisted around her waist, baring her knees and thighs. "Show me that I matter. Please?"

"You matter, *hell*." His fingers moved of their own volition now, unfastening his falls. "You must know." One hand moved between her legs while he used the other to keep his weight from crushing her.

"I don't matter. Show me. Love me." He barely comprehended her words as she pleaded with him.

She would be small, tight.

"Stop me now." He spread her juices along her seam. "Tell me you don't want this."

"But I do. Show me what love is. I need you, Axel." She wound her fingers around the base of his cock, and yet it was her words that excited him most.

"Show me that you need me." She demanded, guiding the tip of his cock to her entrance.

More accurately, it was a combination of her words *and* the fact that he was inches from ultimate bliss that made him rock hard. He was in a place he'd never allowed himself to imagine before. Not with this woman.

"Felicity."

"Axel."

"Stop me."

"*Axel.*"

He was inside of her. A gentle nudge. So tight. Velvety heat clutched around him, luring him deeper. Tight but also open, welcoming. A greater thrust and...

"Oh!" Her exhaled gasp wasn't pleasure. It was pain.

He froze. Experiencing a flash of lucidity, he silently acknowledged that a decision made over the course of less than two minutes had decided both of their futures.

Because, of course, they would marry.

"Felicity?" He lifted some of his weight off her, still inside. When she didn't respond immediately, he began to withdraw slowly. "God, I—"

"No." Her calves wrapped around his thighs, halting him. The enormity of his impulsive actions summoned an unusual flood of feelings, and along with the lust he'd experienced

19

seconds before, his heart squeezed and a strange thickness filled his throat.

"I hurt you." His voice came out sounding gravelly.

"No." Barely allowing himself to breathe, he studied her face in the soft moonlight. Her lips were shiny and parted, her cheeks flushed, and her eyes closed.

One tear escaped, hovering on her lashes.

"What do you want, Felicity?"

She'd told him already... *"Show me what it feels like. What does love feel like? Show me that I matter."*

She'd been distraught and had been in no condition to make such a decision. What the hell kind of person was he that he'd gone ahead and made it for her anyway?

"Finish." Her eyes opened, and her usually lilting voice sounded harder. "I want to finish what we started."

A battle waged in his mind. He moved his hips to withdraw, but her legs clenched around him.

"Please?"

What the hell was a man supposed to do?

He made a half-thrust, watching her eyes which no longer reflected pain, but... hunger—desire.

"You're sure?"

"Yes. Oh, Axel, how does this hurt and feel so... wonderful at the same time?"

In answer, he pushed deeper, prompting a soft moan.

"Again."

He accommodated her request.

Deeper. So damn good.

Again.

He seated himself completely, and then she was moving with him, clutching him, urging him with both her body and her words.

When the beginnings of his release threatened to slide down his spine, Mantis wedged his hand between the two of them. He'd brought her this far; he'd be damned if she wouldn't experience all the benefits of lovemaking.

"Axel, Axel..." She was panting now, tensing. Ten seconds. He closed his eyes and claimed her mouth, driving his tongue past her lips with the same rhythm he moved his hips, the same beat of pressure he applied with his thumb.

Only after she arched her back did Mantis relinquish control. Deeper, hold deeper. Exquisite pleasure no longer slid but shot from the top of his spine to every last nerve in his body.

Fuck!

He jerked his hips back, grasping himself in one fist, but he'd spent some inside. Not a tremendous amount, but...

Fuck.

Their labored breathing hovered in the space between them. Felicity had closed her eyes and thrown one arm across her forehead.

His arms shook from keeping his weight off her.

But not as much as his insides.

Because he'd gone and done the unthinkable. And for all intents and purposes, just gotten himself engaged.

DUTY BE DAMNED

elicity wasn't dead inside, not really, even though she'd wished she was as she'd escaped from the card room, running away after watching Jules propose.

The magnitude of what she'd just done threatened to topple what remained of her sanity, and yet, her heartbeat slowed.

She could still feel him hovering over her--their breaths bouncing between them, his arms bracketing her head, his giant thighs relaxed between her legs.

Perhaps if she kept her eyes closed, he would go away.

"Felicity?"

She could not look at him.

She'd wanted to be ravished. More than that, she'd demanded it.

And now, she was indeed compromised. Ruined, and this time, the fault was strictly her own.

Even if no one else ever discovered what had happened just now, she would know, and eventually, a husband would as well.

Which made her unmarriageable.

It was as though she'd ripped away any remaining hope she might have had for a happily-ever-after for herself.

It was… terrifying.

"Felicity?" His fingertips stroked her cheek, and she turned away. She was going to have to face him—a fallen woman now.

A jezebel.

A choking sound tore through her chest.

"Look at me." The insistence in his voice was impossible to ignore.

This close, even in the shadows, she could make out a myriad of colors in his eyes—eyes fringed by impossibly thick lashes. His thick hair sprang out wildly, ironically making him seem more handsome than when it was combed.

Unbidden, the memory of silky strands threading through her fingers taunted her. His hair was surprisingly soft.

"I'm sorry." It was all she could think to say. Because…

She had used him, and that was unforgivable. She'd taken advantage of his compassion and his willingness to comfort her.

"That's what I'm supposed to say," he said.

So odd, having this conversation with him now. In truth, Manningham was little more than a stranger to her—an acquaintance.

"I… You…"

"You needn't worry. We can marry, a formal wedding if you'd like, but in light of…" Manningham glanced down, "I can obtain a special license."

She was shaking her head, though, and then squirming. No! No! That wasn't what this had been about. She'd simply needed to break the rules—*not trap an unsuspecting husband.*

"Let me up." She pushed at his chest and he immediately moved off her. It was then that she got a glimpse of his manhood, which was smaller now than it had been before, and her thighs, streaked with blood.

Mortified, she shoved down her skirts. Her gown was in tatters, much like her soul.

"There's no need, Manningham."

"There is every need." He wasn't looking at her but tucking himself back into his trousers and sounding impatient.

"No. Please." Men, she was coming to believe, could be ridiculously impossible.

"You are a proper lady, and I am a gentleman—who normally exhibits considerably more honor, mind you. Unmarried people of a certain age don't simply lie with one another and then pretend it never happened."

"But that's exactly what we're going to do." Of course, he would offer to marry her. She would be tied to Manningham, an unsuspecting gentleman. The viscount, she knew, would actually marry her but...

He'd do so for all the wrong reasons. "I...Thank you. That, just now, was lovely. It was precisely what I... needed. But I have no intention of marrying." A wave of shock crested and then rolled over her.

The idea of marrying anyone but Westerley was... inconceivable!

Manningham sat facing her, but she couldn't meet his gaze.

"I *will* take care of you, Felicity."

She steeled herself against the affection in his voice. Because he'd not been with her tonight by choice, he'd merely been in the right place at the right time. Or perhaps it was the opposite. He'd been in the *wrong* place at the wrong time.

She scrubbed a hand down her face.

"I don't have a dowry. My father lost it." In case he hadn't gleaned that from her father's wagers earlier—what now felt like a lifetime ago.

He shrugged. "I know. That's neither here nor there, however. I took your virginity. It's my duty to marry you."

Duty!

"Duty?" Red encroached on the edges of her vision, and she would have spat if she knew how. "Would you like to know how sick and tired I am of hearing about duty?" She'd depended on Westerley fulfilling his duty to his father's promise. She'd counted on duty to compel him to love her. And, always the dutiful daughter, she'd *dutifully* loved him back. She would never trust in duty again.

Dutiful actions only resulted in illusions.

Manningham lowered his brows. "Not only out of duty." But the words were tentative on his lips. Oh, no. He might even convince himself for the moment. Because, well, they had just laid together.

She was no longer a virgin.

Felicity inhaled a calming breath and then stared down at her hands. "This... I am grateful to you." He'd not only extracted her from the thorns but allowed her to seduce him.

Why had she never thought to seduce Westerley? She dismissed the perplexing thought before she could analyze it too closely.

"My lady—Felicity," he groaned, tugging at the back of his neck. "I can't pretend this didn't happen."

"I can't marry you, Manningham." She held his gaze. "Once you've considered it rationally, you'll realize you have no real desire to marry me anyway. Aside from the minor issue of my non-existent dowry, I love Westerley. And I don't know when or if that will ever change."

His mouth tightened. Perhaps that hadn't been the best thing to tell a man who had just been inside of you.

Not that love was necessary for marriage, but—it mattered to her.

Or, it had.

"You are close friends with him. Surely, you must understand how awkward that would be?" He sat silent as though mulling over her argument.

But then he shook his head.

"Doesn't apply in this situation." He sat straighter now, his chin up. He was such a sweet man and far more handsome than she'd realized.

And her private places still ached from where she'd joined with him.

But he wasn't Westerley.

"I'm afraid that it does. Even if it didn't, I've no wish to marry... you." Her explanation came out harsher than she'd intended. "Or anyone, for that matter. I have no choice but to travel to London for the spring and pretend to be husband-hunting—for my mother's sake. But I won't be, really. Come summer, I'll return to Brightland's' Manor and settle into the quiet life of a spinster. My mother will appreciate having her daughter's loving care as she enters her golden years."

He made an odd sort of strangling sound.

"Please. Don't take this personally." She touched his hand to offer him some consolation.

"Rather hard not to, don't you think?" He grimaced.

Less than an hour ago, she'd considered herself incapable of attracting a suitable husband. Being thrown over for another woman tended to shake one's confidence. Now here she sat, refusing an offer from a viscount, heir to a relatively prosperous earl, no less.

And it wasn't fair—it wasn't honest for her to allow him to believe her refusal had anything to do with him.

"But… it isn't personal." She stared back at him. "I should accept you. All my life, I've done everything I should, and look what that brought me."

How could she explain this?

"Until tonight." Her huff of laughter was more of a trembling sound. "I made my own choice—because I wanted to."

"We," he corrected her. "We made a choice."

"Yes. I'm sorry. Of course."

The long breath of air he exhaled revealed that perhaps she was convincing him. And that mattered. She was going to need his cooperation in keeping their indiscretion a secret.

"You won't tell anyone, will you?"

"What kind of man do you think I am? Wait, no, don't answer that. I don't want to know."

"You are… an honorable gentleman… I think. But I don't really know you."

"No, you don't."

Ah, yes. She had either pricked his pride or hurt his feelings. Possibly both.

"You don't truly wish to marry me. That isn't the sort of decision a person makes hastily. And I refuse to become yours, or anyone else's, *duty*, ever again."

"And if you're carrying my child?"

"I thought you…" She was lucky enough that one of her governesses had explained the mechanics involved in conception. Left to her mother, she'd still believe that babies were found hiding under a cabbage leaf.

She frowned.

Manningham had withdrawn. She knew this because the sticky fluid streaking her legs had not been all blood. Not even close.

His wince was not a favorable response.

"But—"

"I wasn't entirely successful."

"You weren't... what?"

He closed his eyes. "As embarrassing as this is to admit, I pulled out. But not before I'd already spilled—"

"Oh!" She held up a hand to stop him, not wanting to hear any more details.

He'd spilled some of his seed inside...

Inside of me!

"Oh!" she exclaimed a second time.

"My sentiments exactly." His gaze held hers. "I don't like this." Did he mean he didn't like the possibility that she was carrying his child? That he might have to marry her? Or did he mean he didn't like her refusal?

Most likely, all of it.

"If I am..." With child. She couldn't even say it out loud. But he was right.

If she was, in fact, *enceinte*, neither of them would have a choice but to marry.

It would change everything. Her fingertips felt numb. Her lips felt numb. Her entire face felt numb.

"If necessary, we'll marry by special license."

"The house party is over in two days," she pointed out. Her father's home, her home, wasn't far, but... "I imagine you'll be returning to London—"

"I won't leave Westerley Crossings until we know."

He didn't sound happy at the prospect. "I'm sorry." Her voice was little more than a whisper.

"So am I." He tugged at the back of his neck again and then rose, looking distant, which was the opposite of how he'd been before she'd refused his dutiful proposal. "I'll locate your maid." He'd tried to take his leave from her before...

And she hadn't allowed him to go.

No, she'd begged him to stay with her. To hold her. *To show her what love felt like.*

And now she knew.

She pinched her lips together rather than insist she could find her way back to her chamber on her own.

She'd already said enough.

"Make yourself scarce if anyone else comes." He looked uncomfortable as he glanced around the orangery, which had always seemed to be such a peaceful place before but suddenly felt... sordid. "It's not safe for you to linger here alone."

"I rather think it was you who wasn't safe."

"Don't make light of it, Felicity." He closed his eyes. "Believe it or not, there are men far worse than me..."

And she knew that. "Most, I would say." She jerked her chin up, refusing to appear more pitiful than she already had. "Go. I'll be fine. And yes, I'll hide if anyone comes. Tell Susan I'll need—" She swept her hands down her front with a grimace. She'd been about to say her lilac silk. How unimportant that seemed now. She could not return to the ball tonight.

"New clothing," he finished for her.

Yes.

He was almost out of sight before he turned one last time.

"Felicity?"

"Yes?"

"This isn't over."

SUSAN DRAPED the cloak around Felicity's shoulders and drew the hood over her head.

"What if somebody recognizes it?" Felicity stared at the familiar garment. It was something she'd worn on much happier occasions—in a life she'd left behind.

"We'll enter through the kitchens and make use of the servant's stairwell."

Susan tied off the front of the cloak and fastened every last button so that no one would have even a glimpse of the gown beneath the billowing folds of the wrap. Her maid, who was only five years older than Felicity, clucked sympathetically, her touch compassionate. Susan took her responsibilities quite seriously, for which Felicity was incredibly grateful tonight.

"I lost my shoes." Waiting alone in the dark had left her feeling brittle. Felicity hugged her arms across her chest, feeling separated from herself. Her actions tonight had been those of a stranger.

Only, that stranger was herself.

She shivered.

"I'll take care of that later. His lordship is ordering a bath prepared. Let's get you safe inside first."

"Westerley did?" But... how did he know?

"Not Westerley—the viscount—Lord Manningham-Tissinton."

But of course Westerley hadn't ordered her bath! The flush creeping up her neck was one of both humiliation and shame.

Felicity huddled in her cloak while Susan steered her around the house. With her chin dipped low, Felicity kept her gaze on the floor, watching her feet, bloodied and filthy now.

The sensation of dripping between her thighs had her increasing her pace—his seed.

Don't think about that!

She would wash the night away in the bath. *Like a baptism.*

Her knees nearly gave out, and she would have fallen if not for Susan's support. "What have I done?"

"None of this is your fault," Susan whispered from behind her. "Hush until we get you out of sight."

But it was!

What was she thinking?

She wasn't thinking at all. She hadn't been thinking clearly since the moment Jules told her he didn't wish to go through with their betrothal.

No, he'd not told her that he did not *wish* to go through with it; he'd told her he did not *intend* to go through with it. She'd fooled herself into believing otherwise.

"Our parents, I realize, have had longstanding expectations that the two of us should marry." More than expectations, she'd wanted to correct him, but she'd said nothing.

"But they never came to an official agreement."

"I had thought—"

"Not even a verbal one, and I've hesitated to act on their expectations for quite some time because I have not sensed romantic inclinations on your part, nor have I experienced them on my own."

He'd been quite blunt about his feelings for her—or lack of them, rather. At that moment, she had realized that the attention he'd given Miss Jackson had been motivated by more than his desire to be an attentive host.

"Unless I am mistaken?" he'd added.

That had been her opportunity, her chance to object, to tell him he was wrong. Because, of course, she'd had romantic inclinations toward him. She was in love with him!

But she'd been mortified. Shocked.

And she was embarrassed to feel waves of pity rolling off

Bethany, her good friend who'd sat beside her to act as an intermediary.

"You are not mistaken, Jules." She'd lied. And in an attempt to have him deny his feelings, she'd added. *"You are in love with Miss Jackson."*

He'd not denied her suspicion. *"I am courting her."*

But he had been wrong on one crucial detail. There *had* been a written agreement. When Felicity had gone to her father, he'd insisted it would be honored. *"Westerley is just sewing a few wild oats. No man in his right mind would marry that Jackson girl. No man with any blunt, that is."*

And her father had chuckled, almost as though he'd found the situation humorous.

That lack of concern had given her hope.

"Let's get you into that tub." Entering the chamber Lady Westerley had always reserved for Felicity's frequent visits, Susan helped her out of her cloak and ruined dress. Her maid gasped, however, when she peeled off Felicity's stays. "Oh, my lady, your poor skin."

Felicity's skin was the least of her worries. "I just want to go home."

"I usually keep my opinion to myself, you know, and I realize that your father is my employer, but what he and Westerley did tonight was unforgivable."

"Jules didn't want to marry me, Susan." Felicity shook her head. "He didn't want me."

"Good riddance then. He's a fool."

Felicity lowered herself into the filled tub. The water was hot, almost too hot. It was perfect.

"What...?" Susan, who normally fluttered around her efficiently, stilled and was staring into the tub. Felicity glanced down and quickly splashed water onto her thigh in an attempt to erase such damning evidence: dried blood and something translucent and white.

Manningham's seed.

"Oh, my lady. What have you done?"

Felicity raised her hands to her face and burst into tears.

WAITING

antis balanced his cue on one end, vaguely listening to Chaswick, Westerley, and Stone Spencer negotiate their latest wager over the billiard's table. Peter Spencer, Stone's brother, coaxed interesting melodies from his cello, where he sat playing at the opposite end of the room.

One week had passed since the house party ended—one week since most of the guests had returned to their own homes or, in some cases, traveled directly to London in anticipation of the spring season.

And nine days had passed since he'd taken advantage of Felicity. Since he'd released inside of her.

Nine days since she'd declined his offer of marriage. Mantis released the cue and watched it hover for a most satisfying ten seconds. He caught it before it unbalanced itself.

She wasn't all that distant, physically—less than two miles. Her father's property most conveniently bordered Westerley Crossings, but she might as well be in the America's, what with the ocean she obviously wished between them.

She'd avoided him the morning after, leaving for home before daylight, and when he'd presented himself as a visitor at Brightland's, she'd declined to meet with him. Her mother had been ill; she'd relayed this information through their butler. Felicity refused to leave her side.

Lady Brightley was well known for suffering a variety of malady's, but even so, Mantis had seen through Felicity's cock and bull story for what it was; a convenient excuse to avoid speaking to him.

His only solace came from knowing she was safely ensconced in the comfort of her own home. And she hadn't been abandoned.

For as long as he'd known Westerley, the earl's sisters had treated Felicity like family.

And neither had quite forgiven their brother yet—even if they did like Miss Jackson, whose father had just returned from his tour of the distilleries to presumably bestow his blessing on the newly engaged couple.

"Stone insists you cannot balance two balls on top of one another." A cigar hanging from his mouth, Chase taunted Westerley from where he lounged sideways on a plush leather chair near the hearth. Mantis had never known a gentleman who was more comfortable in his skin than Chaswick.

"Doubting me, Spencer?" Westerley cocked a brow, looking all too satisfied with himself.

Mantis was happy for his friend, but he was also conflicted. For all intents and purposes, Felicity Brightley had been groomed to become the man's countess.

Given, Westerley had treated Felicity with respect and affection, but he'd never once looked at her the way he looked at Miss Jackson—like the world revolved around her.

And Felicity insisted that she'd loved him—*loved him still.*

Which left Mantis feeling another inconvenient emotion—an ugly one that he'd rather not acknowledge.

He returned the cue to its shelf, and then examined the balls Westerley had lined up on the billiard table. "It's physically impossible." Mantis scoffed. Even he knew that two perfectly spherical objects could not balance upon one another.

"What outcome are you wagering on, Stone?" Arms folded casually across his chest, Greys, as per usual, was dressed to the nines; lace at his sleeves, and an embroidered satin waistcoat beneath his perfectly fitted emerald jacket. "And how many attempts will Westerley be allowed?" He would ensure all pertinent details of any bet were declared and noted.

"One attempt," Stone declared. "And once you've failed, I want unlimited access to your baby for the duration of the season." Westerley's *baby* was a new curricle he'd purchased just before the holidays. Was he willing to put it up over such an idiotic bet?

"When I succeed," Westerley produced two billiard balls from the pocket nearest him on the table, "in balancing these two balls atop one another, I'll expect a boon."

"So long as you don't expect me to act as your butler," Stone laughed, because another fellow in their group had bet just that... and Lost to Greystone. The Duke of Blackheart had returned to England ahead of schedule to put his affairs in order. Presumably, once he stepped into the role of Grey's butler, he wasn't allowed to reveal the terms of the bet to anyone. The trouble was, Blackheart was a bloody duke. It might be impossible to keep his identity under wraps for long.

"Speaking of butlers," Mantis turned to Greys. "When do you expect Blackheart to join your London staff?"

"One week before the season commences."

Mantis nodded thoughtfully. Because he, too, had a stake in the duke's success. If Blackheart failed or gave up, *which he would not*, he and Chase would lose a different bet, one which would compel them to run through Hyde Park wearing nothing but the splendor God gave them. If Blackheart succeeded, Westerley and Greys would be obligated to make the invigorating sprint.

Furthermore, added as an even more outlandish addendum to the bet, if Blackheart failed to complete the stint, then Greys would win the dubious distinction of choosing a duchess for their duke.

Which provided Mantis confidence enough to wager on his success. Blackheart would never allow that to happen.

By that time, Mantis might be a married man himself.

Watching Westerley wave the colorful balls around with a flourish, Mantis absentmindedly drew his index finger down the length of his scar, the uncomfortable memory of Felicity's adamant refusal niggling at him.

She'd been distraught, devastated by Westerley's rejection. Had he merely provided a convenient surrogate to absorb her grief?

"Show me what it feels like. What does love feel like... show me that I matter." She had called him Axel more than once.

Staring at the top of Westerley's head as he bent over the billiard's table, Mantis almost didn't recognize the unsettling emotion that squeezed his chest.

By God, she had not imagined herself with anyone but him.

Westerley cradled the balls stacked atop one another and stepped away.

What the hell? They didn't fall. Showing off, the blasted earl lined up the cue ball and collided it with the bottom sphere, knocking it free and sending it into a side pocket.

"What the hell?" Stone's words echoed Mantis' thoughts.

Trick balls. It seemed his old friend was coming up with a few new ruses. Was that what love did to a man?

"A bet's a bet." Westerley made no attempt to hide his duplicity. Nonetheless...

"He did say, and I quote, 'balance these two balls on top of one another,'" Mantis pointed out.

Mantis racked the balls while Westerley negotiated his prize. It seemed the earl had known the boon he wanted all along. As he intended to take his new bride on a tour of Scottish distilleries rather than be in London for the season, he enlisted Spencer to act as escort and protector for Lady Tabetha. The girl was a ridiculous flirt, but only so long as the gentleman in question was titled.

Which ensured that Stone, who was the second son of an earl, would be safe from her attempts.

"What of Lady Bethany?" Mantis asked. Because Westerley did, indeed, have two sisters.

Chase laughed. "Jules doesn't have to worry about Bethany. She'll be more concerned that her hostess's chairs line up perfectly than filling her dance card. Last night I caught her measuring the distance between her mother's candlesticks."

Mantis frowned, but it was Greys who disagreed aloud. "Would you care to wager on that, Chaswick?"

None of them accepted Grey's wager, which meant, no doubt, that Lady Bethany was going to get herself into trouble.

A stuttering knock was followed by Miss Jackson's invasion of their very masculine abode.

"My father is prepared to meet with you." Looking smug, she requested Westerley's presence.

Her appearance circled Mantis' thoughts back to Felicity.

For the thousandth time that day.

His failure to withdraw in a timely manner was concerning, but that wasn't all that troubled him.

The man she eventually married would know she'd given her virtue to someone before him. And he might not be understanding.

The double standard wasn't just, but such was the way of their world.

Men were expected to possess a fair amount of sexual experience, but women…

Were not.

He glanced out the window, and upon spying two familiar ladies wearing bonnets and pretty day gowns crossing the yard in the direction of Brightlands, inspiration hit.

"If you gentlemen will excuse me." Mantis pushed himself off the wall and strode purposefully toward the door.

"Where are you off to in such a hurry?" Peter Spencer stopped playing his cello long enough to ask.

"Ladies Bethany and Tabetha appear to be in need of an escort for their afternoon stroll." And with that, he stepped out the door, glancing to the left and then the right.

Westerley had his fiancé pinned against the wall, and she seemed not to have any complaints in what ought to remain a private moment.

"So that's what they call meeting with one's father now, eh?" Mantis couldn't help himself.

Miss Jackson hid her face, and Westerley shot him a scowl.

The left it would be.

Because he had an afternoon call to make, and today, he refused to accept defeat.

~

FELICITY SNIPPED the thread and studied the fabric in her hands, a linen handkerchief, rounding out the dozen that she'd begun working on at the end of last season.

Because Jules had kissed her twice, once almost passionately, she'd presumed to embroider the Westerley crest onto twelve lovely linen handkerchiefs. She folded the last one into crisp quarters and added it to the small basket where she'd stored the others.

"I'm so pleased you didn't destroy them," her mother said.

The always serene Lady Brightley sat across from Felicity, embroidering small flowers onto a square that she would likely have framed. Looking younger than her seven and forty years, Felicity's mother wore her blonde hair in an elaborate coiffure. A smile of content danced on her lips. She was either ignoring Felicity's turmoil, or she was oblivious to it.

Nearly a week had passed since Felicity's mother had caught Felicity poised to cut one of the handkerchiefs in half. She'd demanded Felicity give up the scissors at once. Such a vengeful display of temper was both unrefined and wasteful.

"Lady Westerley will appreciate such a thoughtful gift." But her smile fell when she caught Felicity frowning. "Oh, come, dear, there are plenty of other eligible bachelors out there for you. They may not be as handsome as Lord Westerley or as wealthy but, be that as it may, I do wish you would set aside your melancholy."

How many times had her mother dismissed her feelings like this? At the end of every season they'd spent in London, she'd promised that Westerley would make his offer the following year. Or the following. Or the following after that.

Felicity had waited. She had smiled through each disappointment, and for what? To be humiliated and betrayed.

But since being a good girl was so thoroughly ingrained in her, Felicity lifted the corners of her mouth. "I'm trying," she answered, relieved to be finished with the last of the hankies.

And, indeed, shredding them would have been wasteful. Perhaps Bethany and Tabetha would like them. Although, Tabetha was coming out this spring and was likely to land a husband in no time at all.

No, not a husband, Felicity marveled. Tabetha insisted she was going to marry a duke.

Bethany, however, had been out nearly as long as she had. Bethany might make good use of them.

"Guests from Westerley Crossings," Mr. Nelson, the butler who had worked at Brightland's Manor longer than Felicity had been alive, announced from the door. "Lady's Bethany and Tab—"

"But of course," Felicity smoothed her skirts and glanced at her mother. "I think I'll send the handkerchiefs back with them today." She'd be grateful to never see them again.

Mr. Nelson disappeared, and her mother set her handiwork aside. "Splendid notion. You and I will visit Westerley Crossings tomorrow. Good manners demand we offer our felicitations to the new couple."

Felicity had expected this, but not yet. It was too soon.

Usually, she would have taken turns visiting her friends. Then again, on a typical visit, she would not have had to face Westerley's American fiancé. She would have imagined *herself* in that position.

Furthermore, she would not have had to face a gentleman that she'd—

She blushed at the memory and stared at her skirt, pretending to remove a non-existent piece of lint. Lord Manningham had not yet taken his leave from Westerley Crossings. She knew that because he'd called on her more than once.

And each time, she'd made up some excuse to avoid meeting with him.

Of course, he'd offered to marry her. He was a gentleman —albeit the gentleman she'd allowed between her legs. She winced.

It was all just too mortifying. Hearing footsteps, she touched her hair and sat up straight. Perhaps Bethany would have news that he'd returned to London. Yes. He couldn't remain at Westerley Crossings indefinitely, could he?

Perhaps he could. Because as far as Felicity knew, gentlemen did pretty much whatever they wanted.

The door opened, and Tabetha all but flew in, blond ringlets dancing, bringing with her the freshness of the cool March air. Her dark-haired sister, Bethany, followed, showing far more restraint.

And behind Bethany—the last man she wanted to see.

Lord Manningham.

"My lord. What a delightful surprise." Felicity's mother was on her feet, shifting a glance to Felicity and looking rather pleased with this turn of events. "It's Lord Manningham-Tissinton, Felicity." She raised her brows at her daughter as though to say, *'Wasn't I just telling you there were other gentlemen out there?'*

Manningham's height and physique were even more imposing in the confines of their modest withdrawing room.

Staring at the carpet, Felicity rose and then dropped into a curtsey. "My Lord."

She couldn't see his face without looking up, but she felt his presence.

Acutely.

It was impossible to dismiss the fact that she'd welcomed him between her thighs—dear god, begging him to—

"His Lordship offered to escort us this afternoon. Growing weary of my brother's besottedness with Charley, I imagine." Tabetha laughed, and then her eyes flew open wide, apparently realizing what she'd just said and to whom she'd said it.

Bethany winced. "My lady, you are looking well today." She addressed Felicity's mother in an attempt to change the subject, completely unaware of the part the viscount's unexpected presence played in Felicity's turmoil.

"I tire easily, though, my dear. I'll likely take to my bed again tomorrow. But such a delight to meet with the three of you today. My lord, won't you sit down?"

"The weather is gorgeous, Fel." Tabetha didn't waste any time on formalities. It wasn't as though there was anything particularly unique about a visit from her dearest friends. Aside from Manningham's presence, that was. The younger girl lowered herself into the only single chair in the room while Bethany took the seat beside Felicity's mother, leaving Manningham nowhere to sit but beside Felicity.

"I'm looking forward to spring," Felicity answered, sounding almost unnaturally cheerful as she addressed the room in general.

"You really ought to come walking with us." Bethany frowned. She'd apologized more than once over the past week for her brother's faithlessness. And she was tapping her fingers against her thumb—a peculiarity she displayed whenever she was less than comfortable. "Please?"

"Go ahead, dear," her mother answered for her. "No doubt this mild weather is merely teasing us, and one last winter storm is just waiting to blow in. Perhaps the sun can add some roses to your cheeks." She tugged at the bell pull and, when Mr. Nelson appeared, ordered him to fetch her daughter's wrap and bonnet. "Susan will know what she needs," she added as though the man hadn't performed this task hundreds of times in the past.

But before he could leave, another knock sounded from the front door. Within moments, their small withdrawing room was buzzing with enthusiasm when Lord Chaswick and Mr. Spencer invited themselves to join the outing.

"Thought you'd have all these ladies to yourself, eh, Mantis?" Mr. Spencer joked with his friend.

"Westerley's tied up with his future father-in-law, and Greystone had business to attend to, so we've come in Lady Westerley's barouche. Seeing as it's just warm enough to keep the top down, how does everyone feel about a trip to the village?" Lord Chaswick's charm was most persuasive.

"That sounds marvelous!" Tabetha, of course, was already on her feet.

"I'll fetch your things, my lady," Mr. Nelson disappeared.

It seemed they would be going for a drive.

Felicity didn't need to turn sideways to know Manningham was watching her.

"You are amenable?" He, it seemed, was the only one who didn't take her acquiesces for granted. All the colors in his eyes were noticeable with the afternoon sun slanting into the room.

"It seems I have no choice," she answered.

"But of course you do." And for a moment, she felt as though they were discussing something entirely different than a journey into town. "But that doesn't mean I won't attempt to persuade you otherwise."

His voice, low and quiet, sent a shiver down her spine.

"Please," she said in a low tone, grateful for Tabetha's exuberant chatter about, of course, the weather.

Manningham dipped his chin, and her gaze flicked to his mouth. What conversation did a lady make with a gentleman under such circumstances?

"Horses will be getting impatient. Shall we?" Mr. Spencer edged toward the door.

Within five minutes, all six of them were standing outside beneath a bright blue sky, this time discussing various strategies for arranging their group to fit a four-person barouche.

Did men not consider these details?

"I'll stay behind," Felicity volunteered. The quandary allowed her the perfect opportunity to excuse herself.

"But you're the reason we came!" Tabetha said from where she'd already perched herself in the plush vehicle.

Felicity glanced at Bethany, who stood beside her looking torn. "I can stay with you.

"No, no, you go on." For as long as they'd known one another, Bethany had secretly adored Lord Chaswick. And even though the baron was something of a rake and likely would never glance twice at her dear friend, Felicity knew Bethany would enjoy such an outing more than most.

"I will come to Westerley Crossings for tea tomorrow," Felicity said.

Bethany stared at her with eyes the same blue as her brothers, clutching her reticule in front of her. "You promise?"

"Of course." Felicity was going to have to visit at some

point. She reassured herself that if her mother came along, she could avoid speaking privately with Lord Manningham.

She turned to Mr. Spencer, who stood off from the others, pacing and bouncing as she'd often seen him do. When he met her gaze, she sent him an inviting smile.

The Earl of Ravensdale's second son immediately realized Felicity's intent. "I will remain as well. As you've already prepared for an outing, my lady, what do you say to a lazy stroll?"

"Not so fast, Spencer," Manningham stepped forward. "I believe you have a duty to perform for Westerley." He flicked a curious glance toward the carriage. "I'll walk with Lady Felicity."

"And what exactly has my brother roped you into, Mr. Spencer?" Tabetha narrowed her eyes suspiciously. "Come along, Mantis, I am no one's duty."

But rather than be cowed by Tabetha's suspicions, Mr. Spencer sprang into action. "Right you are, Mantis." He leaped onto the barouche and took the empty seat beside Tabetha.

Smiling tightly, Manningham stepped away, allowing Chaswick to assist Bethany into the vehicle and then, with a wave, sent them off.

A weighty discomfort settled in the silence that ensued.

"Let's walk." It was Manningham who broke it, offering his arm.

Already, she'd been inexorably rude to him, and he'd done nothing to deserve it.

Her guilt won out. "Very well."

She could walk with him, and make inane conversation, even. Perhaps they could move past that night in the orangery and pretend it never happened.

But the moment she slid her hand into the crook of his

arm, her innards flipped, reminding her that the night in the orangery, had in fact, happened. Pretending such an event away would require tremendous effort.

And more than one week.

Neither spoke again until they'd covered half the distance of the lane leading to the road.

"I cannot believe you are still embroidering his monograms on handkerchiefs."

His comment was most unexpected. But of course, he would have seen the carefully folded stack.

She sighed.

"My mother insisted I finish the dozen. I'm going to give them to Lady Bethany."

"But they are a gentleman's style."

"Yes, well. I could always add some lace." This conversation was ridiculous.

"Careful." He steered her around a steaming pile, doubtless left by one of the pair that had just departed. As such a large and muscular gentleman, he'd never seemed as sophisticated and cultured as the sort with whom Westerley consorted. It had been an unfair assessment for her to have made.

Like other titled bachelors, it seemed that Manningham possessed an equally inflated sense of honor. More, it seemed, than she'd credited her former betrothed.

Would there ever come a time that she didn't compare all gentleman to the Earl of Westerley?

"How are you?" The question wasn't a casual one. The sincerity of his concern wrapped around her like a cloak. He'd had the same effect on her in the garden. And later in the orangery.

"I'm sorry for sending you away this past week. It's just that I—"

"No need to explain." His voice rumbled low from beside her. "Change is always difficult. Even when that change is for the better."

She'd not viewed her broken engagement as change. She'd considered Westerley's betrayal a great loss.

"Have you ever been in love, Manningham?"

DÉTENTE

Had he ever been in love?

Mantis didn't answer right away. But he was happy, at least, in that she was finally talking with him, so he contemplated an acceptable answer.

"Once, but," he finally said, "love is a convoluted emotion. There was one girl in the village near my home. At the time, I believed she had captured my heart. But my affections were fleeting at that age."

"How old were you?"

"Five and ten." He smiled fondly, remembering the kisses he'd managed to steal behind her father's store.

"And after that?"

After that, he'd had a few flirtations. However, lust had motivated him more than love.

But he couldn't tell her that. Or… could he?

"I chased skirts, as they say."

"Oh…"

He didn't need to explain. Westerley's rakish ways before his father's tragic death hadn't been kept much of a secret.

And still, she had waited for him.

"I may have fancied myself in love a time or two. But—" He stopped himself from adding that he had never felt strongly enough to consider marriage to any of them.

"But...?"

"My emotions weren't all-consuming." He did not return the question because she'd already answered it. She'd answered it both before and after he'd plowed her on the chaise in the orangery.

"Are you enjoying your time at Westerley Crossings?" It seemed she, too, had no desire to persist in that conversational direction.

"I am." But aside from preparing his father's London townhouse for his family's arrival, he had other responsibilities.

"What do you gentlemen do when you are not riding, wagering, drinking, and hunting?" Her voice sounded sweetly beside him. This woman was perhaps the most refined lady of his acquaintance.

Except for when she lay beneath him.

He tamped down the thought immediately so as not to embarrass himself. Because truth be told, he'd relived the experience more than once in the nine days that had passed.

"I enjoy exercise. I spar with Blackheart whenever possible." What would she think if she knew he practiced an eastern form of fighting and meditation? "I fence with Greystone, and exchange blows with Spencer."

"Boxing?"

"Yes."

"What else? Do you like to read?"

"God, no." The answer came without thinking. Sitting, focusing on words, trying to force them into some fictional scenario, resulted in more frustration than was ever worth any enjoyment he could take from it.

"You don't enjoy reading?" She sounded incredulous. "I thought everyone enjoyed reading."

Ah, he'd disappointed her.

"Not me."

"Not even a good adventure story?"

He shook his head.

"You are missing out."

She was not the first person to point out what he lacked by not devouring the tomes his contemporaries did. On occasion, he still berated himself. For the most part, however, he'd gotten over it. He'd discovered other avenues to learn about humanity.

"I enjoy walking, running, swimming." Hell, he even climbed trees on some occasions. Amazing what one could see perched thirty or forty feet off the ground.

"And sparring," she added indulgently.

"Yes." Both the physical activity and the breathing techniques enhanced his life in ways he couldn't explain.

"I meet with a handful of street urchins—to teach them to fight." He hadn't meant to tell her this.

But she had said she wanted to know more about him and the lessons were something he cared about.

She raised her brows. "In London?"

"Near the docks." Mantis focused on the road ahead once again. "I have occasional business in White Chapel. Two years ago, I stumbled upon a gang of ruffians thrashing one of their own—bullies. There were five against one. I pulled the lot of them off the little tramp. He was a pathetic creature and I realized that scenario hadn't been the first and wouldn't be the last. So I taught him a simple fighting technique to help him avoid future thrashings."

"A single technique could make a difference?"

"Yes. But when I returned a few weeks later, the urchin caught up with me, along with three of his friends, asking me to show him other tricks." Mantis shrugged. "So now I teach them."

Those meetings had since developed into regular sessions in a warehouse he'd rented. Mantis had even purchased traditional gi for the more dedicated students to wear while practicing.

"That is commendable," Felicity commented quietly.

"I enjoy it."

Mantis did it for himself. He hated bullies and took satisfaction knowing that the smaller boys could defend themselves. Although his valet had remained in London to ensure lessons continued in his absence, Mantis had told the boys he'd be away less than a month.

He was running out of time if he was going to keep his word.

To uphold his end of the conversation, he asked, "What do you like to do?"

"A little of everything, I suppose." She stared off the side of the road into a small cluster of trees. "I read, of course, I play the pianoforte, I sing. I paint, I sew, I knit, I crochet. I ride. I practice my French." She exhaled a heavy sigh.

But of course, she likely excelled at all those things. No doubt, she was also well versed in managing an Earl's household. Contemplating the details involved in mastering such a variety of tasks made his head swim.

"But what is your favorite?" He persisted.

She must have something she enjoyed more than all the others.

"I—" Little lines appeared on her forehead. A good half minute passed before she answered. "I don't know, Manningham."

Manningham. Not Mantis. Not Axel.

"Why don't you call me Mantis?" Due to his title's length, it was the name nearly every one of his acquaintances used. But it wasn't how he got the name.

Her eyes flew wide. "Horrid creatures. I don't like them at all."

Mantis countered. "But they don't attack humans."

"I know of at least one particular mantis that does, in fact, attack humans." She held up her hand, her pointer finger extended. "The devious creature latched onto me while I was picking flowers. Not at all as harmless as they appear. You think they are like leaves or butterflies, but I assure you, they are quite the opposite."

He refrained from laughing, just barely. "I'm sure he attacked you on accident. He must have felt threatened since they normally show surprisingly sophisticated discernment when they hunt. Although..." He grimaced. "The females are known to practice cannibalism." He shot her a sideways glance.

"Just the females?"

"It is part of their mating ritual."

"You are telling me that they eat...? That's disgusting."

"Only the ladies, though." He was rather enjoying her reaction.

"Please, stop." But she was smiling. He would not add that she'd practically taken his head off when he'd offered marriage after—

Best to stop while he was ahead.

Instead, he covered her hand with his. "So, you don't hate me then, just the insect?"

"I do not hate you. I do hate the bug."

He'd never seen this side of her. Stubborn and... cute. He ought to have realized there was a good deal more to this woman than what she presented to the world. Wasn't that true about everyone?

"Then you must call me Axel."

She stiffened and he wondered if she, too, was recalling how she'd gasped in passion, all but chanting his name...

"Only in private," he added, although that may have made her even more uncomfortable.

"You said your family calls you Manningham." It was one of the first times she had willingly mentioned anything about that night. "But that you don't like it."

"I don't." He didn't expand on his answer because his family was... complicated. "Believe it or not, no one called me Mantis until Blackheart did. Many of the kicks and grabs we use while sparring, in fact, originate from the bug."

"You're joking."

"No," he laughed.

"It'll have to be Axel, then. However, I don't know that I'll have many opportunities in the future. You must be leaving for London soon?"

"That depends. You still intend to be in Mayfair for the season?"

"Yes." She exhaled a long sigh. "Will your family be there?" She would discuss his sister, the world of insects, everything but that which stood between them like an elephant.

He stopped, wanting—no—*needing* her full attention. "Felicity." He grasped both her hands. "Please. I... I realize that

I am not Westerley. I'm not the man you love. But I *am* the man who's taken your innocence, and I cannot reconcile that with the idea of…" he shook his head as he searched for the right words, "leaving you unprotected."

Because as a single woman mingling with Mayfair's elite, despite what she'd told him, bachelors would court her. And, he knew, it was possible she would answer another proposal differently.

However, many gentlemen would not appreciate that she had… experience, and if their indiscretion was ever exposed, it could be more than a little troubling for her.

And damn his eyes, he could prevent such a scenario. He stared at her with all the determination he felt. She would eventually consent to be his viscountess, ultimately his countess. She would be his *wife*.

As though reading his thoughts, she straightened her spine, stiffening even more than when he'd asked her to call him Axel.

"You are kind," she began in an almost cold voice. Felicity Brightley excelled at inserting distance when she was feeling threatened.

"Damn it, this isn't about kindness." He realized a moment later that swearing likely wasn't the proper way to go about proposing marriage.

"No." She pinched her lips together and met his eyes with a hard stare. "It's about duty. And I believe I already told you—"

"*It's not only that.* It's about doing the right thing." And then he paused, his gaze falling to her midsection, hidden beneath the various layers of periwinkle fabric that made up her gown and covering. "What if…?"

"I'm not." Her answer was quick and short.

Ah, so her courses must have arrived. Good Lord, was that

why she'd avoided him all week? His twin sister, Cordelia, sometimes locked herself inside her chamber for the duration, but he'd not even once considered that scenario for Lady Felicity. In the past, she'd always seemed so... controlled.

But for some reason, his heart sunk a few inches. He ought not to have experienced disappointment at Felicity's announcement, and yet—

He did.

"You're quite certain?"

She stared everywhere but at him.

"*Fairly* certain." This answer jolted him nearly more than her first one had. Because, what the hell did 'fairly certain' mean under these circumstances? "You've had your courses?"

She jerked her hands out of his and turned to stride purposefully back in the direction from which they'd come.

"Felicity?" He caught up with her easily.

"I'm not discussing this with you." Eyes straight ahead, she marched away from him with an almost militant purpose. "This is not something a lady discusses with a gentleman."

This time, Mantis couldn't contain his bark of laughter, even though, in truth, there was nothing remotely humorous in their situation.

His response, however, only served to double her determination to get away from him. "Felicity," he didn't know what else to say. "I need to know!"

"And I will tell you if anything pertinent occurs."

The woman was talking in circles. "So, you have not had your courses?"

She raised her hands to cover both ears, shaking her head. "We are not discussing this."

Mantis caught her by the shoulders this time, forcing her

to a halt. She pinched her eyes closed, quite obviously wishing him away.

"I'm not going anywhere, Felicity." He inhaled. He'd known the reason Cordelia locked herself away on a monthly schedule, but it was not something ever spoken aloud. "I've no wish to ignore your sensibilities."

Her cheeks were flushed now.

"*Felicity,*" he willed her to meet his gaze, and when she did, the full effect of her beauty struck him. "I don't want you to be scared. I know that, what we did, it wasn't planned. But it happened." She tried to look away, but he kept himself in her line of vision, leaning forward and holding her gaze.

And then she was shaking her head, looking panicked. Her eyes--eyes he'd always thought had been blue—appeared more emerald than anything else. "I don't even know why, but I wanted it to happen. I wanted to be someone else. I thought it could stop the hurting." She gulped.

He tucked away the notion that she would ever wish to be anyone other than the beautiful person she was and instead focused on comforting her.

"Wanting to fill that need is perfectly natural. You shouldn't be ashamed." He gathered her into his arms. This woman was not known for theatrics or tears. She'd held herself tall and proud all those years waiting for Westerley. "Everything is going to be fine. I promise." If only she'd allow him to take care of this!

He inhaled, and when that mixture of lavender and citrus hit his senses, he ignored an onslaught of lust.

"I—" she sniffed. "I didn't do it to trap you."

He pulled away to meet her gaze. "I know that." He'd not suspected it even once. Any other woman and he might have considered the possibility, but not with her.

She dabbed two fingers at the corner of her eye. "I'm sorry. You didn't ask for any of this."

He hadn't asked. No. But he hadn't stopped it when he had the chance either. In fact, he'd made a conscious decision to keep going.

"It's just that... I don't want to marry—you or anyone—not like this. You have to understand."

They had been over this before. If Felicity was with child, he could "understand" all she wanted but that wouldn't change what they needed to do.

He made a decision. "I won't press you—for now. But you must promise to keep me informed." His hands had slid to her shoulders, where he gently massaged the muscles at the base of her neck.

"I promise." Her voice came out little more than a whisper, and then she licked her lips.

This wasn't the promise he'd hoped to extract from her today, and yet he leaned forward and touched his mouth to hers, tentatively, and drew back before she could either respond or push him away.

"Thank you."

FELICITY RAISED her fingertips to her lips. Was this weak feeling in her knees one of relief, or did it have to do with having this man's attention focused solely on her?

Not on her dress, or her hair, or what she could do for him, but...

It was as though he could see inside of her.

And his kiss... How was it possible that such a small

gesture could convey tenderness and protection, and also promise?

"You will return to London soon, then?" Her voice sounded strained.

Felicity experienced an unexpected sense of loss at the prospect of him leaving, and yet, she wanted him to go. Every time she saw him, she was reminded that despite her careful upbringing, despite everything drilled into her regarding propriety, her character was flawed.

She possessed a shortcoming she'd not realized before. And now Manningham—Axel—was aware of it as well.

It made her feel exposed. Already, he knew her more than most. And now he wanted her to share other very personal information with him.

Although, if her courses didn't come, he would, indeed, have every right to know. Black crept around the edges of her vision at such a possibility. They had to come!

"Greystone wants to leave for London the day after tomorrow." She felt him watching her closely. His hands remained on her shoulders, his thumbs sliding back and forth along the base of her neck. She wanted to squirm, but she also longed to lean into this giant of a man and accept the comfort he offered.

Comfort that he only offered out of duty. Another illusion.

"I'd stay longer, but I promised I'd be at the docks." He looked sheepish and all Felicity could think was that her silly little endeavors seemed meaningless in comparison.

"Of course you must go. And I wish you a safe and pleasant journey."

He was leaving and she could put all of this behind her.

But if that was what she wanted, why did the prospect of his departure shake her? With him gone, she could begin to salvage some of her dignity, prepare to face the ton. This year would be her last season, not because she intended to land a husband, but because she was done.

The idea that any of it mattered had ever only been an illusion. Felicity would not be the first hopeful lady to end up broken-hearted.

Betrayed.

"You will come to London soon?" he asked. His thumb crept up the side of her neck to stroke the line of her jaw, but he kept his eyes locked with hers.

Did he even realize he was doing that? She resisted the urge to tilt her head into his hand and instead nodded.

His gaze shifted to the tip of his thumb, where it barely grazed the corner of her mouth. Was he going to kiss her again?

She stepped back, jerking herself from beneath his hands. "I wish to go home now."

Thankfully, he didn't argue or try to stop her this time. Neither did he offer his arm, choosing to stroll with his hands clasped behind his back all the way to the entrance of her father's house.

"I shall call on you once you've arrived in town." Without taking her hand, he bowed, and when he rose, an errant strand of hair fell along his cheek. Hair that she knew was thick but also soft.

"I look forward to that," she answered out of habit. And by the look on Axel's face, she realized he knew she wasn't being truthful. She dreaded their next meeting. Because when the time came, he would expect her to confirm her condition one way or the other.

An ache settled in her chest. She'd always wanted babies, but not like this. And she barely knew him.

Axel.

"As will I."

When it became apparent that he wasn't going to take his leave until she'd entered the manor, she nodded and rushed past Mr. Nelson, who then quietly closed the door behind her.

THE JOURNEY TO LONDON

"*H*ow do you think Lady Felicity will fare with the ton this spring?"

Greys' question had Mantis sending him a curious glance. "Why do you ask?"

"No reason. Although, in my opinion, she and Westerley both made a lucky escape."

Mantis and the Marquess had made their farewells and best wishes to Westerley the night before and departed at dawn. By now, they'd been on the road for at least a few hours. Mantis hoped he wasn't making a mistake by leaving without going to see her one more time. Although...

He'd promised not to press. Best to leave well enough alone.

In return, she'd assured him she would be in London for the Season.

"But she was in love with him," Mantis pointed out while feigning disinterest. He had no wish to appear overly concerned with her situation but wanted Greys' opinion.

"Lady Felicity only *fancied* herself in love. Free from what has always been a doomed betrothal, she'll have bachelors throwing themselves at her before the Willoughby's ball concludes."

It wasn't what Mantis wished to hear. Not the part about her only fancying herself in love with Westerley, but the part where numerous gentlemen lined up to secure her affections. Such an unpleasant prospect might complicate his objectives.

"My cousin, Posy, along with my mother's youngest sister, Violet, and my Great Aunt, Iris, will be staying with me at Knight House this spring," Greys changed the subject.

"That should be... interesting," Mantis answered.

"Not too interesting, I hope."

Mantis vaguely remembered Greys mentioning a guardianship over an orphaned cousin nearly a decade before. The girl must be of marriageable age by now. "You intend for your cousin to make her come-out?"

"Posy loathes the idea. Over Christmas, she wrote begging permission to forgo a season altogether. Unfortunately, Violet insists she make her bow to the queen."

"Should liven things up for Blackheart."

Greys waved a hand in the air. "He's not the one I'm worried about." He grimaced. "But Posy is, well..."

"An antidote?"

"No. The last time I traveled north, Posy exhibited the makings of a pretty girl, but she's incredibly naïve. Her reluctance makes me wonder if rather than leave her to my aunt's mercies, I ought to have sent her to school somewhere—even that Miss Primm's seminary..."

It wasn't at all like Greys to second guess himself.

"You were all of what, one and twenty when her parents were killed?"

"Two and twenty."

"And I imagine your aunts had something to say about her education?"

Greys chuckled. "I all but threw the poor gel into their capable hands. What the hell did I know? Violet isn't much older than me, but at least she knew something about a young girl's needs."

Mantis didn't comment but instead considered his own maturity—or lack thereof—when he'd achieved his majority. He'd been nowhere near ready to take on such a responsibility, and Greys, the cocksure fellow that he was, likely hadn't been either.

He'd better be prepared by now in the event that Felicity was carrying.

Mantis flexed his shoulders but couldn't quite loosen the invisible band squeezing his chest. Would his father be pleased if that was the case?

"Are you worried about her then, your cousin?" Mantis asked.

It was Greys' turn to twist uncomfortably. Mantis marveled that the man persisted in dressing so fastidiously despite the grueling day's ride ahead of them.

"She'll be my responsibility. I imagine I'll be prevailed to escort her and Violet to all the usual places. Perhaps I ought to have made that bet with Spencer." Greys cocked his head to one side. "Although, if you ask me, Westerley's concerned about the wrong sister."

"You think Lady Bethany is itching for a scandal?" Mantis chuckled but then reconsidered and frowned. If such a well-mannered woman as Felicity was capable of such passion, he supposed anything was possible.

"I wouldn't rule it out. I'm only grateful my duties are limited to my younger cousin—and Violet too, I suppose."

"You have Blackheart at your disposal for nearly three months. He's got two sisters. Simply draw on his experience."

Greys nodded, looking slightly less concerned.

"You're a decent sort, Mantis."

Mantis chuffed. He hadn't acted decently with Lady Felicity. But Greys didn't toss compliments out for no reason.

"Eh? Out with it, what do you need?"

"Dance with Posy? Maybe take her for a drive? She'll handle herself better if she has a little confidence..."

"I can make time for that." Because that's what friends were for.

"Are you still working with your group of orphans?"

"Absolutely. A few have dropped out but..." The last time he'd met with them, just before the house party, there had been twelve in all. Teaching the fundamentals of jiu-jitsu to a dozen street urchins wasn't going to change the world, but if he could help even one of them better themselves in one small way, it was worth it.

"One can only hope they don't use their training to become better pickpockets."

"That doesn't concern me. It's not just about the fighting, you know," Mantis said.

"True. Although it hasn't hurt your fencing skills."

"Nor my boxing."

The students were expecting the lessons to resume in two days. Mantis glanced up at the sky. He would arrive in London with no time to spare. And yet, he still felt guilty for leaving Westerley Crossings without first securing Felicity's consent to marry him. Or at least making a more valiant effort.

"To what lengths would you go if you ruined a lady?" He asked the question vaguely. Most likely, Lady Felicity was not carrying his child. And she seemed quite intent on refusing him given the freedom to do so.

But that didn't alter the fact that he'd taken her virtue. There were too many men in the ton who would hold the loss of her innocence against her. Two years ago, in fact, a particularly pompous baron had demanded an annulment from his wife. The church had refused to dissolve the marriage, but the lady had been banished from society.

"Marry her, I suppose."

"But what if she refused?"

"She would not," Greys answered right away.

Mantis had believed the same until recently.

"But if she did?"

"Then she's a fool."

Mantis nodded in agreement, and then Greys went on to actually answer the question.

"I suppose I would court her. Women are odd creatures, Mantis, in that they don't always say what they mean. Nor do they always mean what they say. Such a lack of transparency leaves us miserable males doomed to figure them out for ourselves. And since we are, for the most part, ignorant where females are concerned, we're compelled to resort to sending flowers and prostrating ourselves like besotted idiots."

It wasn't bad advice. And Mantis couldn't help but agree with such an assessment.

"You are asking this question hypothetically?" Greys inquired.

"For an acquaintance. No one you'd know."

"What reasons did this lady give to this *acquaintance* of yours for declining his proposal?"

Had she declined him outright? Mantis searched his

memory of their conversations and could only surmise that indeed, she had. He'd simply refused to accept her answer as final.

"She doesn't want to enter marriage out of duty. Said she was weary of the notion." More than weary. He remembered that quite distinctly.

Greys turned to stare at Mantis. "To what extent has she been ruined? I've not heard of any recent scandals." He shook his head. "Ruined. Ghastly word for it. Damned lucky of us not to have been born female."

"Indeed," Mantis agreed. Then, on a more serious note, admitted, "quite thoroughly."

"Not one of Westerley's sisters?" Greys gave up his laconic demeanor to shoot the accusation across the space between them.

"God, no." He would never. Mantis shook his head. "I--my er, *acquaintance* would have to have a death wish to do something so asinine."

"True," Greys exhaled. "But your friend, he ought not to give up. If she wants romance, he must walk her in the garden, take her strolling through one of Vauxhall's darkened paths. Some ladies prefer a romantic drive in the park. He must send her all those flowers, or chocolates, or whatever it is she prefers. And when he finally proposes, he must do so in a manner guaranteed to make her swoon, declare his undying affection and all that nonsense."

"He should lie to her? In the name of honor?" The advice sounded plausible—if the woman in question was anyone other than Felicity. Especially now, on the heels of Westerley's betrayal.

"If this *friend* of yours went so far as to take this lady's innocence, my guess is that... *your friend*... has feelings for her. Once he acknowledges those, in all likelihood, he'll discover marrying her is what he wanted all along."

Mantis stiffened. He'd lain with her because... he'd wanted to. And presented with the opportunity, he'd taken it.

"One of the Mossant sisters?" Greys persisted.

Mantis didn't answer.

"The eldest Somerset gel?"

"Leave it." Mantis had said too much already. "It was hypothetical."

"Bollocks." Greys slid back into his lazy demeanor. "You're such a tease."

"Oh, but you make it so easy." Unwilling to discuss the subject further, Mantis pointed at some bulls grazing behind a fence near the road. "Twenty pounds if you snag an apple off the tree behind them."

The bulls looked ancient, but bulls were bulls. And the apples... Mantis grinned. The dare was not a fair one, really.

Then again, not many of their wagers were.

"There aren't any apples this time of year, you ass," Greys responded. "But if you'd care to bring me a blossom for fifty, I'm more than happy to take you up on that." Greys glanced over at Mantis, brushing a non-existent speck of dust off his jacket. "Strike that. You're too much of a goliath for me to have to carry into the village. I'd rather not ruin my clothes with your blood. Because I've no doubt, even the slowest bull would have no difficulty goring you."

At the insult, Mantis very nearly accepted the bet. A month ago, he wouldn't have hesitated.

But if Felicity was carrying, he'd be no good to either her or the child dead. And their well-being, beyond even his own mortality, was a sobering thought.

"It's not that I'm too huge. It's that you, my dear Greys, are too weak."

"At least I know how to dress."

And so it went for most of the journey...

*C*rouched on her knees, mostly curled up over the chamber pot, Felicity spit and then closed her eyes as Susan wiped the cool, damp cloth across her lips.

"This is not a stomach bug, my lady," her maid sighed. "Nor is it driving sickness."

Susan's gentle comment only served to remind Felicity of how difficult the journey to London had been. Her mother, never comfortable when she herself was not the patient, had been overset, and when she'd asked her ailing daughter to ride in one of the coaches reserved for servants, Felicity hadn't had the energy to argue.

And that arrangement had left her father's valet to ride in one of the baggage coaches.

All in all, despite the lovely spring weather, the four-day journey from Leicestershire to London had been miserable for more than just herself.

"This is morning sickness," Susan insisted. "You're with child."

"But I bled." Not as much as usual, but blood meant she'd

had her courses! Which proved that she'd not conceived. The trouble was, if she wasn't enceinte, then what was the matter with her? Was she dying? She may have momentarily wished her death in the hours after Westerley jilted her, but she'd not meant it. Facing such a fate now had her sending off a quick prayer to negate previous feelings she'd had on the matter.

Of course, she hadn't wanted to die! The idea of death had simply comforted her at the time.

Susan touched Felicity's shoulder gently. "A lady's body doesn't always get the message right away."

"It has to be something else," Felicity moaned, partly because another bout of nausea threatened and partly because…

"You're going to have to tell him."

"I'll wait. I have no wish to alarm the viscount prematurely. I'm expecting my courses again next week. If they aren't here by Mayday, I'll tell him then."

"But that's over two weeks away."

"There's plenty of time."

"But, my lady…" Susan sighed, and Felicity closed her eyes. "Here. Having something in your belly will help." A delicate slice of toast appeared in front of her. She made a most unladylike chuffing sound. If only a piece of toast could fix all of this!

Although, not quite an hour later, as she descended the staircase and caught a glimpse of herself in a convenient-looking glass, Felicity could not help but admit that the toast had done wonders.

Enough anyway, that she was capable of meeting with Bethany, who awaited her in the drawing room.

"You're here! London has been even more tedious than usual without you, and I'm sure you can guess that Tabetha has near driven me to Bedlam." Bethany rose and greeted her with a quick kiss near Felicity's ear before dropping onto the settee dramatically. "If she doesn't capture a duke, I may have to find one for her myself. Because I'll kill her before submitting myself to another season of her preening and fussing." Lady Tabetha was all set to enter society this year and was quite prepared to take the ton by storm. Bethany tilted her head. "Your color is off. You aren't ill, are you?"

"I'm fine." Felicity lifted the corners of her mouth a little higher.

"You're not pining after my brother, are you? You needn't worry about seeing them this spring, you know. They're off touring Scotland for their honeymoon."

Oddly enough, Felicity hadn't thought about Westerley and his, by now, new bride, hardly at all.

But, shouldn't she have? If she had been in love with him?

"I haven't been pining." She studied Bethany, who was not quite a year younger. Her friend had always been pretty but never drew attention to herself. "I know Tabetha is intent on husband-hunting, but what about you?" Discussing familiar topics such as this was precisely what she needed.

Normal. That's all Felicity wanted—to feel normal.

"Oh, heavens no." Bethany blushed and stared down at her hands. "I'm thinking of making this my last season. People already consider me to be on the shelf."

"If you are, then I most definitely am."

Bethany shrugged, drawing Felicity's attention to the cut of her gown and the practical style of her coiffure. Most noticeable, however, was the look of hopelessness in Bethany's eyes. Felicity may not be pining after Westerley, but Bethany was most definitely still pining for Lord Chaswick.

Was unrequited love worse than having never loved at all?

"It's different for people like you." Bethany wrinkled her nose with a chagrined smile. "But that's neither here nor there. I need you to come with me to Cedric's. Holden Hampden's latest book was scheduled to be published over the winter. I've been dying to get my hands on a copy."

Cedric's Shop of Tomes, neatly tucked between a solicitor's office and a tea house, was their favorite of all the shops on Bond Street. "Of course I'll come with you, but what do you mean—*people like me?*" She scowled.

"Just... beautiful, confident people," Bethany spoke as though this ought not be new information for her. "Your gowns are always fashionable but not pretentious, perfectly pressed and never too tight or too long, or too short. And then there is your hair, golden, even more perfectly golden than Tabetha's, and let's not even get started on your shape. In addition to all of that, you are always proper and graceful. I can't remember you ever embarrassing yourself—over anything. You, my dear friend, and I say this with only a small amount of jealousy, are perfect."

Bethany would be sorely disabused of this opinion if she'd seen Felicity outside after Westerley proposed to Miss Jackson. "I am not." Far from it, in fact.

"But it goes beyond all of that," Bethany went on. "And I wish I understood how you do it, but... men see you. *All men*, gentlemen, and rogues alike."

"They see you," Felicity protested, her heart weighed down by guilt.

"As a friend, or a sisterly type, perhaps. But not as someone to court. No need to deny this as I've quite come to terms with the notion." But a hint of sadness lurked in Bethany's eyes. "Let's embark on our shopping adventure, now, shall we? I'm hoping we have time for a visit to Gunter's."

"For tea or ices?"

"Both. But we'll need your father's carriage and driver as I arrived on foot." As was usually the case. Having been acquainted for over half their lives, the two girls had made this exact outing on numerous other occasions. Sometimes with Tabetha in tow and occasionally with Westerley's escort.

Yet another change...

"Do you really think Tabetha can land a duke?" Felicity asked as the carriage pulled into the street. It was not as though the younger girl would have many dukes to choose from. Aside from Blackheart, Felicity could count the number of eligible dukes she knew of on one hand. And of those, she couldn't recall a single one who was young and handsome.

"I wouldn't put it past her. Can you remember any time Tabetha didn't get what she wanted?"

Felicity could not.

They drove along in silence, Felicity feeling more like an imposter with each second that passed. "I'm not perfect, Bethany, far from it, in fact."

"Well," Bethany stared out the window. "You're as close to perfect as anyone I know. You aren't overly fussy with unimportant details like I am, and don't pretend you haven't noticed that I'm a little particular about unimportant things. Nor do you fumble for words while conversing with people." She raised her hand. "P-I-C-K-Y." She tapped her thumb to each finger and then folded her thumb down as she counted out each letter. And then "C-L-U-T-Z."

"You may be a little fastidious, but you're much smarter than I am," Felicity interjected.

"Perhaps," Bethany sighed. "And I apologize for calling you

perfect. It's a terrible burden to have to live up to." The grin she sent Felicity's direction was a teasing one.

Felicity rolled her eyes. "If you say so."

"Oh, look!" Bethany leaned closer to one of the windows. "It's Mantis and Greys, but they aren't alone. I don't know either of those ladies. Do you suppose Chaswick is in town as well?"

Felicity leaned forward in surprise. For all of Manningham's insistence that he would call upon her, she'd arrived in London three days ago and not heard a peep. Perhaps he'd forgotten all about his promise.

Slowing their steps to match their companions, Manningham and the marquess strolled along the walk, navigating a path amongst similarly fashionable people. On Greystone's arm, a tall, elegant lady and on Manningham's a shorter, rounder lady who all but bounced along beside him. Felicity got a glimpse of their faces, but neither seemed familiar. The taller woman was older and held her head high. The shorter woman was younger and seemed far less concerned with maintaining her dignity.

Felicity touched her lips with her fingertips. Had he moved along so easily?

She inhaled and then released a long breath. Good for Manningham. He'd wanted a wife, and perhaps he had found one.

Yes. *Good for him.*

And yet, a sick feeling settled in her belly. This scenario was precisely what she'd expected.

She'd been right not to trust in his sense of duty. Even the kindest of men were inclined to shift their affections at the drop of a hat.

"Chaswick isn't with them." Bethany was miserable at

hiding her feelings.

"He'll turn up." Of course, Chaswick would, but he'd never be the man Bethany wanted him to be. He was likely worse than Westerley and Manningham put together when it came to charming ladies.

Both of them released heavy sighs with a hint of longing and then turned to smile ruefully at each other.

Because for a moment, Felicity had hoped Manningham might be different than those other gentlemen.

She'd already pined after one man, and she wasn't about to pine after another.

Please, God, bring my courses before Mayday. She sent up a silent prayer and then leaned back on the carriage bench, determined to summon enthusiasm for the afternoon and then for the dizzying round of activities planned for the weeks ahead.

"Now, tell me about this Hampden fellow's books."

FIRST BALL OF THE SEASON

"*H*ow many times have we done this?" Felicity glanced around the Willoughby foyer, feeling much older than her five and twenty years. Lord and Lady Willoughby had hosted the first ball for longer than she'd been alive. And every year, the decorations sparkled more than the year before.

"Too many, for certain," Bethany grumbled from beside her as Lady Westerley conversed with Lady Ravensdale in the reception line ahead of them. Felicity's parents followed behind her. Three years ago, before Lord Westerley's untimely death, the two earls would have been chatting together, leaving the ladies to one another's company.

The death of Bethany's father had hit the family hard, but that was also when Westerley had finally put off his wild ways. Everyone had assumed that he'd propose at the end of the mourning period. But Felicity had gone on to wait two more years.

All for nothing.

She glanced back to watch her father greet another couple,

feeling an unusual pang. As angry as she'd been with him over the debacle with Westerley, she was grateful she still had him.

A brilliant chandelier hung from the ceiling, reflecting candlelight off the shining marble floor and the unrecognizable busts propped on pedestals that lined the corridor.

"Are you nervous?" Bethany whispered.

Felicity didn't need to ask why. Every person she was remotely acquainted with would know Westerley had chosen to marry an American heiress rather than her. They would be wondering if she was devastated. Likely many were disappointed that Westerley and his bride were not in attendance that evening. Because then they could have watched to see if Felicity would slight Miss Jackson—no, not Miss Jackson, Lady Westerley now.

There was nothing like a good scandal to make for a memorable evening.

"Surprisingly, no." She felt a little queasy as she answered. Aside from her breasts aching beneath her stays, she felt perfectly fine.

If not unusually tired.

"That's just what I meant when I said you were perfect. I'd be a mass of quivering nerves if I were you," Bethany shrugged.

"You sell yourself short."

The line inched forward, and after being greeted by their hosts and then handing off their wraps, she and Bethany descended the staircase into the magnificent ballroom.

The guests quieted, but Felicity ignored them. Bethany squeezed her arm.

"Smile and keep walking," Felicity whispered through clenched teeth. And then, as though Bethany answered with something entertaining, she threw her head back and laughed with the perfect amount of inflection.

The room's volume returned to normal by the time they stepped onto the shining parquet floor.

"Felicity, my dear, I have someone I'd like you to meet." Lady Westerley approached with a handsome gentleman on her arm. However, before she could introduce him, she turned to her daughter, handing over her reticule. "Do be a dear, won't you, Bethany, and watch over this. And my shawl as well. There are a few seats available beside Lady Brightley. Save me one of the more comfortable ones if you don't mind?"

"But—" Felicity went to interrupt. This handsome gentleman ought to be presented to Bethany as well.

"Of course, mother." Bethany didn't protest but sent Felicity a weak smile before doing her mother's bidding.

This sort of disregard, Felicity realized, was why Bethany lacked confidence. Felicity would have to do something to help her friend this season—especially if it was to be their last. Bethany deserved a happy marriage as much as anyone—more so, in fact.

"My dear Oswald, allow me to introduce you to Lady Felicity Brightley, Brightley's daughter. Felicity, Viscount Oswald, Lord St. Vincent's heir." The man was tall and slim with olive-colored skin and glossy black hair.

"A pleasure, indeed. My Lady." His bow was low and effortless, and when he rose, he stared at her with ebony eyes. He seemed like a decent sort. But even if she had found him to be attractive, it wouldn't have mattered.

"You are too kind," she returned out of habit.

"Would it be presumptuous of me to request a place on

your dance card?" he asked after a few subtle niceties. "A waltz, perhaps?"

By the time the orchestra was in place, all but the last dance of the night had been claimed. And although a few of the names belonged to elderly and pompous widowers, most of her partners for the evening were pleasant and reasonably handsome gentlemen.

However, rather than be invigorated by the attention, it weighed her down.

And now, in addition to that ache in her breasts, a queasy feeling lurched in her gut. Likely it was the heat and all of the ladies' perfumes and various scents worn by the gentlemen. "You're doing swimmingly, dear." Lady Westerley leaned close and patted Felicity's hand. "And I am so glad. After what my son has put you through, I'd be devastated if you didn't have a successful season. All those years, you waited for him. You must know how disappointed I've been ever since..."

"I'm fine." Felicity hated that even Westerley's mother pitied her. She fought the desire to gulp for air. "Please, you mustn't give it another thought."

"I ought to have known you would handle this with an abundance of grace." But regret lingered in the dowager's eyes. "Shall we sit with Bethany until your first partner claims you?"

"I'm...going to visit the retiring room." That queasy feeling was worse now, and all the grace in the world wouldn't help if...

She did not even allow herself to think it.

"Don't take long, darling. The orchestra is warming up already."

Felicity nodded and, as a cold sweat broke out on her forehead and the back of her neck, summoned all the poise she could muster until she was able to locate a shadowy corridor.

She needed to be alone. Spying a rather imposing door, she pushed it open and was relieved to discover it was a library. The temperature was noticeably cooler inside, and the air was fresh. She could handle the scent of leather and books far better than the cacophony of overpowering floral and musk in the ballroom.

Much better. So much better.

Crossing the small sitting area, Felicity dropped her knees to the floor and buried her face in the seat of a leather settee.

Deep, cleansing breaths calmed her stomach.

In. Out. Felicity gulped for air. This cannot be happening.

"Dear God, help me, please?" she begged.

"Are you praying, Felicity?" The intruding voice had become familiar by now.

Manningham—Axel. She hadn't spoken to him since he'd walked her along the lane at Brightland's Manor. The door clicked shut behind him.

"Are you following me, Axel?" she answered without raising her head.

"As a matter of fact, yes. The last time you disappeared from a festivity, a ruthless rosebush was holding you hostage."

"A gentleman would refrain from reminding a lady of something so embarrassing, thank you very much." She startled when the cushion sank beside her. A peek to her right from beneath her folded arms put taut thighs in a pair of snug breaches in her line of sight. He shifted and then leaned forward, resting his elbows on his knees and staring at the carpet.

"I merely wished to add my name to your dance card—unless I'm too late." He sounded tired and a little discouraged.

Felicity leaned back on her heels. Why did she persist in treating him so poorly? He had done nothing but allowed her advances. She wasn't so hypocritical as to pretend she had not demanded his attentions that night.

No, her reasons for being so unhappy were all her own.

"I'm sorry. My head is aching." It wasn't a lie. But she wouldn't go into the litany of what ailed her like an old woman, or they'd be sitting here all night. "Do you have a pencil?" She held out her hand, presenting the card tied to her wrist.

She was getting too old for this.

"I did earlier." He searched his pockets and then, taking her hand, examined the card.

His touch, ironically enough, sent waves of comfort and warmth through her. And then she caught his scent, that clean manly fragrance she couldn't quite identify.

"Last one of the night, if you don't mind? It's a waltz."

Would she mind having him take her into his arms? "Are you proficient at it?" She teased. There was nothing worse than dancing with a gentleman who didn't perform the steps correctly. Too many evenings, she'd returned home with scuffs on her slippers and bruises on her toes.

He leaned back and grinned. "I may have failed to master many of the finer pursuits, but dancing isn't one of them."

"In that case," she dipped her lashes demurely. "The dance is yours."

She watched him write his name very carefully, achieving a childlike quality.

"Shall I locate some willowbark for you?" Just as he had on

the night of Lady Westerley's ball, he exhibited that same compassion once again.

"I'm fine." However, the idea of willowbark and her bed sounded far better than returning to the ballroom.

The first dance was set to begin any minute.

"Come up off the floor, then." He assisted her to her feet and onto the settee beside him.

The desire to lean against his comforting frame was almost impossible to ignore.

Almost.

"Lady Bethany and I saw you on Bond Street two days ago," she said. "With Lord Greystone." Felicity wasn't sure why she mentioned it. He didn't owe her any explanations of his actions or whereabouts since arriving in London.

"Ah. Yes. Delightful ladies. Lady Posy is Greys' ward, and miss Faraday his cousin. His great aunt is in town as well, for the season, all the way from Yorkshire. It seems Lady Posy's aunts have decided it's high time she enter society."

Felicity's chest loosened for no reason at all. "Oh. How lovely for her." Words that generally would mean nothing more than precisely what she said. So why did they come out sounding petty?

Axel swiped at an unruly lock of hair and then tilted his head to study her. "Greys doesn't have much family."

"Oh."

"I wanted to call on you, but…" he was staring at his hands, his elbows resting on his knees again. "I thought it best to allow you a few days to settle in."

"I appreciate that." But had she?

"You didn't seem overly anxious for my company last month." He glanced at her sideways.

"This isn't a proper time," Felicity glanced around the room, "or place to discuss this."

"A simple, I am, or I am not, would suffice." He set his jaw. And here she was, being snippy again. How did he even stand to be in her presence?

He deserved an answer from her. He deserved to know whether or not he could go on with his life as though nothing had happened between them.

"I'm not sure."

His head snapped around. "How is that possible?"

She certainly was not going to explain or discuss the amount of blood that had signified what she'd believed to be her courses. Nor was she going to provide an account of her morning bouts of retching.

They were at Lady Willoughby's ball, for heaven's sake!

"My mother will be wondering where I've gone off to." But before she could jump to her feet, he grasped her wrist.

"You will tell me everything." It wasn't a question. "We can walk outside rather than waltz if you'd like, but I need to know, Felicity."

She jerked her arm free, even knowing he deserved an answer.

Because if she was with child, she wasn't going to have a choice but to marry him. Everything would change.

"Very well." And knowing she was already late for her dance with Lord Oswald, she all but flew out of the room.

She could only avoid Manningham for a few hours.

But just as Felicity had determined she had no choice but to face the consequences, fate stepped in.

Much later that evening, when she'd looked around for him at the allotted time, while waiting in the chairs along the walls with the chaperones, and then wandered to the terrace door, he was nowhere to be seen. Were all men so fickle?

Because the waltz, the one that he'd reserved, was already halfway over.

"There you are. Your mother is ready to leave but said you had promised this set? Why are you not dancing?" Circles etched beneath her father's eyes, but they were also sparkling. He must have won at cards this evening, and for that, at least, she was grateful.

"I was," she admitted.

"Who is this cad who's stood you up?"

Felicity bit her tongue. She wasn't keen about revealing the name of that cad to her father. He was capable of holding onto grudges forever.

"Felicity?" He demanded an answer.

"Manningham-Tissinton."

"Oh, well, I believe he departed with Lord Chaswick following the garden incident. For the best, though, dear. I'd rather you not encourage that particular viscount." He jerked his chin for her to follow him.

"What garden incident?" She hurried her steps to keep up. "And why would you have me avoid him?" For a man as stocky as her father, he certainly could move swiftly.

"Disgusting. I dare not speak of it with you. No doubt you'll hear all about it from your mother."

Felicity trailed in her father's wake. She'd managed to fulfill all of her dancing obligations, but in between sets, she'd located a chair placed conveniently behind a rather tall plant and made use of it to avoid having to make conversation.

When had attending a ball become so exhausting?

"Why should I avoid Manningham?" She persisted. All her

life, she'd obliged her father's wishes, not once questioning that he knew what was best for her—that her future was set.

"Because I asked you, that is why." His question brought her up short. His word had always been reason enough in the past.

The Willoughby butler awaited them, her wrap in hand as she and her father arrived in the foyer. "Lady Brightley is already waiting in your vehicle, my lord," he addressed her father. Felicity tied her cloak, lost in thought, and then allowed her father to lead her outside to their carriage.

Sitting across from her parents in the dark as they drove home, the niggling annoyance she'd felt at her father's condescending answer did not go away. It became louder. "I'm just curious, that's all," she said.

"About what, dear?"

"Father has asked me to avoid Manningham-Tissinton. I simply wondered why."

"The viscount? I'd thought he was a decent sort, but in the end, your father's opinion is all that counts. He has our best interests at heart—always has."

"The man is simple." Her father's grumbling response surprised her. "Lord Crestwood, his father, has made it known that as a boy, Manningham was intellectually years behind his peers. I have no wish to enter a simpleton into my bloodline."

"But—" That made no sense whatsoever. Manningham was well-spoken, eloquent, clever. She shook her head but didn't argue.

But if something didn't happen quickly… Felicity splayed her hand over her belly, feeling as though all the air swooshed out of the interior of the carriage.

Her father may not have a choice.

TRY FLOWERS

*M*antis tapped Blackheart's arm, who immediately relaxed the hold around his neck, making this his third loss out of four today.

Sprawled on the floor and breathing heavily, Mantis eyed his sparring opponent thoughtfully. He was not accustomed to being bested like this.

"That last toss was unexpected." When did the bloody duke have time to pick up new moves? The two of them were ordinarily dead even, having learned under the same sensei from the age of ten and four. Mantis remembered such a significant time of his life quite distinctly. Blackheart had suggested Mantis join him in his lessons the very day he'd taken a slash to the face—the sword brandished by his own father.

"Masaki used it on me while you were at Westerley's." Blackheart offered a hand and pulled Mantis to his feet.

The reason he'd remained at Westerley Crossings had him frowning.

Since the Willoughby Ball, Mantis had presented himself

at Bright Hall three afternoons in a row now. On each occasion, he had been turned away.

True, he'd stood her up, but he hadn't much choice but to assist Chaswick home after the baron had perpetuated the scandal of the century. In retrospect, Mantis could have sent a message, but time had been of the essence. How long did she intend to hold it against him?

"I wasn't sure you'd have time to spar while in service," Mantis said. With the season underway, Blackheart was already installed as Greystone's butler. God help them all if Blackheart failed and was forced to marry the woman of Grey's choosing.

Of all of them, Blackheart seemed the least concerned of such a possibility.

The duke's lips barely tilted up, giving Mantis the impression that escaping his butlering duties posed no difficulty whatsoever. "Matters at Knight House are well in hand." Confidence lurked in the man's black eyes. "One more?"

Mantis ought to have known his friend took their practice as seriously as he did. Students of Jiu-Jitsu, an ancient Samurai form of fighting, not only benefitted physically but mentally as well.

He nodded and inhaled, drawing on the mental focus he needed to best the other man. Because, in truth, overcoming one's opponent had more to do with achieving heightened awareness than it had to do with size or strength. The idea was to turn an enemy's energy against himself.

And when one lost, he could still win if he could learn the cause of his defeat.

By the end of this last bout, it was Blackheart who lay winded on the mat.

Drawing in a deep breath, Mantis stood up and paced to

the edge of the mat and then back. He'd nearly lost a fourth match but managed to subdue Blackheart in the end.

Mantis was distracted, and he hated that he'd lacked focus for much of this session.

He offered a hand and assisted the duke to his feet. Blackheart eyed him suspiciously.

"What's eating you?"

What was eating him?

"Lady Felicity Brightley." Her name escaped before he could stop it. But Mantis knew that anything he told his ducal friend would be kept in confidence.

"Ah." Blackheart tossed him a clean towel, keeping one for himself and dabbing at the sweat just inside the collar of his gi.

"I need her to marry me." Mantis scrubbed his hand through his hair. It sounded even more ridiculous when he said it out loud. Blackheart merely waited.

"She refuses to even meet with me."

"A conundrum, indeed." At least Blackheart wasn't laughing.

"I stood her up after reserving the last waltz on her card." He wouldn't disclose that they hadn't intended to dance. "At Willoughby's"

"Thanks to Chaswick."

"Yes. And now…" Mantis frowned at the successive rebuttals he'd met with.

Brightley's butler hadn't even pretended to inquire as to whether or not she wished to meet with him. He'd simply stared down his nose and announced that Lady Felicity was indisposed.

"And you must marry her because…?" Blackheart inquired in a soft voice.

"Because." Mantis met the duke's eyes, eyes such a dark blue they might as well be black. "Honor demands it."

Blackheart lifted one lofty brow but then nodded slowly. Such reasoning was something all gentlemen understood.

"Have you tried sending flowers? A note of apology, perhaps?"

He had not. Such a pathetically simple idea, but Mantis had failed to think of it. "Damn my eyes, no."

Blackheart chuckled as he draped the towel around his neck. "I wouldn't put it off much longer." The duke pivoted and strolled across the salon. Without so much as a backward glance, he added, "the servants will be awaiting my inspection. Give my best to Lady Felicity." Of course, even as a butler, Blackheart would have matters well within his control.

Mantis didn't bother answering but instead began mentally composing his note of apology. He wasn't adept at penning romantic sentiments, but if it helped his endeavor for forgiveness, he would make an attempt.

And by the time he had located a flower cart, he'd decided on daisies and lavender instead of greenery. Daisy's because the gold reminded him of her hair, and lavender because the scent evoked exquisitely pleasant memories. And in his note, he asked her to meet him at the park tomorrow afternoon, at a particularly picturesque bank along the water.

He only hoped she didn't use the opportunity to return the favor of standing him up this time.

Even if he did deserve it.

"FLOWERS FOR YOU, MY LADY." Felicity glanced up from reading in time to see Susan enter her bedchamber with a fragrant, if not unusual, bouquet. "I took the liberty of putting them in water."

Rather than bother her recently sensitive constitution, the floral scents refreshed her. She took a moment to appreciate the colorful daisies before breaking the seal on the small envelope.

Manningham's handwriting was easy to distinguish, and she couldn't help but remember her father's assertions. She didn't believe for a second that Manningham was simple. Nor, she knew, would anyone else who knew him. But why would his own father spread such a falsehood?

My lady—the message began. Not Felicity, but very polite and perfectly proper.

Please accept my most abject apologies for failing to meet you as I promised. I beg your forgiveness. Rather than make my explanations in writing, I'd be grateful if you'd meet me in the park, on the south side of the folly near the footbridge tomorrow at two in the afternoon.

Your humble servant,

Ld. Manningham-Tissinton

SHE DREW a deep breath through her nostrils. He'd waited *half a week* to apologize. Had he been too busy squiring Greystone's ward around town during that time?

But that shouldn't matter to her.

She was well aware that he'd involved himself in Chaswick and Bethany's most unfortunate incident. She had gone with Tabetha to visit Bethany the morning after her hurried wedding.

What a whirlwind that had been!

In Manningham's missive, he insisted he wanted to explain. She would meet him.

She'd waited long enough.

Each morning when she awoke to the disheartening knowledge that her courses hadn't arrived, she'd tried to ignore that time was running out.

She would meet him. Of course, she would. Because unless she was greatly mistaken, she no longer had a choice.

THE NEXT AFTERNOON, following her by-now regular bout of retching, Felicity joined her mother in the drawing room, bringing along a new crocheting project to work on—a very feminine set of handkerchiefs.

And these she was making *for herself.*

"I'm going to call on Bethany again this morning." But her friend was no longer simply *Bethany*—she was *Lady Chaswick.*

"Your father wasn't pleased to hear you visited Byrd House. He doesn't want you associating with the baroness until the scandal has settled." Her mother waved a hand in front of her face as though the matter was too harrowing to discuss.

"But she's my best friend, Mother, more like a sister. Father can't expect me to stay away in her time of need."

Her mother eyed her and then frowned. "But she isn't going to be your sister, after all, now, is she?" She raised her brows before returning to her sewing.

Felicity's mother's words evoked a stubborn desire to protect her friend. Bethany had done nothing wrong and needed all the support she could get.

First, her father would take issue with Manningham, and now Bethany?

Felicity didn't argue with her mother. It would only be for naught. But she wouldn't allow this to go unchallenged. She was going to have to speak with her father.

And as though caught in an endless spiral, her thoughts brought her back to her present condition. Her stomach lurched and then the contents seemed to sink like a stone.

Her father was going to be livid. He had expressed his opinion where Manningham was concerned and if she was...

He was going to be livid!

She placed her hand over her abdomen, which was still relatively flat. Her father would have no choice but to give Manningham permission to marry her when he learned that she was carrying the viscount's child.

Her situation was becoming all too real.

Carrying a child.

She tested the flesh beneath her fingers, unable to discern any noticeable difference... and yet. She was...

She was with child. There was no other reasonable explanation for the changes happening within her body—the fatigue, the tenderness in her breasts, not to mention the time she spent staring into the bottom of a chamber pot every morning.

Susan had been correct. She'd barely bled at all last month.

I'm with child.

A baby!

"I'm going to walk in the park this afternoon." She stared outside. The sun was shining, and the sky was unnaturally blue.

"The exercise ought to do you some good. You have looked a little pale lately. But don't take too much sun. And Susan must go as well."

"Of course," Felicity promised, hearing her mother but not caring what she was saying.

A baby.

She stared down at the handkerchief resting in her lap, thinking it was all wrong. She should be knitting rather than embroidering. She should be making something cozy—for instance, a blanket or a tiny hat...

Her heartbeat fluttered. For weeks she'd considered the possibility to be something of a tragedy, but for all the complications it would bring...

It was also rather...

Wonderful.

SHE IS

*M*antis stared across the water. Would she come? A glance at his fob watch showed he was early. It also showed that his hand wasn't as steady as he'd like it to be.

He would finally have an answer, and the implications of that washed over him like a giant wave. When he walked out of this park today, he would either be an engaged man with a babe on the way. Or he would...

Not.

And if that was the case, he might very well be forced to accept that she did not wish to marry him, which was irksome.

Had he only been a convenient substitute for Westerley? She'd told him she loved her former betrothed. Hell, Mantis had personally witnessed the devastation she experienced following Westerley's proposal to Miss Jackson.

A flash of blue on the bridge caught his eye, and his heart lurched.

She had come.

The colors in her hat, pinned at a jaunty angle, matched the complimentary gown that flared from her hips to swirl around her ankles. Her maid walked beside her looking severe, but rather than appear somber for the occasion, Lady Felicity's mouth tipped up at the corners in an expressive smile.

She was not then.

No, she looked...

Happy with the world.

Radiant, *damn it.*

Her steps faltered, and she turned to the woman beside her. Chin held high, she carried a fan in one hand and kept the other behind her back as she approached him alone.

Untouchable. Felicity Brightley had always been unattainable to him. And despite having known her intimately, she would remain just that.

And yet, here she was.

"My lady," he uttered when she was near enough to hear.

She nodded. "My lord." She curtsied.

He bowed.

Rather inconvenient that he wanted to kiss her at that moment. At a temporary loss for words, he offered his elbow and gestured to stroll along the shore.

"I wasn't sure you would come," he said. Mantis matched his steps to hers as they slowly made their way along the edge of the water, inhaling her scent and experiencing a visceral response to it.

"I wasn't sure you would ever apologize to me."

"I would have," he grumbled. "If you had received my calls."

"What calls?" She jerked to a halt, scowling.

A very pretty scowl that had him staring at the cupid's bow of her lips.

"I've called on you daily since the Willoughby Ball. Without fail on every occasion, Your Mr. Michaels has sent me away. *Lady Felicity is indisposed.*" Mantis mimicked the butler's posture and voice.

"Indisposed?" Confusion etched her brow… and then her eyes narrowed. "My father."

Her father? "Lord Brightley doesn't wish you to meet with callers? Even with your mother present?"

"My father can be somewhat…" She winced. "Managing."

Mantis contemplated her explanation even as he reconciled it with the considerable freedom Felicity had had where Westerley was concerned.

Did her father disapprove of Mantis expressly? That would only make sense if Lord Brightley knew of the events that occurred in Westerley's orangery. And he could not.

Rather than dwell on that, he reminded himself of the two reasons he had for this meeting.

"I did not meet you as promised. Regardless of my excuse, that was unacceptable." They had not been going to dance. They'd been going to walk—and talk. "I beg of you to accept my apology."

He stared straight ahead, and didn't notice until she covered his gloved hand with hers that she was watching him while they walked.

"You were helping a friend. I only wish I'd been there for Bethany." She turned her face back to stare at the path ahead. "But I was…" She shook her head.

"What?"

"For the past seven weeks… and three days, I have not been myself."

Mantis kept quiet because she was finally talking to him without bristling. For once, he didn't have to drag information out of her. He'd never considered her talkative in the past, but since finding themselves caught up in these unlikely circumstances, she'd gone relatively silent.

"I've been tired and out of sorts. On the evening that my dearest friend found herself in one of the worst scandals in years, I was… hiding behind one of Lady Willoughby's plants, wishing I was at home in my bed."

Comprehending that Felicity, the most socially responsible lady of his acquaintance, would hide rather than mingle dutifully at a ball—drew him up short.

"You have been ill?"

"Not ill." They'd halted again, and her expression flitted from dismay to chagrin and then to something else as she stared at him. "I'm going to have to tell my father what we've done."

"What we've done?" She must mean—"I don't understand." His words caught in his throat.

She rolled her lips together, her gaze pinned on his.

And then he did understand.

"You mean?" His heart skipped a beat. "You are?"

"I'm so sorry, Axel." She was calling him by his given name, smiling at him. Was she saying that he was going to be a father? "I never intended any of this. You were simply being kind to me that night, and now… I've treated you horribly. I don't know what's wrong with me…"

Which meant he was also going to be a husband.

She was going to be his wife.

He was going to be a *father*.

Taking both her hands in his, he drew her to a nearby

bench. For the first time in his life, he thought his knees might give out beneath him.

Once seated, keeping her gloved hands in his, he studied her face. He needed to be sure. "You are... with child?"

She nodded.

"You do not seem overset by it."

At this, she laughed. "Not now. I've had time to get used to the idea."

"I will speak with your father." It was imperative more now than ever. "Should you be out walking? Are you eating enough? How are you feeling?" If anything, she appeared thinner than she had earlier that spring.

All these weeks, she'd been carrying their child while he'd merrily gone about his daily business. He wanted to know *everything*.

But before he could form any questions, she broke into his thoughts.

"Tell me about your family." She seemed far too calm as she made her request.

"My family?" His mind raced in a thousand different directions.

"You do have one, don't you?" She laughed. "Your father, siblings, perhaps...? I realize that although I've known you for some time, I don't really *know* you."

Mantis nodded, allowing himself a moment to catch up. She was with child. They were going to marry.

She wanted to know him better.

Of course!

"I have two siblings," he began. *I'm going to be a father.*

"Yes?" she prompted. Mantis blinked to chase the fog out of his brain and focus on answering her question.

"My sister is the same age as me: Cordelia."

"You're a twin?"

"I am."

"Does she have children?" *Children.*

"She is unmarried." Mantis pushed away his confusion enough to answer a little more coherently. Cordelia had made her come out several years ago, and finding herself embarrassingly neglected, chose to exit the marriage mart. She insisted that she preferred helping to care for Conner, who'd been an infant at the time. In Mantis' eyes, his sister's failed season only proved how idiotic most bachelors were.

"Is she like you?" Felicity asked.

"She is"—perhaps too much so—"We're of similar height and coloring, but she's smarter than me." Mantis slid her a meaningful gaze. "She actually enjoys reading all those stories of romance and adventure."

Felicity's eyes opened wide. "She is tall then. I think that would be magnificent."

"She *is* magnificent." Mantis frowned. "She's something of a Viking goddess." If only the rest of the world saw her as he did.

"But?" Felicity tilted her head. "If she is your twin, then she is... thirty? Did she not wish to marry?" Felicity realized she would have to put in a little work to get him talking.

"It's my opinion that she scared away any eligible suitors."

"Are the two of you close?" she asked.

"Not as close as we used to be. Although she's in London for the season, Cordelia prefers the country. And I... do not. But as children, we finished one another's sentences."

The only twins of Felicity's acquaintance were the Duke of

Blackheart's sisters. They had made their come out the night before and, although they resembled one another physically, exhibited considerably different temperaments.

"And your other sibling?"

"We have a younger half-brother, Connor. He turned twelve over the holidays."

Felicity vaguely remembered a few details gleaned over the years she'd known him. Tidbits casually mentioned by Westerley, or perhaps Bethany, or other ladies of her acquaintance.

Axel's mother had died when he was born, and his father had remarried nearly a decade later. She hadn't realized the second marriage had produced other children.

"Tell me about your father." She was most curious about Lord Crestwood. Why would the man speak so insultingly about his own son?

"The earl," he began, "is highly intelligent, but he is…hard." Axel stiffened. "He has high expectations for himself and the people that surround him."

Not my father, but *the earl*.

"Are you and he close?"

"No."

When Axel had pulled her to sit on the bench beside him, he'd taken her hands in his. When she'd asked about his father, his body went still.

"My father and I." Felicity changed the subject. "Are not as close as we once were." And then she swallowed hard. "I have no idea what he'll say about the baby."

Baby.

Saying the word out loud sent a warm protective sensation shooting through her. It also succeeded in launching a thousand nerves.

Manningham had not been looking at her but staring across the water. He shook his head. "You don't have to tell him until after we're married. I'll speak with him this afternoon."

"He'll be at his clubs." Felicity exhaled. She hadn't considered keeping her condition from her parents. And yet, it would be much easier to wait until after she was married—until she was already a wife, until her child's legitimacy was assured—before telling them.

"First thing tomorrow morning then." He was watching her now and looking somber. "Would you prefer to elope?"

"No." She couldn't do that to her parents. They were far from perfect, but she loved them. And her mother would be bereft. "A church wedding. We have time..." She splayed her hand over her belly, and his gaze followed.

He cleared his throat. "Can you feel it?" His question magnified the intimacy of their situation—not only the physical, but also the notion that their two lives would be linked together forever. Eventually, they would know one another better than anyone else.

Wouldn't they?

"I can't feel it yet." But it was there. The idea of it not being there, now that she'd accepted the truth, was something she didn't even want to consider.

"How are you feeling?" he asked. A particular quality in his voice made Felicity feel safe—protected. She hardly knew him, yet she did not doubt that he was going to make an excellent father.

"The mornings are difficult." She wanted to be honest with him without going into too great of detail. "My maid, Susan, says it's typical for the first few months, but I'll be quite happy to move beyond this phase of my confinement."

"Have you seen a physician or midwife?" But he dismissed his question before she could answer. "Of course, you have not. I'll make arrangements. No one needs to know, but I'm going to seek out the best available in all of London."

So very protected...

She hadn't expected this relief that came with finally sharing her burden.

"But first—"

"Your father."

"Yes."

When silence fell this time, it was a comfortable one. The birds singing in the trees and the water gently lapping along the shore soothed her nerves, which had become considerably frayed.

Or perhaps it was just him.

Axel. He was a large, almost gruff sort of man, but he was not insensitive.

Still holding her hand between his, the tip of his thumb drew lazy lines along the back of her wrist. The air between them grew heavy, and the memory of that night infused her thoughts. The memory of him kissing her, of him holding himself above her and then pressing inside of her.

She'd anticipated pain. Had she initiated it as some sort of punishment to herself?

But it had not been like a punishment, even the painful part. She'd expected to feel degraded, used, but instead, she'd felt worshipped by him. And it had been... wonderful.

Until the guilt set in—and the shock of what she'd done had sent her reeling.

But during... Felicity tightened the muscles in her thighs as the moment's restful mood transformed into awareness.

Protected.

He squeezed her hand.

"Everything is going to work out. I promise."

But she couldn't depend on his optimism.

"I hope so." She was unable to simply trust in the future. She'd done that before, and look how that had ended.

DENIED

"*I* was beginning to think this day would never come." Susan was tidying their chamber while Felicity paced from the window to the door and then back to the window again.

"I needed to be sure..." Felicity murmured.

Axel had arrived over half an hour ago. From what the housemaid had told them, her father had welcomed the viscount into his study almost immediately. Her mother ought to arrive at her door any minute now, saying the viscount wished to meet with her downstairs.

What was taking so long? Her concern heightened with each minute that passed.

Her father could not possibly deny Axel the opportunity of offering for her. She was five and twenty, for heaven's sake! There was no guarantee that anyone as suitable would come along... besides, her father was the one who'd given up her betrothal to Westerley...

Only, that wasn't the real reason her engagement had ended.

Westerley had been in love with someone else.

She inhaled, happy to note that her heart didn't hurt at this admission as it had initially.

In fact, the pain she'd felt from his rejection seemed relatively insignificant now—now that she was expecting another man's child.

The door sounded from below, drawing her gaze down to the street.

Was Axel leaving? But... if he was going, that meant...!

She turned and flew to the door, down the stairs, and without bothering to knock, burst into her father's study. "Why is he leaving?"

Her father finished writing his signature on something and set his pen aside before looking up from his desk to acknowledge her.

"Manningham-Tissinton? You knew he was coming then? You cannot seriously believe I would have allowed him to offer for you?" Her father seemed utterly unconcerned at her dismay.

"It is my life. I ought to be allowed to decide for myself who I wish to marry." This was not the first time she'd had a meaningful discussion with her father in this room—so very masculine in its furnishings.

However, it was the first time that she had ever argued with him there.

Or anywhere.

"I told you already. The viscount's blood is tainted—his mother was not right. You don't want simple children, do you?"

Felicity was shaking her head. Such an excuse was nonsense. "He is not simple, Father."

Her father's eyes narrowed, and his jaw tightened at her

defense of Axel. "I've made my decision, and it is final. Furthermore, I forbid you to have anything to do with the man. Don't try me on this, daughter."

She knew that tone.

"But I—"

"Now go."

"You don't understand." Once he knew the truth, he'd have no choice but to reverse his decision. "I'm—"

A loud thump echoed off the walls when her father's fist landed heavily on his desk. The sound of his displeasure must have echoed throughout most of the house.

"What in God's name has come over you? Go to your chamber and contemplate all that I do for you. One more word, and you can stay there without dinner."

Her father was overbearing, more than most, but he hadn't shouted at her since she'd wandered off into the woods as a child, and the entire household had had to go searching in the dead of night.

And that morning last winter, after he lost heavily at cards.

Felicity inhaled a deep breath through her nostrils.

She'd very nearly told him the truth. She would tell her mother instead. And then, he'd have no choice but to allow Axel to make his offer.

But she would speak with Axel first.

When they'd parted ways the day before, they had not made arrangements to see one another. They'd expected to be engaged by this time today.

"Very well." She backed away from her father's desk, feeling like a soldier withdrawing from battle, intent on refortifying his strength to fight another day.

She would send Axel a message requesting him to meet

with her in the park again tomorrow. Susan could make sure it was delivered into his hands.

And after that, Felicity would go to her mother.

As she closed the door to her father's study behind her, she rested her hand low on her belly. It wasn't as soft or as flat as it had been the day before.

Time, most definitely, was not on their side.

$\sim$

"GOOD DAY, MY LORD." Mantis backed out the door just before the butler slammed it closed.

Blinking in confusion, Mantis stood, frozen, on the front stoop of Felicity's father's house.

What the hell just happened? Had he entered an altered dimension?

Shocked, he shook his head then forced his legs to carry him along the walk.

And as the truth of what his father had done hit him, a heavy pit formed in his gut. Mantis was well aware of his father's feelings of disappointment. He'd been pummeled with the knowledge almost daily for as long as he could remember. But he'd never imagined the earl would share those criticisms outside of their family.

Born a twin, he'd been the weaker baby. Cordelia, the girl, had been almost twice his size, pink, and loud. Mantis had been scrawny, practically blue, and mostly silent.

His father, unwilling to waste his given name on a still-born, had named him Axel Royce Lupton after his mother's father. He'd saved Connor Delbert Lupton, IV, for his second son.

On the third day of his life, his mother had passed, but

while the household mourned, Mantis had inexplicably clung to life.

The first time he'd disappointed his father, he'd eventually realized, was when he'd lived.

He'd rather gotten used to disappointing the earl.

But he'd always believed that his father's poor opinion of him was something kept within their family.

This morning, by non-other than the father of the woman he intended to wed, he'd learned this was not the case.

Lord Brightley had barely allowed Mantis to finish presenting his request before objecting.

"I'm afraid the answer is no." Lord Brightley had been quite matter-of-fact.

Mantis hadn't been sure he'd heard rightly. "No?"

Mantis wasn't misleading himself to believe that he was considered quite respectable, perhaps more so than many of his acquaintances. He not only held a decent title but was in line to inherit an earldom. And truth be told, Mantis was relatively well off. Was the Earl of Brightley repulsed by his scar?

That would be ridiculous.

"Don't take it personally, my boy," Brightley's attempt to console him had sounded slightly apologetic but mostly condescending.

"Might I ask your reason?"

"Your father and I play cards from time to time. Crestwood is a good man. Knew your mother too. A shame about her passing... Nonetheless, your father was good enough to share the nature of your deficiencies with me." Mantis had sat frozen, all but reeling from what he was hearing. "My daughter, Lady Felicity, is... of the finest lineage. Not only my ancestors but her mother's. She must marry a man with equal, if not superior, intelligence."

Earlier that morning, Mantis had taken the time to spar with Blackheart, as he usually did, and he'd gone to meet with Brightley feeling focused and confident. The earl's rejection sent his mind into a swirling vortex of... outrage and shame.

And betrayal. Mantis should hate his father. Why didn't he?

He walked unseeing through the genteel streets of Mayfair for what could be minutes or hours, at some point he'd lost track, before arriving at Knight house.

The door opened a fraction of a second after Mantis sounded the knocker.

"It didn't go well then?" Blackheart cocked one of his slashing brows.

Mantis had told his friend where he was going that morning. He'd felt rather confident, in fact. He scrubbed a hand through his hair and entered. "It did not."

Blackheart closed the door and gestured for Mantis to step into the small office allocated for Greystone's butler. Set behind a secret door in the foyer, it was rather cozy, really.

Dropping onto a wooden chair, Mantis momentarily forgot Brightley's rejection as Blackheart took his place behind the serviceable desk. The duke crossed one leg over the other, entirely at ease in his position. Mantis could almost believe he would be safe from running through the park come the end of the season.

"Your father?" Blackheart asked.

"Yes," Mantis answered and then glanced sideways to the tight entrance.

"It's you." Greystone peaked inside. "I thought I heard the door, Mr. Cockfield." He glared sternly at Blackheart but with laughter lurking behind his eyes. Both of them were enjoying the results of this wager far more than Mantis would have expected.

To provide Blackheart a real challenge, Greys ought to have required the duke to act as a footman.

"Why so glum?" The marquess stared down at Mantis, folding his arms and leaning casually against the door frame.

"I went to offer for Lady Felicity this morning. Her father refused to allow it."

"Disappointing," Blackheart said. "But I'm not all that surprised."

"Good to see you have so much confidence in me," Mantis groused.

"Brightley is tight with your father," the duke explained.

How the hell hadn't he realized this?

"One would think that would work in a gentleman's favor," Greys offered with a frown.

"But not in mine," Mantis added.

"No." Blackheart tapped his chin and then leaned forward. "Not in yours."

Both men were aware of the struggles Mantis had experienced in school, and at one point, had no doubt witnessed any of Crestwood's thinly veiled barbs. They rarely spoke of them, however, and it was his friends who had helped him successfully finish out his schooling.

"Were either of you aware that Crestwood's been disparaging me publicly?" The back of Mantis's neck burned with a combination of white-hot anger and embarrassment. That his father would go so far was mortifying. Such a public humiliation would affect their entire family.

Blackheart's jaw ticked, but it was Greys who answered.

"I'd heard rumblings but hoped them to be isolated incidences."

111

The duke pinned his gaze on Mantis. "It isn't true. You know that."

Mantis clenched his fists. "I thought I did. What the hell am I missing?" He got by well enough but knew his limitations.

His friends exchanged a loaded glance. Greys exhaled loudly and announced, "He's a bloody cocksucker. That's what you're missing. I cannot comprehend why you've chosen to reside at Crest House. You're more than welcome to stay here. Or take bachelor's quarters, for God's sake."

Greys had the right of it, but Mantis couldn't help wonder when he would see Cordelia and Conner if he moved out. Cordelia would be perfectly fine without him, but he worried about Conner.

He pressed his fist against his forehead.

Moving out would be the beginning of the end. The end of what?

Rather than begin to answer such an unanswerable question, Mantis chose to address his more urgent problems.

"Lord Brightley poses something of an obstacle." One he could overcome, but that could prove troublesome long after Mantis and Felicity married.

Marry they would, though, and soon.

They could elope. He could take the decision out of her father's hands, but Mantis deplored the idea of robbing Felicity of a wedding.

"Tell them the truth," Blackheart stated baldly. "The earl will have no choice but to concede his blessing."

Grey's brows rose. "The truth?"

Neither Mantis nor Blackheart expanded because, of course, Greys could figure it out.

"When Brightley discovered Westerley intended to call off

his betrothal to Felicity," Greys pointed out, "Lady Felicity's father did not take it lying down. My advice is that you be prepared to elope regardless. The man seems pleasant enough, but…" Greys shrugged. "I wouldn't take his approval for granted even after he's aware… well, when you meet with him again."

Mantis nodded. "I need to talk with Felicity, but—" Unfortunately, that wasn't going to be as easy as it sounded. "He's ordered me away from her."

"That reminds me." Blackheart opened a drawer and removed an envelope from his desk. "Your valet delivered this just before you arrived."

Mantis stared at delicate handwriting. Had her father directed her to write to him demanding he leave her alone?

Her scent on the envelope teased his senses as he broke the seal.

The missive was short and to the point. "She wants to meet me in the park tomorrow afternoon."

A BENCH IN THE WOODS

*F*elicity clenched her hands in her lap, seated as she was, in the exact spot, on the exact bench where she'd seen him last.

She hadn't slept well the night before and had then spent half the morning staring into the bottom of a chamber pot. She'd been so hopeful yesterday and hadn't been prepared for the despair that settled on her today.

"Felicity?" His hand dropped on her shoulder and squeezed from behind. "We aren't afforded privacy here. Follow the path around to those trees, and I'll meet you there."

Why hadn't she thought of this? She nodded, ignoring the urge to turn and glance up at him, and then rose. What would her father do if he discovered she was going against his wishes? She smoothed her skirts and then glanced across the lawn, just barely catching the back of the viscount before he disappeared down a different walking path.

Sure enough, a handful of strolling couples, two nannies with prams, and a few gentlemen on horseback were present. A shiver of unease shook her—and guilt. In all her life, she'd never defied her father, not knowingly, anyway. Not deliberately.

On knees weaker than she'd like, she strolled in the direction Axel had instructed her. An elderly lady scowled at Felicity because she was alone. She'd left Susan to wait for her near the bridge.

Entering the shade of the trees, Felicity shivered. The path was overgrown, and the air was cooler. She hadn't even realized this section of the park existed. She often walked alone while at home at Brightland's. But that was her father's property.

This was a public park in the city.

So when Axel's large figure appeared in front of her, she jumped.

"Sorry about that." He sent her a half-smile. One she hadn't noticed before but was finding to be quite attractive. A few leaves clung to his hair.

"You're fast."

"I didn't want you to be alone for long." He took hold of her hand, leading her deeper into the hidden forest.

"I've never ventured this way before."

"So, you prefer the straight and narrow?" His question was an ironic one. She'd thought so at one time.

"I... don't know." Felicity kept her head down and watched her feet, not wanting to trip over the roots that meandered across the trail. "I thought I did. But it involved an awful lot of patience and waiting—of which neither were rewarded...Oh!" He'd led them to a charming wooden bench someone had built under the trees. Trunks extended in all directions, vines hanging down from them.

"I come here alone sometimes." Axel held the branches back so she could step inside.

It wasn't a large bench. It provided enough space for two people to sit. When Axel lowered himself beside her, his arms and legs pressed along hers and she shivered.

"Are you cold?" He leaned forward to remove his jacket.

"No. I'm fine."

But he worked his arms out of the sleeves and then settled the warm garment around her shoulders. *Protected...* the sensation washed over her even as the word flitted through her mind. "Thank you... Axel."

"I'm so sorry—"

"I ought to have—"

They both began to speak at once and then stopped at the same time.

"Do not apologize for your father." He was cradling her hands in his.

"What did he tell you?" What reason could her father have possibly given a wealthy viscount for sending him away? Surely, not that nonsense Lord Crestwood had told him?

Axel's nostrils flared. "I'm not good enough for you. Not that I don't agree wholeheartedly, mind you. I just didn't expect that it would be my own father making that argument."

"My father told you that he spoke with your father...?" Felicity winced.

"I'm afraid so."

"It isn't true. I told him that."

"I'm not simple," his tone sounded indifferent, but Felicity didn't miss the ticking of his jaw.

She hated that Axel felt compelled to give her any explanation or defense. "I find you to be quite intelligent." She had joked with him about not reading and now felt sorry for it. Not all people were the same.

"My father would be the first to disagree with you."

She stared into his eyes. In the trees' shade, the green flecks nearly overwhelmed the brown—like the color of the forest itself. "When I absented myself from Lady Westerley's ball, it was you who followed me." She had not been crying, and she'd been sure to smile and to greet people she'd met on her way out of the room. And yet...he'd realized something nobody else had.

"Westerley proposed to her right in front of you."

"It was horrible." Although she no longer pined for the Earl, the memory was one she'd like to forget someday.

"You were caught in a thicket of thorns." His smile was kind. He'd never made fun of her. He'd listened to her. He'd given her distance when she'd needed it, and then when she needed... him.

He was there.

She had misjudged him before. "You saved me that night." In more ways than one.

"You would have saved yourself," he tilted his head, "eventually." The white of his teeth flashed, and she found herself appreciating another thing about this man.

A brilliant smile. Felicity realized she was staring at his mouth and raised her gaze to find him staring at hers. And just as it had two days before, the air grew heavy between them.

She wanted him to kiss her.

In the orangery, she could make excuses for having made advances toward him... for all but throwing herself at him. She would have no such excuse today.

She licked her lips and forced herself to focus on the discussion they were supposed to be having.

"I'll tell my mother the truth. She can tell my father, and then he'll have no choice but to give us his permission." Her voice came out breathy sounding.

"I'll go with you to tell them." Axel grew serious again. "I cannot risk…"

"You cannot risk?" She wasn't sure she understood.

"My father has convinced yours that any child of mine would be born with defects." He swallowed hard.

And then it struck her.

He was worried her father would refuse permission even after hearing the truth. Was he also concerned her father would somehow keep him from their child? Or worse? It was preposterous!

Wasn't it?

"Surely you don't think…?"

Axel watched her closely. "I don't think it likely, but with even so much as the possibility, I… I need to be there. We can tell your parents together."

"You're afraid he'd send me away."

Don't push me, daughter. She'd wondered what her father had meant. More than anyone, she had seen the two sides of the seemingly mild-mannered Lord Brightley. One, a caring family man, a man who had weaknesses and made mistakes— and the other, an ill-tempered earl struggling to protect his legacy.

Axel nodded and Felicity made no attempt to argue otherwise.

Because this babe, this invisible little being growing inside of her, was Axel's child, too. It was *theirs.*

Her insides felt like they were shaking. "Very well. When?"

Axel released her hands to pull her closer. It was as though he knew what she needed. Closing her eyes, she soaked up his tenderness, burrowing into the warmth of his jacket, memorizing the scent of his soap and cologne... Good heavens, she was crying!

She brushed a hand over her eyes. "I'm sorry. I'm never weepy." How many times had she cried to him since that night in March?

"Everything will be fine. I promise you that. I won't allow anything else."

His fingers lifted her chin so she had no choice but to stare into his eyes again. "I hope so." When would she believe that?

He studied her as though looking right into her soul.

"I'm going to take care of you," he whispered. "I'm going to make you happy."

Could he? Yes. Felicity inhaled. Yes. It was possible.

"Then kiss me."

His eyes widened, but he gathered her closer with only a moment's pause. "You'll never need to ask twice."

All his strength, all his power, his maleness... wrapped around her. Felicity closed her eyes, unable to bear the mixture of emotions threatening to spill over. And when his mouth claimed hers, her hands slid up and she wound her arms around his neck.

SOMEDAY, Mantis vowed to himself, he would kiss this woman when she wasn't on the verge of tears.

"Felicity," he growled her name even as he claimed her willing mouth.

How many times had he relived that night? Hundreds?

Her fingers worked their way to his hair, tugging, sliding, demanding. Any hope he had of subduing his erection fled when she hummed softly in the back of her throat.

He remembered that sound, practically had it memorized from when she'd made it over and over again while he'd worked himself inside of her.

"Axel."

They could still elope. He palmed her breast over her bodice, and his heart raced. She pressed closer, and he deepened the kiss, exploring the tender flesh behind her teeth, the roof of her mouth, sparring with her tongue. He wanted to taste all of her.

He slid off the bench and turned to face her. Kneeling on the damp ground, he gripped her thighs.

"I want to take care of you."

She nodded, her eyes sleepy, her hands on the sides of his face.

"Yes," she whispered.

"Right now."

"Yes." Her hips twitched, unknowingly inviting him. Or was it knowingly?

He slid his hands up her thighs, dragging her skirts along with them, around her waist and then beneath her, squeezing her buttocks, lifting her, and hooking her knees over his shoulders.

Once he had her settled, he moved one of her hands from his hair to the edge of the bench. "Hold on."

Her eyes widened as he dipped his chin and buried his face between her legs. She was wet, glistening.

Mantis claimed her intimately, just as he'd kissed her mouth moments before.

"Oh," she gasped from above. And then she moaned.

"So perfect." He flicked his tongue inside of her, at the same time clutching the backs of her thighs and then the soft mounds of her buttocks.

"Axel." She widened her legs, clasping the edge of the bench with both hands now.

"Too good for me." He rubbed his chin along her seam.

It was true. Felicity deserved someone better than him. Someone who would seduce her slowly, on silk sheets in an elegant bedchamber, someone who would take his time pressing kisses up the length of her leg and teasing her gently. Not a giant of a man who would ravish her in a public park.

"I'm not."

Feeling her sliding off the bench, Mantis adjusted his arms around her thighs and spread her wider, rewarding himself with the prettiest sight of his life.

He was lost, wanting to explore her with his hands, his tongue, but also bury himself inside again.

"What's wrong?" Her words jolted him.

"I'm—" He flicked his eyes up to meet her gaze. "I don't deserve you."

"Don't stop." She closed her eyes, tipping her head back. "Take care of me, Axel." And then, *"Please?"*

Drinking in the sight of her, he drew two fingers along the most tender of flesh. And then he was sucking her into his mouth, stroking her inside and out, listening for what she liked while gratifying his own carnal desires.

Tremors rolled through her, her hands tugging at his hair. When she finally stilled, breathing heavily, he gave her a few seconds of respite before beginning again, building that wicked tension once more, drawing it out, patting her, rubbing her, massaging her inner flesh until she arched, writhing to be closer.

And again.

And again.

"I can't..." She was gasping. "Axel... I want... but I..." She lay limp, causing him to draw back in concern.

"Felicity?"

"Um-hum..."

"Are you alright?"

"Um-hum..."

The delicate curve of her satiated smile gratified him more than anything had in recent memory. The sight of her lashes fanned out on alabaster skin seemed more intimate than it should.

Ignoring the discomfort of his rock-hard cock, he tugged her skirts back down. He would wait to find his satisfaction. He withdrew a handkerchief from his jacket pocket, swiped it across his mouth, and then arranged himself beside her on the bench again and then chuckled softly.

She had fallen asleep in his arms.

If left up to him, he'd hold her like this all afternoon. Her maid, however, was waiting near the bridge for her.

And the two of them needed to confront her parents.

JUST A NAP

"Are you sure I look all right?" Felicity brushed at her skirts. One last glance at the wooden bench had her pressing both hands to her cheeks, which felt much hotter than usual.

Axel reached out and removed a fallen leaf from her sleeve and then lifted his gaze to hers, a light in it that she'd not seen before. "You look beautiful."

"And you look dashing, as usual, but are you sure we should do this today?"

He smirked with a nod, and taking her hand, led her along the path she'd followed earlier—much earlier. Susan was going to be in a panic. "You shouldn't have let me sleep!" But she felt better than she had in days.

So very much better.

"The sooner we tell them, the sooner we can have banns read, and the sooner you'll have my protection."

His hand was warm around hers—assertive. She was nervous. Her father would hate her for this, for making him go against his own decision.

But she wasn't going to have to face them alone.

Axel would be at her side.

Axel.

"I'm not too good for you." He'd told her that, while he had his head... while he was...*taking care of her*.

"You've been too good for me since the day you were born." They were emerging from the trees by now, and he pulled her even with him, dropping her hand and then placing his on the small of her back.

It was more likely that he, in fact, was too good for her, too pure of heart. She blinked away tears as the two of them stepped into the sunlight.

"Oh, my lady!" Susan charged toward them, her hair looking frazzled and her cheeks pink. "I've been sick with worry! I cannot imagine what his lordship will say if he discovers we've been away for so long. I'm a horrible chaperone—utterly useless." Susan's hand was on her chest as though she needed it there to keep her heart from jumping out even as she narrowed her eyes in Axel's direction.

"I'm so sorry. We sat on the grass, and..." Felicity slid her gaze to his, noting that his eyes were a lighter cinnamon color in the sunlight. "I fell asleep." She smiled ruefully.

Her maid knew she hadn't been sleeping well, making the weak excuse somewhat believable. "Susan, I'd like to present you to the Viscount Manningham-Tissinton. He will be escorting us back to Bright Place."

Since her father wasn't likely to admit him as a guest, they had decided to arrive together.

Felicity had no choice but to overcome the particular weak feeling in her lower extremities after...

"Axel, Susan is my most valued maid. I don't know what I would do without her."

Axel bowed over Susan's hand. He didn't have to—she was a maid—and yet by doing so, he revealed another layer of his character.

"We've met before," Axel reminded her. "Miss Susan. I beg your forgiveness for keeping your mistress so long. I didn't have the heart to wake her, but it was not my intention to alarm you." This man. He was powerful in every sense of the word, but, Axel's true strength, Felicity realized, was in his *goodness.*

"It's my honor to meet you." Susan's suspicions evaporated under his charm, which was quite telling. For weeks now, her maid hadn't a single kind word to say about the man who'd bedded her mistress while she'd been feeling unhappy following Westerley's betrayal.

But it seemed he was to be forgiven, which was bolstering in itself. Because having the support of a servant was of far more value than most realized.

"Shall we?" Axel offered his arm, and Susan fell into step behind them.

Felicity hadn't bargained on spending so long at the park, and familiar gentlemen of the ton were already driving ladies in elaborate day dresses and feathered hats.

"My dear Manningham." An incredibly handsome woman had her driver halt their open barouche before their trio could escape unseen. "Such a surprise to see you out and about, escorting Lord Brightley's daughter, I believe?"

Axel stiffened beside her. "Felicity, may I present you to my father's wife, her ladyship, Countess of Crestwood. Louisa, this is my... This is Lady Felicity, my... very good friend."

"Pleased to meet you, my lady," Felicity dropped into a

curtsey, anxiously realizing that this woman was her future mother-in-law.

"Likewise, I'm sure." Polite words, but Felicity couldn't help but miss the chill in the woman's cool grey eyes.

"Hello, Conner," Axel addressed a small boy seated proudly in the corner of the barouche.

"Manningham." Nothing in the boy's appearance would have had Felicity guessing he was Axel's brother. Nothing in his looks, nor what was almost a condescending demeanor.

"You missed dinner last night. Cook would appreciate it if you would show some consideration and inform her before-hand. Do you intend to join us tonight?" Lady Crestwood's smile softened her criticism.

"Not this evening," Axel's voice came out tight sounding. "But I'll speak with Cook later myself. It's never my intent to be an inconvenience."

"You might as well take a room at one of the Lodging houses for as much time as you spend with your family." She ignored him a moment to wave across the park to another vehicle and then looked down at him again. "Poor Cordelia is feeling quite abandoned by you."

Axel cleared his throat. "I suppose I can join the family for dinner this evening if you'd like. Although I highly doubt Cordelia would ever allow anyone to abandon her."

"She is a lady, after all. But don't change your plans for your family. We have guests coming, and the numbers are already set. Another time. Connor, you always enjoy Manningham's visits, don't you?"

"Yes, ma'am." The boy sounded incredibly solemn for being only twelve. And then his mother's gaze fell back on Felicity.

"Incredibly kind of you to allow our Manningham to escort you this afternoon."

"I am the fortunate one," Felicity responded honestly. "No doubt the new debutantes are wishing me to perdition about now."

Lady Crestwood's brows rose, and then she threw back her head and laughed. "Oh, my dear. Aren't you simply delightful?" However, her lip curled, and, if possible, her eyes turned even cooler.

"We mustn't dally, though. Do come around more, Manningham." The woman smiled again and then dropped back into her seat. "Drive," she ordered, and with a jerk, Axel's stepmother and half-brother moved along.

Felicity would have stared after them, lost in thought, if Axel wasn't urging her away from others who might wish to stop them.

He had told her once that he didn't like being called Manningham—because it was how his family addressed him. Now, although Lady Crestwood hadn't been outwardly rude, Felicity understood.

Away from the park, their trio had the walk mostly to themselves.

Felicity had not been joking when she'd told Lady Crestwood that the debutantes of the ton would be disappointed. His burly good looks notwithstanding. Because any time a titled and wealthy gentleman was scooped off the marriage mart, a handful of ladies—and their mothers, of course—fell into mourning. Did his family seriously believe that Axel lacked intelligence? It seemed preposterous—no, in fact, it *was* preposterous.

"Your father was wrong to tell my father what he did," Felicity announced abruptly.

Axel was an intelligent, charming gentleman. Her father ought to have realized this. But at the sight of her home, Felicity's insides flipped. Her father was the most stubborn person she knew, and he had chosen to disapprove of the man she was going to marry.

He was going to have to get past that.

~

MR. MICHAELS, the same gentleman who'd all but thrown Mantis out the day before, must have been watching for the daughter of the house to return home safely. They'd barely arrived at the front steps when the door swung open.

"Her ladyship was growing concerned, Lady Felicity." The butler spoke to Felicity but then skipped his gaze to Mantis, holding up one hand presumably with the intent of barring him from entering. "I'm afraid you are not welcome here, my lord."

"Lord Manningham-Tissinton is my guest, Mr. Michaels." Felicity's spine stiffened beneath Mantis' hand. "Has my father returned from his club?"

"Not yet." This Michaels fellow glanced behind him. "I have orders, my lady."

"If you won't allow us to enter, then the two of us will await him on the front step."

"The three of us." Susan crossed her arms. "I wonder what the neighbors would think about that?"

"Don't be foolish." The butler addressed the maid and then turned back to Felicity. "Please, my lady. If you would just come inside, perhaps the Viscount could visit another time."

Mantis considered pushing past the servant, but the ladies' strategy might prove more effective. He stepped back and merely crossed his arms. He'd do whatever was necessary.

"All of us, or none of us, Michaels." Felicity and her maid presented a united front.

Felicity, it seemed, a woman he'd once mistakenly considered to be mostly delicate and feminine, possessed the strength of a soldier. Mantis bit back a grin as he watched her stand up to a man more than twice her size.

He didn't deserve someone like her—someone so possessed of grace, poise, and an organic gentility.

He didn't deserve her, but by some unlikely twist of fate, she'd agreed to marry him. And he'd be damned if he let her go now.

"You'll be sure to inform his Lordship that this was not my choice." Mr. Michaels moved back. "And I'd appreciate a recommendation when I'm sacked." Mantis almost felt sorry but couldn't quite get past feeling vindicated as Mr. Michaels had all but shoved him out the door the day before.

"No one is going to sack you, Michaels." Felicity touched the man's arm reassuringly as she and Mantis passed into the foyer. "Is my mother in the drawing room?"

"She is."

"If you would be so kind as to tell my father that we're waiting to meet with him there, I'd be grateful."

"Of course, my lady."

"And tell him it's important."

"As you wish." The butler bowed, stepping back so they could climb the steps to the main floor.

"Thank you, Susan." Felicity sent her maid a grateful grin.

"You're welcome." Susan then touched Felicity's arm and then curtsied. "And best of luck to you both."

"We're on our own now," Mantis whispered once Susan

was out of sight. Felicity squeezed his hand, smiling over her shoulder. The sudden warmth in his chest wasn't something with which he was familiar.

But walking with Felicity, talking to her, conspiring with her…

She just made him happy. His gaze followed the slender line of her neck where golden tendrils curled to rest on her shoulders.

Her taste had been uniquely addictive.

He jerked himself back to the present. Now was not the time to relive what had perhaps been one of the most sensual encounters of his life.

When he'd visited Bright Place the day before, he'd noticed the elegant floor and tasteful moldings but had been too preoccupied to consider the empty places on the wall where paintings were noticeably absent.

A thought struck him. "Refresh my memory," he spoke softly again. "Did you tell me your father had lost your dowry?"

She nodded. "Is that going to be a problem?"

"Not at all. In fact, I think that might work in our favor." The closed door to her father's study, from where he'd been kindly ejected the day before, was on their left. The doors to the right were opened wide.

"Is that you, Felicity?" A feminine voice called from inside. "I've been worried sick for your whereabouts. What on earth was Susan doing, allowing you to stay out for so long." Felicity stepped inside first, with Mantis one step behind her.

"Lord Manningham!" Lady Brightley halted her knitting needled as she stared at him from the far end of a long settee. "Felicity?" She seemed horrified by his presence but not so much as to challenge him outright.

"Mother, you remember Lord Manningham-Tissinton?"

"My lady," Axel bowed to his future mother-in-law. "You are looking lovely this afternoon." He would do all he could to win her mother over—to win her family over. Because regardless of the outcome of this meeting, he would marry Felicity.

It was the proper thing, the honorable thing, and he would settle for nothing less.

And in addition to all of that, it was what he wanted.

"But…" Lady Brightley's brow furrowed. "Did you not remember what your father said?" This woman was not comfortable defying her husband's rules. At one time, Mantis might have thought Felicity was similar in temperament.

By now, he'd learned to presume nothing where she was concerned.

"We have come, together, to speak with father."

"Dear me." Her mother had gone somewhat pale and was waving a hand before her face. "He's not going to be pleased at all. Must you do this today, Felicity? I don't mean to be rude, my lord, but we have been told in no uncertain terms that my daughter is not to associate with you, and my husband is going to be terribly angry if he discovers you here."

"May I?" He moved slowly into the room and gestured toward the smaller settee that sat opposite the countess.

"Oh, no! But of course. Be seated. But this is not good, not at all good."

Brightley had pointed out to Mantis the day before that Felicity's mother was the daughter of a duke. Although not nearly as poised as her daughter, she possessed the same regal bearing.

Felicity lowered herself to sit beside her mother, and

Mantis noticed both the similarities and the differences between Felicity and the older woman.

"Mother, please don't be upset. It'll only make matters worse." Felicity turned a pleading gaze to Mantis.

"My lady. We're here to reason with the Earl." If that was at all possible. "I do believe the yarn you're working with is the same shade as your daughter's eyes." It was the color of the Mediterranean.

"That's why I chose it. Felicity inherited her eyes from her father."

"And what is it that you are knitting?"

"A scarf. One can never own too many scarves, isn't that right, darling?" She touched Felicity's leg. "I tried making mittens, but the patterns are too complicated."

Seemingly forgetting how her husband was going to respond to Mantis' presence, whether by accident or choice, Felicity's mother was more than happy to discuss the difficulty involved in knitting, the cold weather they'd experienced the past winter, and even the newest color debutantes were wearing this year. "Catmint," she enthused.

But when heavy footsteps approached outside the drawing-room, Lady Brightley fell silent.

"What in the devil are you doing here?"

Bracing himself, Mantis turned to stare at the man who'd sent him packing the day before. Her father could fight him all he wished, but he wasn't about to win.

The Earl of Brightley paced back into the hallway and then inside once again, to where Mantis, Felicity, and her mother sat. Red-faced, he then raised one arm and pointed toward the door.

"Out. Now. Before I have you thrown out."

CONFRONTING THE PARENTS

*F*elicity burst to her feet. "But Father—"

"It's imperative we speak with you and Lady Brightley," Axel turned his hazel gaze to land on Felicity's and added, "together." His voice carried calmly from where he'd risen from his seat across from her.

Nodding, Felicity carefully picked her way around the table to stand at his side.

"My lord, I think that perhaps you ought to hear them out." Rather than panic, as Felicity half expected, her mother seemed to have realized that this meeting was of considerable import. Perhaps it was because Felicity had never outright defied her father like this before. Perhaps it was the pleading look Felicity sent her.

Or perhaps she'd noticed some of the changes Felicity had gone through over the past almost two months.

Her father's scowl deepened, and she could only guess at the struggle waging inside of him. He was not a person to back down.

Was that why she'd never defied him before? Because she'd known it was all but impossible to act outside of his will?

"I would not have come if it was not of the utmost importance," Axel added.

"Come," Felicity's mother patted the space beside her. "Just for a moment, Milton."

The room was silent but for the ticking clock on the mantel, which had to have gone on for some thirty seconds before her father nodded and then crossed the room.

Felicity lowered herself onto her seat, but Axel didn't join her until after her father was seated.

"Very well." Her father fingered the fob watch hanging from his jacket. "You have five minutes."

The air flew from Felicity's lungs because this was the moment she'd been dreading for weeks now.

"I need," Axel paused meaningfully, "I *need* to marry your daughter."

"I already told you—"

"I am not asking, my lord. It is of the greatest importance that I marry your daughter and, allow me to be perfectly clear; time is of the essence."

Axel took her hand in his, and Felicity was finally able to breathe. Her mother's mouth had fallen open, and her father, if anything, appeared even more enraged.

"I'll meet you on a field of honor, sir. How dare you take advantage of my daughter!"

"He did not take advantage of me!" Felicity decisively found her voice. Only... she couldn't expose what had transpired in the orangery, or how, or that she'd hardly known Axel before that. And yet, her parents would expect an explanation. "We fell in love months ago. After Westerley broke off the betrothal—*after you lost my betrothal in a game of cards—*"

she could not help but add, "I was so relieved, and Axel proposed, and well… It's not only that we have to get married, but that we want to. I cannot wait to spend the rest of my life with him."

Everyone in the room, it seemed, was stunned by her declaration. Perhaps Axel more than either of her parents. To emphasize her point, she lifted both their hands to her mouth, pressing a kiss to the back of his.

Axel cleared his voice. "Please, sir, your daughter will be distraught without your blessing."

"Is it true?" Her mother asked. "You are with child?"

Felicity could only nod. *Your daughter will be distraught without your blessing.*

She'd told him she wanted an actual wedding. He understood that her father was beyond overbearing, but he'd also known this was important to her.

"Hell and damnation." Her father slumped against the back of the settee. "I thought we taught her better than this," her father grumbled into his collar.

"You gambled away my betrothal, Father. How is that teaching me better?" She'd not ever challenged him on anything. "You built up a future for me and then threw it away with a turn of the cards."

And he'd never bothered to apologize for it. Felicity straightened her spine. *Yes,* she'd made a mistake, *yes* she was lying to him about having fallen in love, but…

He was not without fault, either.

"You told me Lord Crestwood belittled his son to you. But I am your *daughter,* and on more than one occasion, you've complimented my intellect, my talents, and my abilities. I am telling you that my, my *fiancé,* has impressed me with his intellect, his talents, and his abilities to no end. Lord Crestwood is wrong, and I have no concerns whatsoever that our..." heat crept up her neck, "our child will be born anything but perfect."

Axel shifted beside her, and she guessed that he did not like being discussed like this. She would not either if she was him, but she needed to set both her mother and father straight on this count right now.

"Why would Crestwood lie?" Her father directed the question to the man sitting beside her.

Axel exhaled and ran a hand through his hair. "I was born small. No one expected me to live. From what my governess told me, my twin sister, Cordelia, talked for both of us until I was nearly four." A tick pulsed at his jaw. "I struggled in school. However, I did graduate, and I assure you I am not simple. And you have my word that no one will take care of your daughter better than I intend to."

A most inconvenient heat pooled between Felicity's legs when she recalled how he had "taken care" of her earlier that afternoon.

Silence again. The clock ticking might as well be an active participant in this conversation.

Felicity squeezed Axel's hand. He was such a worthy person. He didn't deserve any of this.

"She has no dowry," her father finally grumbled. She'd suspected this but not been entirely sure. It wasn't the sort of information her father would be willing to share with her.

"Perhaps you and I can discuss the specifics in private?" Felicity stiffened, and this time, it was Axel who squeezed *her* hand.

Her father leaned forward, clasping his hands between his knees. "Very well." He pushed himself to stand. "In my study, Manningham."

Axel tightened her hand in his one last time before releasing it to rise as well. She nearly burst out laughing, however, when he turned his head and winked at her.

The worst was over.

In the wake of their departure, Felicity met her mother's eyes, which held a twinkle she hadn't expected.

"He'll get over it," her mother said. "It's not as though we waited before our nuptials."

Which, Felicity thought in horror, was not something she had ever wanted to hear.

"CHEROOT?" Lord Brightley opened a box and extracted two cigars without waiting for an answer. Mantis was no stranger to the habit—Chaswick was constantly introducing him to new blends.

"Thank you." He accepted it, willing to wait while the earl gathered his thoughts.

He, himself, was grateful to allow a few moments to pass while the earlier tension subsided.

Felicity had declared that the two of them had fallen in love even before Westerley broke off their engagement. She'd kissed Axel's hand and then defended him to her parents.

Even knowing the first part wasn't true, hearing her say those words had shaken him.

She liked him. She needed him. And she appreciated what he could do for her sexually, but he doubted someone like her could ever love him.

Because despite everything she'd told her father in that room, Mantis did not deserve her. A man who failed to garner his own father's respect and affection could hardly expect either from Felicity, a diamond of the first water.

Not when she was forced to defend his blasted intelligence.

"You are willing to marry her, even without a dowry?" Brightley had finally settled in behind his desk, the red in his face from earlier a considerably softer shade of pink.

"Absolutely," Mantis answered. "In fact," he leaned forward, "I am willing to pay off your vowels to do so."

The earl's brows rose. "What do you know of my vowels?"

"Enough."

"And you have the funds to do so?"

Mantis' father might hate him, but access to the Mannington-Tissinton estate ensured funds were never a problem. By residing at Crest House, limiting his gambling, and spurning the practice of keeping a mistress, he lived relatively frugally. Even with the expense of his project on the docks, he barely put a dent in even the interest most months.

In addition to all of that, his investments had proven more successful than he'd deigned ever to imagine.

"Would twenty-thousand pounds cover them?"

Brightley swallowed hard, staring at him from across the desk. "And then some. You love her."

"I do." The words came out sounding gruff.

Mantis ought to have realized this about himself before that moment. Because if he'd found any other woman in the orangery that night, he doubted the outcome would have been the same. Nor would he have been nearly so eager to put an end to his bachelorhood under such circumstances.

Because he wasn't the sort to randomly take advantage of distraught and innocent ladies.

Just Felicity.

If he didn't love her, he sure as hell was infatuated with her.

"I've listened to your explanation, but I still have questions. Why would a man spread such falsehoods about his own son?"

It was simple, but not something Mantis enjoyed acknowledging. "I have always been a disappointment to him. If not for the bravery of my mother's maid, he would have tossed me out with the rubbish. I was a feeble and pathetic infant, and every servant at Stonegate Manor knew he'd have preferred me to die. I did not."

"His disregard for you will affect my daughter… and your children."

"Something I will mitigate to the best of my abilities."

Lord Brightley's gaze remained pinned on Mantis. Lady Brightley had been correct. They were the same startling blue as Felicity's.

"Crestwood's opinion might change after he learns you've won Lady Felicity's hand." The earl suggested. "But if it doesn't, how do you plan to protect my daughter from his ill will?"

The prospect of garnering his father's respect caught Mantis unaware, igniting the slightest flicker of hope, and one he just as quickly doused before answering Brightley's question.

"We'll associate with them only when necessary—aside from my sister and my younger brother, of course." Cordelia would welcome Felicity with open arms. "In addition to being heir to the earldom, I've Tissinton Towers, my estate near Exeter. Being as Stonegate Manor, the Crestwood Country seat, is in Norfolk, avoiding them shouldn't be a problem."

"And when you and my daughter are in London…?"

"I'll rent a suitable townhouse for as long as necessary." No way in hell would he expose Felicity to his father's abuse.

Lord Brightley rubbed his chin, and then apparently coming to some decision, lifted his pen and opened a drawer. "Let's get this in writing, then."

~

SIGNED contract tucked safely into his pocket; Mantis followed Lord Brightley out of the study back to where they'd left the ladies a little over an hour before. Mantis had been given permission to make his proposal formally, even though he already had her answer.

There was no reason to argue with her father on this, and, more importantly, Mantis wanted to propose to her properly.

His swagger easy, rubbing his hands together, Brightley entered the room looking considerably more at ease.

Mantis met Felicity's gaze with a reassuring one of his own.

"Roberta," Lord Brightly addressed his wife. "Lord Manningham-Tissinton requires a moment alone with our daughter."

Lady Brightley grinned as she set her knitting aside. "But of course. But of course!"

Mantis thanked them both as they exited and then, most ironically, found himself beset by an attack of nerves.

Ridiculous.

"Do you wish to sit down?" Her voice posed a serious question. Should he sit beside her? Help her to her feet?

"No." He strode across the room and, for the second time that day, dropped to one knee before her. Only this time, instead of raising her skirts, he took her hands in his.

Meeting her gaze, his confidence wavered. She'd not wanted any man to marry her out of duty. Allowed the opportunity, in time, he would prove to her that his reasons went far beyond the notion of honor.

Marrying her simply felt… right.

"Will you make me the happiest of men? Will you marry me?" It didn't matter how they had arrived at this place, he would do this properly.

She was blinking and shaking her head side to side. "You don't have to do this."

"You don't want to marry me?"

"No, I mean, of course, I'm going to marry you. But you don't need to…" Her fingers tightened around his. "You said I was too good for you. But it's the opposite."

Mantis raised a finger to her lips, stopping her before she went any farther.

"A simple yes would suffice."

"Of course." She blinked away tears. "Yes. Would you believe that I never cry?"

"I've no reason to doubt such an assertion," he answered biting back a grin.

She cared about him. He didn't doubt that. She would be a perfect wife. And he would have her in his bed.

He clasped behind her neck and pulled her toward him. "I realize I'm not at all what you expected," he said, his face inches from hers. "But I'm going to kiss you anyway."

She wasn't crying. She wasn't upset. Mantis simply wanted to kiss his fiancée.

Her hands landed on his shoulders. Her mouth was on his. An unfamiliar possessiveness roared through him. His wife. His woman.

To have, to protect, to defend.

And to love.

By the time he released her, both of them were breathless.

"What kind of marriage will this be?" She touched her lips.

"What kind of marriage do you want it to be?" His question was a challenge. He stilled, waiting for her answer.

Because he knew exactly what he wanted.

"As real as it can be?" She captured her bottom lip with her teeth, a lip that was rosy and swollen and glistening. "I will be faithful to you. I didn't allow you much choice—"

"We will both be faithful." Anything else would destroy him.

With that settled, Mantis rose to stand, pulling her up to join him. "We can tell your parents that you are amenable to my offer."

"My mother is happy already. I can tell." Her hand was on his arm. No one had ever touched him the way she did—a casual brush seeking comfort, a soothing stroke to provide it.

"Will you allow me to drive you tomorrow?"

"I believe my father will allow that." The girl he'd known before ventured out in her teasing answer. "Will you have dinner this evening with your family?"

"Greystone is expecting me." Since he doubted he'd be allowed much time alone with his fiancée until after their wedding, touching base with his friends would have to fill the gaps.

"Will Lord Greystone's cousins be there? Lady Posy and Miss Faraday?" And then her eyes widened. "I'm not—I mean —" She stared at him, looking almost horrified. "I have no right to—"

"You have every right." He caught her mouth again, unable to help himself. And his heart leapt just a little, imagining that she might feel a fraction of the possessiveness he felt for her.

"And in answer to your question, I believe so. And they will be thrilled to hear of my engagement."

"You'll notify the papers."

"First thing in the morning."

"And your parents?"

"Are number two on my list of chores."

Sounds of footsteps approaching warned that they only had a few moments of privacy remaining. "Driving you will be my reward."

And before her parents could join them, he stole one more kiss.

SHE SAID YES

"*T*he Marquess is in his billiard room." Blackheart slipped into his butler persona like an actor playing a favored role.

"Alone?"

"Indeed, my lord."

Considering it was in his best interest that Blackheart fulfill the terms of the wager, Mantis kept himself from scoffing as he made his way down the familiar corridor and into the masculine abode.

Greystone glanced up before taking his shot, which he missed, and Blackheart picked up an abandoned cue and studied the table.

"Where is everyone?" Mantis asked. It was unusual for neither of the two Spencer brothers to be present, if not Chaswick, or Westerley, despite their recent marriages.

"Peter has taken up his apprenticeship with Sir Bickford-Crowden in Brighton." Greys folded his arms across his chest and scowled at Blackheart's perfect shot.

Ah yes, Mantis recalled hearing about the younger

Spencer's brother's opportunity to advance his career as a world-class cellist.

"Stone, Chaswick, and Westerley are tracking Lady Tabetha down. Gretna Green. She's run off with Culpepper."

"What the devil?" Culpepper, a duke, was also an ass. Caught up in his own affairs, Mantis had undoubtedly missed a good deal of goings-on.

"Don't ask." Greys' scowl deepened as Blackheart sunk another solid. "I don't imagine they'll be back for a few weeks."

The duke finished out the table, returned his stick to the shelf, and tipped a non-existent hat. "I'll leave the two of you now. Cook will want my approval of this evening's courses."

"She said yes," Mantis sauntered around the table, collecting the balls for another game. He was feeling particularly lucky that evening. "But even more importantly, so did her father."

Blackheart spun around, opening the door as he did so. "In that case, I'll bring up a case of Greystone's champagne."

"Excellent, old man," Greys chuckled. Once the door closed behind him, the marquess met Mantis' gaze. "I'm going to miss having such an excellent butler. He will be most difficult to replace."

"Do you think he'll endure the entire season?"

Greys allowed a slow smile—a slow, *sly* smile. "We'll see."

What the devil did the marquess mean by that?

Greys waved a hand. "So you won't be following Spencer and Westerley to Gretna Green?"

"Not at all." Mantis racked the balls and then stepped back, watching as Greys tossed a crown in the air.

"Heads," Mantis said automatically.

Heads it was.

"My fiancé wants a traditional church wedding." Felicity would have all pomp and circumstances. He lined up the cue and broke, resulting in a satisfying scatter with two striped balls dropping into corner pockets. "Banns are to be read at St. George's beginning this week."

Smirking, Mantis lined up his next shot.

"Brightley gave his blessing, eh?" Greys scowled as another striped ball dropped.

"With some inducements." Fourteen thousand, two hundred and fifty of them, to be exact. The Earl's debt hadn't been quite as large as Mantis had assumed, as it turned out. Brightley had insisted, however, that another twenty-five thousand be put in trust for Felicity and any children they had.

Mantis planned on fifty anyway.

"And what of your parents? Crestwood's reaction ought to be interesting."

"I'll tell them tomorrow morning." It would actually be the third item on his list. First, he would spar with Blackheart, then go to the papers, and then face his family—which was always an ambiguous proposition.

He looked forward to introducing Felicity to Cordelia, who would be happy for him. Louisa would enjoy planning the wedding, and Mantis only hoped she was considerate enough not to step on Lady Brightley's toes.

Which left his father.

Mantis never knew what to expect of the man who'd sired him. Would Crestwood be happy for him? Mantis doubted it.

Greys rubbed his chin. "Why interfere with your marriage prospects? Doesn't he realize it's his own lineage he's sabotaging? I've said this before, and it bears repeating. Crestwood is an ass."

Mantis ought to agree with his friend wholeheartedly. However, that particular ass also happened to be his father.

Feminine shuffling at the door effectively prevented Mantis from having to respond in one way or the other. Greystone's great Aunt Iris entered first, clutching Miss Violet Faraday's arm, with Lady Posy tucked in behind them.

Although at least thirty years of age, Miss Faraday, tall and elegant, with dark hair and olive skin, was a stunning-looking woman. Lady Posy, petite and curvy, might someday be equally as pretty in her own way if not for her lopsided spectacles and head of unruly ebony curls, which refused to be subdued in even the most severe chignon.

Greys and Mantis set their cues on the table. "Ladies."

"Manningham-Tissinton," the elderly lady nodded in Mantis' direction.

"My lady."

"Hello, Mantis," Miss Faraday dipped her chin.

"Brandy?" Greys lifted the decanter questioningly.

"Much appreciated."

"I'm starving," Lady Posy announced in general.

"In that case, dinner is served." Blackheart had silently arrived to stand in the doorway, a smirk on his ducal mouth as he glanced around the room. If Mantis didn't know better, he'd think the duke was teasing Grey's youngest cousin.

The evening could only have been more enjoyable if Felicity had been at his side.

After partaking of an extravagant ten-course dinner, excellent company, and copious amounts of champagne, Mantis and Greys reclined at the table to enjoy their port.

"I've been meaning to take my cousins to Vauxhall," Greys declared. "Might as well make it a celebration."

Mantis hadn't been to Vauxhall for a few years. "A private box?"

"What else?"

"Count me in."

"You're an attached gentleman now. Don't promise your time until after you've spoken with her. Who knows, she may have already made plans for the two of you?"

Mantis blinked.

He was an *engaged* man.

By god, he was getting married! Before he could so much as lift his glass, Blackheart appeared to refill it from over his shoulder.

Bloody duke was setting out to get him drunk.

"Dɪᴅ you enjoy your session this morning, my lord?" Cornell, the young valet Mantis hired at Blackheart's suggestion six years earlier, set aside the Hessian he'd just finished buffing to a high shine.

Not only was the man excellent at his profession, but he'd plenty of fighting experience as well.

Handy that was, having a valet who wasn't the grandfatherly type.

"I did." Although Blackheart had been on his toes and the two of them had split bouts.

"The new mats are to be delivered to the warehouse today. And two more boys have expressed interest in joining up."

"Excellent." Cornell often seemed as invested in the dock project as Mantis was. In fact, if Mantis and Felicity spent the summer at Tissinton Towers, he was going to have to hire himself a new valet.

Mantis struggled with one boot while Cornell assisted him with the other.

"Have the betrothal notices been sent to all the papers?"

"Delivered them myself."

All that was left now was his meeting downstairs this morning. Mantis tugged at his cravat.

"I'll only have to retie it," Cornell's voice halted him from loosening the knot altogether.

"Pigeon-liver'd loon." Mantis dropped his hand. "Wish me luck." He grimaced.

"Luck." Cornell pinched back a smile. "You loathsome boil." His valet was well-aware of the earl's animosity toward Mantis.

"Addlepated pizzle."

Cornell bit back a grin, and Mantis shook his head. Might as well get this over with.

He usually avoided the morning room this time of day, but it was as good a place as any to deliver his news.

He was marrying Lady Felicity Brightley.

Felicity.

The thought alone was enough to puff out his chest.

And yet another good sign when he nearly ran into his sister at the landing.

"My, but you look fine today. Don't tell me you're joining us this morning." She leaned forward and bussed him on the cheek.

"I am." He gestured for her to precede him down the stairs.

"I do wish you were around more often. I think Louisa might be softening him."

Even Louisa didn't have that kind of influence. "I don't know how you do it, Cordy." Only, he did. Because although their father wasn't thrilled that his daughter towered over him, he didn't hate her like he did his heir. "You're looking fetching yourself."

Mantis smiled at the pink creeping up the back of her neck. And yet, she wasn't so easily distracted. "What's the occasion? And don't tell me there isn't one because I know you better than that." Cordelia had always had the ability to read him. And since he would be telling them all anyway, he might as well practice on her.

"I'm engaged," he muttered.

"To be married?" She halted midway down the stairs to turn and gape at him.

"That's what the term usually implies, yes." But he couldn't help smiling at her because she appeared surprised, yes, almost stunned, but also happy for him.

"Who?" She whispered and glanced around. "No doubt someone whose father is unacquainted with Crestwood."

Even Cordelia knew? "What the devil is that about anyway?"

They resumed their descent until Cordelia pulled him aside at the landing. "I only became aware a few days ago."

Mantis scowled. "From who?"

"Father has mentioned his concerns to Miss Faraday. She's met you, of course, so she knew them to be patently untrue. She questioned me, though, in case you had set your sights on Greystone's younger cousin—the bouncy, curly one."

Mantis tensed and then relaxed his shoulders. His father's indiscretions wouldn't affect him much longer. And whatever his reasons were would be rendered moot by his and Felicity's engagement.

"Lady Posy is quite safe from me."

"Who, then?"

"Lady Felicity Brightley."

"Westerley's betrothed?"

"*Former* betrothed."

"That's right." Cordelia twisted her mouth into a familiar expression. Familiar because he recognized it from his own reflection. "I do hope she didn't agree only because Westerley jilted—"

"She did not." And since Felicity, herself, had resorted to claiming a love match for her parents' sake, Mantis added, "We've been in love for some time. Now that she's free, we wish to marry as soon as possible. Banns will be read beginning this Sunday."

Cordelia, of course, couldn't take his explanation at face value, and her expression held more than a trace of suspicion.

"You never mentioned her before."

"Of course I didn't. She was betrothed to one of my best friends." Handy explanation, really. And it made all of this so much easier.

Louisa appeared almost magically from the door to the servant's staircase.

"What a special treat this is. Let's go inside, shall we? Your father came down ten minutes ago."

She took a great deal of pride in managing the household going's on and would have, no doubt, wished to ensure breakfast was served precisely as his father liked it.

"Good morning, Louisa," Cordelia nodded. "After you."

Crestwood was already seated at the head of the table, his newspaper opened, an empty cup of tea at his elbow. Connor rarely took a meal with adults and would already be well into his studies in the nursery.

Cordelia and Louisa each took up a plate to fill at the sideboard. Mantis bided himself just inside the door, waiting for the ladies to be seated before finding his own.

"To what do we owe the honor of your presence, Manningham?"

Mantis supposed he ought to consider himself lucky his father acknowledged him at all.

He met Cordelia's gaze and then flicked it back to the one man in his life that he'd not once presumed to impress.

"The occasion of my pending nuptials. Lady Felicity Brightley has consented to become my wife in a little over three weeks."

The shattering of glass had everyone turning toward the sideboard where Louisa stood amongst the ruins of broken porcelain, eggs, toast, and jam. Mantis wasn't sure if her look of shock was from his announcement or the fact that she'd just broken a piece of two-hundred-year-old dishware.

"Take care of it," the earl snapped at the footmen, who'd frozen at the commotion. An uncomfortable silence settled in the room until both Cordelia and his father's wife were seated at the table.

Mantis remained standing.

"We received an invitation to dine with Lord and Lady Brightley just this morning. I imagine that's what this is about," Louisa offered before taking a delicate bite.

"How'd you manage to land such a piece as Brightley's chit? Knock her up?"

Mantis stiffened but remained impassive.

"We've held an affection for one another for some time now. Now that Lady Felicity is free, she's agreed to become my wife."

"So, she is not simply a friend," Louisa smiled. "How wonderful."

"When is this dinner?" His father cut in.

"Tomorrow evening." Louisa provided.

Mantis remembered Lady Brightley saying she would host his family to celebrate the pending nuptials and begin formalizing arrangements. Still, he hadn't realized she would initiate it so quickly.

"I imagine," Louisa met Mantis' father's stare, "Lady Brightley wishes to discuss wedding details. Three weeks, you say?" This to Mantis. "A church wedding then. How proper of you both."

"My fiancé is a very proper lady." As well as compassionate, exciting, beautiful, and all-around... breathtaking.

"You will accept the invitation." His father lifted his cup for one of the manservants to refill.

"Of course." Louisa sipped at her own tea. "I quite look forward to becoming better acquainted with your future in-laws, Manningham."

Mantis cringed. Because making pleasant conversation wasn't something his father had ever aspired to.

Being spared what promised to be a problematic evening would have made a trip to Gretna Green worth the trouble.

But Felicity wanted a proper wedding, and so a proper wedding she would have.

"Lord Brightley and my father are already acquainted," Mantis mentioned casually. Would his father admit to having warned the earl away from his own son?

"I was under the impression he and I understood one another." Ah, yes. His father knew to what Mantis alluded. "Apparently, I was wrong."

"And now, it is he and I who understand one another." Mantis locked his gaze with the earl.

He could ask his father why he'd been spreading such exaggerated falsehoods around town. He could ask him if he'd ever see fit to stop hating him.

But the answers weren't likely anything he wished to hear.

Besides, Mantis had won the lady's hand and her father's approval anyway. He'd won this round—perhaps it was the last one they'd play.

And Mantis had an appointment to drive his fiancée in the park in less than three hours on what promised to be a beautiful spring day.

With a single nod, he walked out of the room.

He had his entire life ahead of him. He refused to dwell on his father's animosities.

A PRANK?

"Did you sleep well?" Felicity didn't look as pale as she had recently, whether it was due to the sunshine, or the fresh air, or simply the excitement of riding through the park in a curricle, Mantis didn't care. All that mattered was the smile she sent his direction as he assisted her onto the seat, which was high up and barely wide enough for two people.

"I did, thank you."

He walked around the back and boarded with ease, settling himself beside her and not at all minding the close confines of the narrow bench.

Staring at her for a moment, Mantis found himself caught off guard by her beauty. So much so that he completely forgot what he'd intended to say.

"What?" She touched her hat self-consciously.

"You're beautiful." Cliché and trite, but it was true.

She dropped her gaze and a lovely pink blossomed like roses in her cheeks.

"Thank you." He barely heard her response. "The horses will get restless if we sit here much longer though."

She was right. Of course she was.

He wanted to kiss her but instead he signaled for the horses to pull them into the street.

She seemed nervous today. Was it because of what happened in the park?

"I apologize for making up that story about our courtship yesterday. But I realized I couldn't possibly tell my parents about the orangery..."

"So you haven't been madly in love with me for months?" he teased.

Of course, she had not.

"I just... I never intended... But. You seemed to understand. And... I just needed..." She stopped and cleared her throat.

"I did not take advantage of you, did I? Nor did you of me? It wasn't a conscious decision by either of us. It was what you needed, and what I wanted." He wasn't about to allow her to continue berating herself for it.

She jerked her head to turn and stare at him. "You did?"

"Of course I did." Had he not made this clear to her? "Just as I wanted to taste you yesterday." And now that his mind was going in this direction, his breeches were feeling unusually tight.

"But we are supposed to deny ourselves."

"Whose standards are you trying to live up to? If they are your own, that's one thing. Someone else's?" Mantis cocked a brow as he slid her a sideways glance. "Quite another."

"They are inherent in society. A person who fails to live up to them ceases to belong."

"So, as human beings, we adjust our behavior to reflect

standards set up arbitrarily by a small group of individuals so as not to be rejected?"

"That group may be small, but it consists of the most wealthy and powerful individuals in England, perhaps in the entire world. And it also consists of my closest friends. Society… is my world." Mantis wasn't sure if she was trying to convince herself or him.

He was one of the last persons in the world to embark on a philosophical discussion willingly. And yet when he turned into the park, rather than drive toward the road that would be densely populated so he could show her off, he headed in the opposite direction and then drew the horses to a halt.

"And yet you risked all of that with me, in Westerley's orangery. Why, Felicity?" He thought he knew. He'd thought it was simply because she'd felt dejected. But was it possible there was some other reason?

At first, it seemed she didn't—or wouldn't, rather—provide him with an answer. But just as he was about to turn the horses around, she did.

"Because I didn't care about what society wanted anymore —not in that moment." Her voice caught. "It betrayed me."

It… "Westerley?"

But she was shaking her head.

"Your father?"

She shook her head more adamantly. "The… rules. *Following the rules* betrayed me."

"And by being with me, you could… take your revenge? On the rules?"

"Yes." She exhaled. "Maybe."

Her ambiguous answer summoned Greys' words of wisdom on the road from Westerley Crossings—that women often failed to say what they meant. "Sex with me was your

157

way of lashing back at society," he chuffed. It wasn't a question.

"No!" Her hand covered his and she squeezed. "I wasn't thinking straight."

Neither had he. He refused to feel dejected.

"I cannot imagine I would have done... what we did... with any other person in the world. But it was you who took care of me. And because it was you, I was able to be utterly improper without worrying about..."

"About what?" Mantis held his breath.

She squirmed beside him.

"ABOUT..." Felicity closed her eyes, mortified at the dream she'd had the night before, and how it had made her feel when she woke up. "I'm not supposed to..."

"About what, Felicity?"

She dipped her chin and stared down at her hands, properly clasped in her lap, resting on her knees which were pressed together just as she'd been taught—with her ankles crossed and hidden in the material of her skirts.

"About liking it." Her voice was barely more than a whisper.

Only, she wasn't supposed to like it. She wasn't even supposed to think about liking it.

She'd had a little success making excuses for herself after the night in the orangery. Because she'd been jilted, she'd rationalized that she'd not been in her right mind.

But yesterday... in the park.

She couldn't make excuses for that. And she'd enjoyed it—too much!

She tensed all the muscles in her legs trying to ignore the liquid heat low in her belly.

"There's nothing wrong with liking it, Felicity." Even the warmth of his hand, low on her back, pricked her awareness.

Improper, utterly wanton awareness.

"Yesterday," she began.

He sat silently beside her and she wondered if his memory was as vivid, as all-encompassing as hers.

"You are a large man," she attempted to begin her explanation again.

The horses shifted but all of Axel's attention focused on her.

This was mortifying. Why would she tell him this?

"I pretended that I didn't have a choice… in my mind. And if I didn't have a choice, then… I could…"

"Experience your pleasure free from having to suffer any guilt?" There was no judgment in his question, in his accurate assumption.

"Yes." She squeezed her eyes tighter together.

She had imagined he'd carried her into the woods, tied her to that wooden bench, forced her knees apart, and ravished her despite several heartfelt protests. She'd had no choice but to lift her hips and writhe beneath his invading mouth. And when she'd grasped his hair between her fingers, it had been her last attempt to stop him.

All of it in vain, because he'd captured her, and could have his lecherous way with her.

Mantis' hand rested on her lower back. "So," his voice was gravelly. "If I were to drive you into the woods, bend you over a fallen tree, and lift your skirts to take you from behind…"

Felicity could hardly breathe for all the fiery sensations

elicited by his words. Her mouth went dry, and her heartbeats thundered in her ears.

A loud cracking sound pierced the air around them, and an insect whistled behind her.

"What the devil?" Axel glanced around as though searching for the origin of the noise. But the horses, which had been perfectly mannered until that moment, demanded all of his attention. Startled, one of them threw herself onto her hind legs and the other tucked her head and pawed at the ground.

"Get down, Felicity. And hold on." Mantis was on his feet gripping the reins.

"To what?" She dropped to her knees on the floorboard, her hands searched for anything other than the bench, which was thick and provided little friction to keep from slipping.

"To me."

She'd barely managed to reach an arm around one of his legs before the vehicle lurched into motion, carrying them wildly across the lawns.

Trusting that he could keep both of them safe, Felicity nonetheless squeezed her eyes closed, ducked her head, and sent up a silent prayer.

Because there was more to worry about than hers and Axel's safety. They had a baby to protect as well.

Quite conscious of the muscles straining in his legs, Felicity clung to him, quivering but also a little in awe as he issued stern commands to the horses from above. She ought to fear for their lives but a part of her marveled that he could sound so masterly and forgiving at the same time. She ought to be terrified, but Axel was in control. He would save them. He would protect them.

This man, the most underestimated Viscount Manningham-Tissinton, was anything but simple.

And just as quickly as the chaos erupted, the curricle slowed to a halt and all was silent.

"Are you all right?" Axel's hands were around her, lifting her onto the seat. "Are you hurt?" The concern in his voice was palpable.

"I'm fine. Are you?" Her own hands were sliding up his arms, over the sleeves of his jacket, searching for—what? A bullet? "Was that a gunshot?" Had someone just tried to kill them?

"You two all right up there?" A handful of gentlemen approached on horseback. The Marquess of Greystone, unmistakable in his fashionable apparel of a deep lilac jacket and matching top hat, arrived first. "Did you see where it came from?"

"I did not." Axel had turned and was peering behind them into the woods.

The steel in his voice sent a chill down her spine.

Lord Greystone removed his hat and ran a hand through thick, brown hair. Three other riders arrived as well. A few familiar faces...the Earl of Hawthorne, the Marquess of Rockingham, and yet another that she didn't recognize.

Axel was still gripping the tethers, his attention divided between the horses and the gentlemen who'd arrived to provide their assistance.

And all the while, he kept one hand on her knee as though to assure himself she was whole and safe.

"What idiot practices his shooting on this side of the park?" Rockingham glowered.

"A suicidal one, that's who." Greystone was already turning his horse. "Rockingham, take the west side. Hawthorn and I will investigate the east."

"If you find the blighter—" Axel began.

"Come by Knight House when you're finished," Greystone nodded. "Forgive me for racing away, my lady, but we've a dangerous idiot to subdue." He replaced his hat, tipped it in her direction, and then raced off behind the other men.

Felicity's heart slowly resumed beating at a normal rate.

It had been an accident. No one was trying to kill them.

Axel studied her. "You're sure you're all right?" He brushed a strand of hair away from her face and if she wasn't mistaken, his hand was shaking.

"Yes."

"And the baby?"

"Yes." She gave him a tremulous smile and after a moment, he exhaled a great sigh of relief.

"Blackheart recommended a midwife and a physician. Will you meet with each of them? Once you have a preference, we'll schedule an appointment for as soon as possible."

"I'm inclined to a midwife." She doubted her father had given her mother a choice. "But yes. I'd like to meet with them, too—so long as they are discreet."

"Of course." One of the horses tossed his head and Axel glanced around the park. "Best let these two walk it out. Do you trust me to get you home safely?"

"Absolutely." She doubted she'd ever trusted another person more. She settled onto the bench facing forward, one hand on the seat, the other clutching his arm.

The earlier intimacy between them was lost, but her comfort with him was not. "You spoke with your parents? I'm sorry about the dinner party. My mother sent her invitation without checking with me first. I had no idea how enthusiastic she would be." But she'd wondered how his father and stepmother would react. "Were they happy for you?"

She glanced sideways just in time to see his jaw tighten. So they were not. She was learning these little tells of his.

"They responded no worse than expected, but Cordelia is looking forward to meeting you. And I'm fine with the dinner." He grimaced, meeting her gaze with a sideways glance of his own. "I imagine such a gathering would have come up eventually."

"My mother wished to consult with Lady Crestwood on the wedding details. A breakfast at Bright Place, of course, but she is wishing to give your parents the opportunity to host the prewedding ball." She sighed. Normally, she would have been just as excited about such details herself, but... she seemed tired all the time and couldn't seem to thrum up much enthusiasm at all.

"Greystone is arranging an evening at Vauxhall." Axel sent her a glance. "Is that something you'd be interested in attending?"

"I'm always interested in Vauxhall," she sighed and leaned into him.

"In that case, we'll reward ourselves once we've survived dinner with our parents."

SURVIVING THE PARENTS

*T*wo nights later, Felicity met Axel's eyes from across the drawing room and shrugged. For all she'd dreaded the gathering between their two sets of parents, the evening had been surprisingly uneventful.

Axel cradled a snifter of amber liquid and leaned casually against the mantel, for all appearances, looking as though he was following their fathers' conversation. But he had a thoughtful expression in his eyes that told Felicity his mind was otherwise engaged.

While taking tea with her fiancé the day before, her mother had brought up the gunshot incident in the park. Her mother had heard about it from her lady's maid—who had heard it from another lady's maid who had been walking in the park that afternoon.

Mantis explained that although they hadn't caught the shooter, it had likely been nothing more than an accident. That was the logical conclusion. She hadn't any enemies, and he would have told her if he thought he had.

Wouldn't he?

"I know you are the prospective bride, but I'm fairly certain your presence is not required for any of this."

Lady Cordelia, Axel's sister, whispered beside Felicity, although whispering probably wasn't necessary. Because Lady Crestwood and Felicity's mother had all the wedding plans well in hand. Felicity liked Lady Cordelia enormously, and Axel had described her quite accurately—tall and noble but not at all unfeminine.

Felicity grinned at his sister's comment and then met Axel's gaze.

He winked, causing her grin to stretch even wider.

"I do believe my brother is happier than he's ever been." His sister unexpectedly reached over and squeezed Felicity's hand.

Had he been unhappy before? The unanswered question in her mind was a reminder that there was a great deal that she didn't know about him, and that they weren't, in fact, in love; they were only pretending to be for their parent's sakes.

Even if they were going to marry and his child was growing inside of her.

Felicity noticed the distance between Axel and his father. He regarded the earl with a sense of wariness, and his father occasionally glanced over at him with…disdain.

"We'll serve every delicacy imaginable at the prewedding ball." Lady Crestwood's voice carried across the room from where she jotted notes on a piece of parchment provided by Felicity's mother. "If we were in the country, we could have made a house-party of it. The gentlemen could have hunted fresh game, but we'll simply have to make do. I'll ensure Cook serves the richest meats. She makes this positively delightful parsley sauce. We'll have no less than a dozen courses—or perhaps fifteen. What are your thoughts, Lady Brightley?"

Felicity's mother leaned forward and covered Lady Crestwood's hand, a secretive smile dancing on her lips. "Nothing too rich, my lady. I do believe Felicity's condition has affected her constitution."

"Her..." Lady Crestwood froze, looking confused, and then cocked a brow. "Condition? What condition is that?"

Felicity's mother smiled secretly. "The one that has all of us anticipating a most exciting event come the holidays this year."

In that moment, the lighthearted mood of the evening devolved into something that was almost... insidious. Although Felicity had expected some scorn in that they'd acted outside of society's norms, she also expected his parents to show the slightest relief knowing the heir would waste no time in setting up his nursery.

They were going to be grandparents!

Felicity, the daughter, and only child of an earl, was well aware of the importance of these matters as one of her cousins, rather than a brother, looked to inherit her own father's title.

"Crestwood." Axel's stepmother's eyes narrowed as she garnered her husband's attention. "Were you aware of the circumstances surrounding this betrothal? That *Lady Felicity* is... not quite the genteel lady we took her for?" The woman cocked a brow. "No offense meant, of course."

Felicity ignored the insult in order to watch for the Earl of Crestwood's response.

The muscles in his jaw ticked ever so slightly and his fists were clenched, surprisingly reminding her of Axel. But his eyes, darker than his son's, were cold and hard as they stared back at Lady Crestwood. Had the earl turned somewhat grey at the news?

"I was not."

Axel had pushed away from the mantel. "Lady Felicity is, and always will be, a lady. Louisa, you will apologize at once." His eyes blazed and Felicity could almost feel the anger rolling off him.

On her behalf. But she had no wish to be the reason for any discord between their two families. "No. It's fine—"

"I refuse to allow anyone to speak thusly of my daughter. Most certainly not in my own home." Her own father stepped forward as well.

"But by definition, a lady would not…" As though entering a battle, Lady Crestwood rose from where she'd been sitting. "Find herself in such circumstances."

"Louisa," Axel warned.

"It is true that she is with child." This from Felicity's father. "But casting insults on my daughter's reputation will only harm both our family names."

But, being that she was the woman involved, Felicity knew it would taint her family more than Axel's.

"You are pleased with this turn of events?" Crestwood chortled, astonished.

"I'll not have my daughter insulted in my own house."

Axel's mouth pinched so tightly that his lips were almost white. Sensing that he was about to attack his father physically, Felicity rose and all but lunged to grasp his arm.

"It's not an insult to call a woman a whore if it's true," Lord Crestwood said.

Felicity tightened her hands around Axel's bicep at the same time her mother clutched Lord Brightley's.

"Now, now. I understand the two of you are somewhat taken aback by this wonderful news!" Felicity's mother's voice sounded cheerful despite the brawl that threatened to break out in her drawing room. "And as they are in love, and planning to marry in a few weeks, this isn't something to fret about." She turned to Lady Crestwood. "They certainly won't be the first couple in the ton to give birth to a perfectly normal-sized seven-month baby."

"Your succession is likely to be assured before year's end, Father. Surely you must be grateful for that." Cordelia joined Felicity's mother in doing what she could to deescalate the stand-off taking place. She met Felicity's stare with a sympathetic one before turning to their stepmother. "Given time, both of you will realize what wonderful news this is."

Which finally drew an assenting nod from Axel's father.

As the tension slowly ebbed out of the room, Felicity's father's fists unclenched, and her mother drew in a deep breath.

But beneath her hand, the muscles in Axel's arm remained taut.

"You will apologize to my fiancée." His eyes narrowed as he glared at Lord Crestwood and Felicity couldn't help but shiver. Normally, Axel's size wasn't intimidating, but having caught a glimpse of his temper at the park, she was coming to believe a warrior lurked beneath the façade of what most believed to be a gentle giant. "Or meet me on the field of honor."

He would challenge his own father over her. "But, no!" She turned, intent upon imploring him not to.

"He didn't mean anything by it, did you, Father?" Lady Cordelia stepped in once again. "Did you, Father? You were simply taken by surprise."

The room itself seemed to be holding its breath until the Earl nodded. "My apologies, Lady Felicity."

A whore.

He'd called her *a whore*. And for what? For lashing back at the rules which had failed her? Felicity dipped her chin. Of course, she would forgive him. He was Axel's father.

Nonetheless, Felicity fought the numbness creeping over her. *Lord Crestwood had called her a whore.* The cold feeling spread from her fingers, up her arms, and around her chest.

He wasn't entirely wrong. Axel had kissed her, but only because she'd practically thrown herself at him. And then she'd all but begged him...

"We'd best be on our way. My thanks for a delightful evening. Send me your list to invite to the ball, and I'll do the same for the breakfast." Lady Crestwood moved toward the door, her rouge-colored lips trembling despite her bravado. "Come, Cordelia dear, Crestwood."

Felicity didn't move but instead remained clutching Axel while her parents escorted his family downstairs to the foyer. Only when their voices disappeared did either of them move when Axel shook his head as though escaping an unexpected fog.

"I'll kill him."

"No. Oh, Axel. I'm so sorry."

"You have done nothing wrong. I'm the one who's sorry." He took hold of her hands. "I'm accustomed to his derision but he'll never again speak to you in such a manner."

But she had lain with a man that she hardly knew... and the things Axel had done to her in the woods. The most frightening thing she realized in all of this was that ... She wanted more. More of his touch. More of his mouth. Just...

More.

"Do you think that I am—?"

"No." He raised her hands to his lips. "Never."

For the past few days, they had pretended to be in love.

She knew he cared for her, he'd done nothing but treat her with affection since... since the moment he'd discovered her trapped in the thorns.

"How are you?" His softly spoken question slowed her heart.

He'd ask her this periodically now, looking protective and gentle, but also fierce. "Will you be up to Vauxhall in two nights' time?"

"Oh, yes!" She was grateful for something else to discuss. "I'm quite looking forward to it." There would be no parents on hand to embarrass her, or to harass him. The Marquess of Greystone had arranged for an elderly cousin to attend as chaperone. Lady Posy and Lady Cordelia would be there as well.

Since both Bethany and Tabetha had yet to have returned to London, Felicity was grateful to have met Lady Cordelia and was looking forward to acquainting herself with Lord Greystone's distant cousins.

Because, of course, Axel had not been courting the younger one. She was embarrassed that she'd allowed herself to be bothered by the idea.

"At least tonight is over." Axel pulled her into a warm embrace, and she rested her cheek against his chest. When had his arms become such a place of refuge?

He dropped a kiss on the top of her head, and even such an innocent gesture sent a flood of heat to her core. When had she become so wanton?

She had even told Axel how much she'd liked it, and why she'd been able to like it, but he didn't know the worst of it. He didn't know the thoughts she'd had while lying in bed the night before, or how she'd touched herself while imagining it was—

Whore. The word echoed in her head and she drew back.

She'd quite forgotten who she was: a proper lady, a woman of breeding and culture. Banns had been read the day before and they would marry in just under three weeks.

Axel tipped her chin up and studied her, his gaze shifting slightly as he searched hers. And then he stroked a fingertip just below her eyes.

"You aren't sleeping well."

"I'm fine." She could not tell him what it was that had kept her awake the night before. In that moment, the weight of the evening fell like a giant stone on her shoulders. "I just want all of this to be over with."

"Soon." He touched his lips to hers. Nothing like what she wanted. Not nearly enough. "I wish I could help you sleep. You had no trouble in the park two days ago."

"Please, don't tease."

"I'm not." He tightened his arms around her. "I would help you sleep if I could."

Felicity laughed weakly.

"I am quite looking forward to escorting you and Cordelia shopping tomorrow afternoon," he reminded her.

"I like your sister."

"Louisa will come around as well."

Hearing her parents returning, Axel released her a moment before her father appeared in the doorway, looking grim with more than a single line of worry etching his brow.

Even her mother's eyes showed unfamiliar concern. She met Felicity's stare apologetically. "I'm terribly sorry for mentioning it. I thought they knew."

Felicity, herself, hadn't bothered to verify what her fiancé had told his parents. Why would her mother not make such an assumption?

"My fault, my lady." Axel, being Axel, would put her mother at ease. "And please accept my apology for this."

"You were not the person to blame," Felicity's father ground out before glancing in her mother's direction. "Nor are you, my dear."

"But it is over." Felicity didn't want to talk about this anymore. All she wanted was to put it behind them and curl up beneath her covers. Because those people were going to become her in-laws. Axel had said they would not live on the family estate but when two people married, families joined. She was not going to be able to avoid them forever.

The thought was an exhausting one.

"In that case," Axel straightened. "I'll see myself out so that Lady Felicity can have a well-needed rest." He was always thinking of her. He'd told her he wasn't good enough for her, but Felicity had long since decided it was the other way around. "Lady Brightley, my thanks for a delightful meal."

"Mantis?" Felicity's father broke in.

"Yes, my lord?"

"My door is open if you need it."

Felicity glanced between the two most important men in her life. The offer was an unusual one for her father to make, but Axel didn't seem at all confused by it.

"I appreciate that."

And after dropping a bow in her mother's direction and a chaste kiss on Felicity's cheek, he disappeared down the stairs and into the night.

An emptiness settled around her heart at his departure, and she was forced to acknowledge the truth of her own thoughts mere seconds before.

Axel Lupton, the Viscount Manningham-Tissinton, had

indeed become one of the most important people in her life—if not, in fact, the most important.

He was her child's father. He was the last person she thought of before falling asleep and the first person in her mind when she awoke.

Westerley, and the anemic emotions she'd felt for him, had been relegated to the distant past.

Axel was her today—her now.

Him and her child. They were her future.

CANCELLED PLANS

*L*ying in bed the following day, Felicity was already
awake when Susan opened the drapes to allow the
morning sunshine to flood the familiar chamber.

It was a new day. She was fortunate enough to have a tiny
baby in her belly and she was going shopping with her fiancé
and his sister that afternoon.

All of these ought to have been enough to chase away the
concerns that had plagued her the night before.

The clock on the mantel showed it was almost noon. Axel
was going to collect her in just over two hours. She sat up and
stretched, happy to note the dreadful sickness she'd experienced regularly for two months now was gloriously absent.

And she was hungry. She wanted pastries and eggs and
meats. "Jonquil," she announced. "I think the jonquil muslin
will be perfect for today. The viscount is taking me shopping
on Bond street and I do believe I'm going to insist upon ices at
Gunter's afterward." She slid off the bed. "Or perhaps before-
hand. I'm starving today, Susan."

Her maid moved to the bell pull and tugged. "Cook will be

happy you're interested in more than toast and jam. And I'd much rather have food brought up than a second chamber pot," Susan grinned.

"Likewise. I'm sorry I've been so difficult lately." Felicity stared at herself in the looking glass, pleased that the circles Axel had pointed out the night before were less visible. "Tissinton Towers, the viscount's estate, is near Exeter. Axel has suggested that we might forgo the remainder of the season and go there right after the wedding. You do wish to come with me, don't you?"

Susan had been her maid since the day her governess departed when she'd turned ten and six, and she could hardly imagine finding anyone else.

"My place is with you, my lady, and it always will be. But I am glad to hear we'll not be taking up residence with your betrothed's family," Susan mumbled the last part.

A cold shiver slid down Felicity's spine at the mention of Axel's parents. "The servants heard about it?"

"Smithy and Peters were at the door. Is it true the viscount nearly challenged his father? Pardon me if I'm overstepping. It cannot have been a pleasant situation for you and Lady Brightley."

"It was horrible," Felicity shivered, holding her braid so Susan could untie the strings at the back of her night rail. "And yes, he would have. If not for Lady Cordelia, I can't imagine any other outcome."

"Lord Crestwood should not have insulted my lady like he did, even if he is an earl."

"But I—"

"You are a lady through and through. You have always been a lady and there is nothing in the world that will ever change that."

Felicity appreciated her maid's loyalty. Especially in light of what Susan knew—which was essentially everything. She'd likely even guessed to some extent the nature of what had occurred on that bench in the woods.

"I hope you are right," Felicity sighed. *A whore.* Her fiancé's father had called her a whore. "I didn't think parents like Lord and Lady Crestwood existed."

"They do seem rather unpleasant, don't they?" Susan helped Felicity step into her corset, working it over her hips. Gripping the bedpost for support, Felicity wondered how much longer before she'd require larger undergarments. "Will Madam Chantal notice, do you think?" Somehow, Felicity doubted she could fool the renowned modiste for very long. The stout little French woman knew most of her clients' measurements by heart. Of course, she would suspect Felicity's condition when those measurements began to change.

"She will know. I've already let out the bodice of your evergreen silk." Felicity exhaled as the laces tightened and then glanced down at what she'd always considered to be a somewhat modest bosom. Her breasts were unusually sensitive, and, she cupped her hand around one of them, yes, they were also more prominent.

Lately, it seemed, her entire body was extraordinarily sensitive.

In between dressing, a tray of food arrived, and Felicity consumed more than she had in some time, then went back to dressing.

Her fiancé would be arriving soon, and she would be dressed and ready when he arrived. Even though it was expected of a lady, she had absolutely no interest whatsoever in making him wait.

"Are you quite certain I'm not dead?" Mantis collapsed face-down on his bed. He'd never felt this sick in all his life.

"I'm fairly certain you yet live," Cornell answered.

Sometime just before sundown, after a less than restful night, Mantis had expelled the very last contents of his stomach. The ensuing violent heaving, however, had him wishing himself unconscious.

"No one else is ill?" he asked his valet again, thinking he must have eaten something that had turned. If that was the case, Felicity could be ill as well.

"Not since the last time I checked. I asked Mr. Mortimer to inform me at once if anyone else fell ill."

Mr. Mortimer was his father's butler. Mantis needed to know about the Brightley household. "Check on my fiancée." He barely managed to get the words out.

Perspiration broke out on his forehead even as an icy chill swept through him. Cornell pulled up the counterpane. "I'll send a manservant."

"She's expecting me today." As much as Mantis wished to be with her, he could barely manage to sit upright, let alone squire them around the shops. Damn it. This would be the second time he failed to meet her as promised. "Send my apologies."

What the hell had he eaten? Even on those occasions when he'd drunk himself stupid, he'd never felt this wretched.

"I've also sent for a physician." Cornell tucked the cover around Mantis' shoulders. Ridiculous for a grown man to huddle in bed like this.

"Send my apologies..." Had he said that already? "Bond Street shopping."

"Of course. I'll make certain she knows. Perhaps after you've slept you could scribble her a personal note, my lord."

My Lord, not ape-witted grunt, or addlepated skinflint. Was that apprehension in his valet's voice? "Next time you wake, you can try keeping some tea down."

His last attempt at swallowing anything had ended most unfortunately. Mantis didn't nod, only mumbled.

Nothing to worry about. This would pass—*damn his eyes*. Mantis wasn't about to allow a little food poisoning to result in his untimely demise. He would sleep it off.

Felicity and their child needed him.

Mantis was going to be a father and a husband. Furthermore, tomorrow he'd escort her to Vauxhall where he would dance with her and then take her walking on one of the darker paths.

Perhaps he would whisper that he was kidnapping her and then ravish her against a tree... He fell into a restless sleep, a sleep in which his dreams felt like nightmares and nightmares like death.

"If he doesn't improve by morning, I'll bleed him." Mantis woke to an unfamiliar voice speaking over him. "But he's no longer burning up."

"Like a damn horse, he is." This voice, his father's. "Bleed him anyway."

Of course, his father would presume to know more than a physician. Mantis forced his eyes to open. Darkness had fallen and a single branch of candles cast tall shadows on the wall.

His head still ached, and his body hurt all over, but, he pushed himself up to sit, his stomach wasn't burning.

"I'm fine." Although his mouth felt like a desert. "Water."

"A good sign, my lord." Mantis opened his eyes and recognized a doctor who had attended to his younger half-brother. Poor Conner fell ill at least once a year.

His father crossed the room and poured out a drink from Mantis' private decanter. "This will get you moving."

Mantis was already shaking his head. "God, no. Water, I think. And toast."

"Right here." Cornell, who'd been hovering near the door, leaped into action. Judging by the looks of his valet, the man had not had an easy time of it either.

The physician, meanwhile, was opening a satchel that revealed a collection of treacherous-looking instruments.

"I'm good thanks. Put those things away." Mantis didn't put much stock in the practice. On the few occasions he'd witnessed it, the patient had seemed weaker after the treatment than before.

"Afraid to be cut?" His father's gaze flicked to Mantis' face with a sneer. "I'm not sure we've a drawer big enough for you in the family vault."

"Not when it isn't necessary. Although I thank you for your kind consideration." Nothing unusual in any of this. Why had he remained under the same roof as his father for so long? He'd been kidding himself hoping to earn the man's approval.

Would it be worth his trouble to look into a boarding room for his remaining weeks in London?

Cornell ushered the doctor out, thanking him and promising he'd call if his lordship took a turn for the worse.

Mantis downed the water in two swallows. "If you allow them to bleed me, consider yourself sacked." The threat was an empty one, but just in case his father saw fit to bring the physician in a second time, he'd make his wishes perfectly clear.

Even if it put Cornell in a difficult situation.

But his valet seemed to agree. "It's a senseless treatment," he said.

"Lady Felicity?"

"You're the only person who took ill, my lord. She sent word back earlier this afternoon. Right here, in fact." Cornell handed over a small envelope, recognizing the same pretty handwriting from the missive she'd sent before. Just a few days ago, but so much had changed since then. The hint of her perfume teased him as he tore it open.

Moving the candelabra closer, he studied the words on the page.

Dearest Axel,

I'm dreadfully disappointed to be denied your company this afternoon, but our outing is not worth risking your health. Please send word tomorrow if you are not greatly improved. Vauxhall isn't going anywhere.

Regardless, I will count the hours until I see you again.

Yours,

Felicity

I WILL COUNT *the hours until I see you again.*

He read the words three times over until deciding that she must have added the last part in the event someone other than he was to read it.

Because the narrative was that they were in love.

Even so, the words elicited a humming feeling in his heart.

Yours.

In three weeks' time, she would be just that—his. Even in his weakened condition, that buzzing, tingling sensation moved from his heart to his lower regions.

If the physician returned to bleed him, Mantis doubted he'd have any success. All the blood seemed to have gone to his cock.

And on that thought, Mantis brushed a hand down his face, too weak to laugh at his own joke.

"What should I do about tomorrow's lessons? I considered posting a sign but none of those urchins can read." Cornell handed Mantis a plate that held a single slice of bread.

"Blast and damn." Not fulfilling his obligations wasn't something he wanted to teach his little charges. "Why don't you fill in for me?"

Cornell frowned. "Who'll protect you from the leaches?"

"I think I can manage to protect myself." He'd already disappointed his betrothed. "I can always lock myself in here." He spoke the words in jest but didn't expect the spidery sensation that trailed down his spine. "Just be back in time to help me dress for Vauxhall." He'd be damned if he stood her up again.

He was going to have to give Cornell another raise. Before years end, it was likely his valet would be the highest paid in all of England.

Exhausted, Mantis was asleep almost before his head hit the pillow again.

SOMETHING'S OFF

"*Y*ou look like death." Blackheart didn't hold back when he opened the door for Mantis and Cordelia, who was joining them for this evening's festivities.

"Why thank you, *Your Grace*." Mantis didn't even try to keep the sarcasm out of his voice. Even before these butler tomfooleries, he doubted any of them had "Your Graced" Blackheart in over a decade. Not that they didn't respect him, rather the opposite really.

Because the man behind the title, the person, was so much more than your run-of-the-mill duke.

Blackheart held the door wide with a flourish. The plan was for Mantis, Cordelia, Greystone, as well as the two cousins, to collect Felicity from her home and then ride the boat over to the pleasure gardens, where they would meet up with the rest of their party.

Breathless after climbing a simple flight of stairs, Mantis cursed his recent malady.

"You ought to be in bed," Cordelia scolded as she turned around to watch him.

"I'm fine," he answered, determined not to disappoint his fiancée on what was planned to be a most enjoyable evening.

The stomach upset was gone. He could endure the residual aches and weakness.

"I'm going upstairs." Cordelia was already halfway up another flight of stairs. "Miss Faraday said she wanted to try something new with my hair."

"First door on your left," Blackheart instructed her from behind them.

"Don't take too long," Mantis added. He was happy for his sister to enjoy some female company but was determined to arrive on time to collect Felicity. He'd drive to Bright Place on his own if necessary.

"Good God, what happened to you?" Greys' greeting as Mantis stepped inside the drawing room was no less encouraging than his butler's had been. Blackheart followed him inside and made no move to return to his post.

Mantis waved the question off. All he cared about was seeing Felicity, even if he wasn't really feeling up to a night of revelry.

"Ate something bad." The memory of the violent retching sent a tremor through him.

"When was this?" Blackheart asked.

Last night? The night before? Where had he been? A simple question and yet Mantis' brain struggled to isolate an answer. He hadn't meditated or sparred in two days and that was often the result. Too many thoughts in his head.

"Two nights ago. Dinner at Bright Place. With my parents," he added. "Not the most enjoyable evening I've spent, but a man does what a man must do."

"I thought Brightley had come around."

"He has." More than Mantis could have hoped for, in fact. "The evening was ruined by Crestwood and his wife." Admissions such as this made it difficult to refer to his father by anything other than his title. "My father quite lived up to my expectations."

He had only inferred the nature of Felicity's condition to Blackheart, and he presumed Greystone had guessed. Still, Mantis wasn't willing to openly discuss the details of such a sensitive situation.

Although...

In light of a brush with his own mortality, it might be best to have two of the people he trusted more than anyone else informed of his current circumstances.

"A gathering of the future in-laws. Can't say I'm sorry I wasn't invited." Greys crossed one leg over the other. For tonight's festivities, the marquess's evening wear went beyond the height of fashion. Elaborate lace peeked out from the sleeves of his emerald velvet jacket, and matching trousers and a mint green waistcoat rounded out the ensemble. Despite the ostentatious choice of eveningwear, Greys appeared perfectly elegant and at ease in his masculinity.

Mantis ran a hand through his hair. "Lady Felicity's parents were aware of her condition, but mine were not. At the end of the evening, Lady Brightley allowed it to slip and my father..." *had called his fiancée a whore* "and his wife did not take it well."

Blackheart stepped sideways and closed the door.

When he turned around, his expression reminded Mantis of one of the exotic cats he'd once observed at The Royal Menagerie. "What did Crestwood say?"

Mantis couldn't repeat it. "He disparaged Felicity, but when I challenged him, he backed down."

Greys had leaned forward in his chair, looking more alert as well.

"An earl learns his heir is setting up his nursery earlier than anticipated and he is *unhappy* about that? It's not as though Crestwood has ever been a stickler about upholding societal standards."

Blackheart stared at Mantis as though working some sort of mental puzzle.

"Nothing I do satisfies him." Mantis' own words struck him like a sword. But it was true. And it was high time he stopped trying. "Aside from that, I don't know what the hell is going on." And then he finally voiced that which troubled him the most. "Is it possible someone intentionally poisoned me? Was the shot in the park really an accident?" He allowed himself to utter all the questions that plagued him while he lay in his bed. It hadn't helped that he'd felt too weak to do anything about it.

"If something happens to me before my wedding, I need to know one of you will ensure Felicity's protected."

"Of course," Greys answered immediately, and Blackheart dipped his chin in agreement.

"But I've no intention of losing one of my oldest friends to an unfortunate accident mere days before his wedding." Blackheart planted his feet wide, hands clasped behind his back. "My Lord," he turned to Greys. "It seems I might be absent from my post this evening."

Greys shifted his attention to their ducal friend. "You don't say, Mr. Cockfield?"

"I have a friend in need of assistance."

Mantis exhaled. He, too, had realized that the chaos of

Vauxhall would be the perfect setting for another attempt—if, in fact there was some insidious plot behind the recent events. Having Blackheart and whatever resources he chose to put into place milling about couldn't hurt.

"Chaswick is returned from their flight to Gretna Green. He and his baroness will be joining us this evening as well," Greys provided. "Westerley and Spencer are back in town but have other matters to attend to."

"Excellent," Mantis said. With four of them present, he could almost trust the evening to be uneventful.

Shuffling outside the closed door, and then Lady Posy's voice interrupted their discussion.

"Must I go? Really?"

"Vauxhall is nothing like the garden parties and balls. Trust me. You cannot help but enjoy yourself there."

"I don't see how—"

Miss Violet's shushing sounds carried from behind the door, followed by Cordelia's laughter.

Before they could knock, Blackheart held it open and gestured for the ladies to enter. Greys and Mantis rose in deference to their arrival but also in anticipation of making their departure.

Mantis, perhaps, showing more impatience than the others. Because they could finally leave to collect Felicity.

Even though Felicity had anticipated the evening, Axel's appearance had her wondering if they shouldn't have perhaps postponed the outing. His normally robust complexion lacked color, and the steps he took were slower than usual—almost cautious.

How did he still manage to look more handsome than every other gentleman in London?

She didn't make her opinion known, however, when Cordelia, Lord Greystone, and his cousins followed them inside.

Instead, she greeted the arrivals, complimenting the ladies' dresses, accepting their compliments in turn, and then pondered what sort of wrap to bring. When the marquess insisted the evening promised to be a warm one, with everyone in agreement, Felicity sent Mr. Michaels to collect the silk cloak Susan would have had ready.

The gold material perfectly complimented the deep red of her gown—one which she would never wear to any official ton event but had dared to bring out for the Vauxhall excursion.

Vauxhall was the only place in London, it seemed, where proper ladies and gentlemen were practically encouraged to ignore a few of society's proprieties.

Furthermore, she and Susan had reasoned, the cut of this particular gown ensured that it wouldn't fit her much longer.

With transparent puffed sleeves, the gown allowed for an almost indecent amount of cleavage if not for the fichu Felicity had decided upon. The scarlet silk material hugged her bosom and ribcage and then flared out just below her waist. The moment Mr. Michaels opened the door, a breeze swirled the fabric around her legs.

"I don't understand how you manage to look more beautiful every time I see you. But tonight, Felicity, you have outdone yourself." Axel offered his arm for escort and they made their way outside to Lord Greystone's carriage.

If his almost poetic compliment wasn't enough, the appreciative look in her betrothed's eyes deemed Susan's efforts worthwhile. In the past, she'd dressed to please the members of society, but this gown had been purchased to please herself. That it also pleased her future husband sent an excited shiver dancing down her spine.

The look she saw in his eyes when she turned to thank him stole her breath. She had seen that look in his gaze before, just before he'd dipped his head and—

"Positively stunning." The tip of his tongue wet his lips.

This close, she could make out the individual whiskers around his mouth, and the thick fringe of lashes framing his hazel eyes, and... an almost imperceptible sheen of perspiration on his brow and upper lip.

"You are still unwell," she whispered as they waited for the marquess and one of his outriders to assist the other ladies into the luxurious carriage. "You ought to be in bed."

"I look worse than I feel." The warmth of his breath caressed her cheek when he half-growled his response.

She only wished the tiredness around his eyes didn't contradict his claim.

"*How are you?*" he asked.

She had quite missed the tenderly spoken question. He had only come tonight because of her.

Which gave her an idea.

He was obviously unwilling to take the evening to rest for himself but would undoubtedly make accommodations if she claimed to grow weary. She would simply cut the evening short by offering a complaint on her own behalf.

"I am a little tired," she answered, punctuating her admission with a soft sigh. She'd wait until after supper, and perhaps a dance or two, to request they make an early evening of it. But first, she simply wanted to be with him. When he'd sent word that he was ill, all she'd wanted to do was go to him.

She'd wanted to sooth his brow and sit at his side. She'd wanted to return some of the comfort he'd provided her in the past.

"Tell me when you've had enough." His arm felt strong beneath her hand. *She had missed him.* "And I'll escort you home."

Over the past two months, he'd proven to be steadfast over and over again. His physical strength was only rivaled by the steel of his character. Until she'd received the message that he was too ill to escort them shopping, she hadn't truly considered that he could ever be vulnerable.

And tonight, despite not being fully recovered, he had come anyway. How ill must he have been to have cried off?

The realization, the reminder that he was not invincible, was a sobering one.

Because not only did she need him, as the father of her child, but also, she... simply needed him!

"You are looking far too serious for a lady *en route* to the pleasure gardens," Lord Greystone commented after they were all seated. Felicity, Posy, and Cordelia shared the front-facing bench and the Marquess, his older cousin, and Axel shared the opposite.

Felicity summoned her smile. "I've been looking forward to this outing all afternoon. Thank you so much for including me."

"As one of the guests of honor, I'd be more than remiss not to have. I'm more than happy to celebrate the betrothal of my good friend to one of London's most sought-after ladies."

At such an over-the-top compliment, Felicity couldn't help but smile. "I am the lucky one." She met Axel's eyes, feeling a need to convey her sincerity. Because she was, in fact, very, very lucky.

What if some other man had found her in the thorn bush that night? She dismissed the thought as quickly as it came. Because...

Going through all of this with anyone but Axel was unthinkable.

"Have you been to Vauxhall, my lady?" Lady Posy asked from beside her.

"Please, call me Felicity." Vauxhall was not a place to be formal and in a matter of minutes, the ladies were all on a first-name basis with one another. Felicity told a few stories of previous trips she'd made to the pleasure gardens, and her excitement grew as she embellished on the romance of the setting. Because most of all, she remembered the almost surreal lowering of inhibitions that, matched with the general excitement of the prospect of fireworks at the end of the night and the free-flowing champagne, left one feeling that anything was possible.

She and Axel would dance together for the very first time, and for no reason that she understood, it seemed more appropriate that they do so away from the eyes of the ton.

His gaze caught hers from across the carriage. Was he imagining the same? Holding her in his arms, twirling her beneath the night sky filled with stars overhead? She pressed her thighs together when she dared imagine being alone with him again.

Their courtship had been quite unconventional up until tonight and she saw no reason for it to change now.

Was that what this was? A courtship?

She held his stare for as long as she dared. Already her blood was thrumming through her veins. Felicity shifted uncomfortably in her seat.

Ten minutes later, standing beside him on the barge,

floating across to the island, that familiar magic settled over them like a gentle caress.

Never, in all her years as Westerley's intended, had she felt so protected, so *cherished.*

A cool breeze stirred the air, and when the boat lurched, he steadied her instantly.

Stepping onto dry land, Axel's hand at her back, Felicity could forget all the unpleasantness behind them. She forgot about his illness, his father's insults, and even the wait between now and their coming nuptials—because the air was sweet and soft, and the evening promised romance and indulgence.

The evening couldn't be any more perfect, she thought, until they rounded the corner to the entrance to the private box reserved by Lord Greystone. Both Bethany and Lord Chaswick sprang to their feet to greet them, and Felicity couldn't quite hold back a squeal of delight.

"You are back!" Only a few weeks had passed since Felicity had last seen her dear friend, but so much had happened in that time, making it feel like she'd not seen her for years!

"I have so much to tell you!" Bethany drew her into an exuberant embrace until, catching herself, she stepped back. Etiquette required introductions be made all around.

Having been raised in society, almost right alongside Felicity, manners took over in both. While enjoying the thinly sliced ham, strawberries, and champagne, they enjoyed the first part of the evening becoming better acquainted with the other ladies. Despite an occasional stern glance toward Lady Posy, Miss Faraday was soft-spoken. She had made her come out over a decade before, but then taken on the responsibility of raising her deceased sister's daughter. This was the first time since that she'd returned to London. In contrast to her petite niece, she was tall and slim, with the same dark eyes and straight golden-brown hair.

Whereas everything about Lady Posy was round and curvy —which included her personality. She made certain no one made the mistake that entering the marriage mart had been her idea.

She was, Felicity decided, something of a breath of fresh air.

Felicity also decided that although her future mother and father-in-law posed a considerable challenge, she was going to enjoy having Cordelia as a sister. Like Posy, she admitted to preferring country life to the city but valued the occasional visit to London. Doing so, she said, merely enhanced her appreciation of the fresh air and vast skies when she returned home.

"You are enjoying yourselves?" Axel touched her elbow from behind. All evening, she'd felt as though a secret line of communication existed between the two of them. She'd catch his gaze from across the box, and he'd send her a subtle grin or a sardonic lift of his brow.

"If I hadn't told you already, Mantis, I'm telling you now that I whole-heartedly approve of your choice of wife." The warmth in Cordelia's eyes was similar to that of her brother's.

Axel clutched his heart and wiped an arm across his brow. "Phew." He blinked in mock relief before sliding a teasing glance in Felicity's direction. "You don't know how I've worried that we wouldn't be able to go through with the wedding."

Felicity was happy to note that the tired look was absent from his eyes, replaced with simple enjoyment.

She'd only had rare glimpses of this side of him since the

incident in the orangery—untroubled, laughing, and at ease amongst people who cared for him.

He tucked Felicity's arm through his, stroking the back of her hand in a most disconcerting manner. "Shall we join the merrymakers?" Chaswick appeared beside Bethany, as did Lord Middleton and Major Lockbridge, gentlemen of whom, Felicity presumed, the marquess had invited to even out the numbers.

Enthusiastic agreement had all of them setting aside champagne glasses, collecting wraps, and making their way out from beneath the tent.

Felicity and Axel lingered, watching the others pair up and also waiting for an opening in the parade of revelers. Several in the crowd wore brightly colored masks, but one particular gentleman dressed in all black, a cloth tied around his head with slits cut for him to see through, appeared and seemed to be watching them. She caught his eye a moment before he was swallowed up by the crowd.

"Was that Blackheart?" Felicity asked when she realized Axel was looking in the same direction. Aside from appearing at his twin sister's come-out ball, the duke had been suspiciously absent this season.

Axel blinked but then shook his head.

"I'm certain it was," she pondered. No one else walked like the duke. But it was his black eyes that gave him away. "Have you and Greystone had a falling out with him?" Because in the past, Blackheart had often accompanied Axel and the formerly elusive cocksure bachelors that he'd run with.

"Not at all." Axel dropped his arm around her shoulders. "We meet to spar almost every morning." But he did not elaborate, choosing instead to peer over the heads of those who'd crowded around them—which wasn't difficult since he was taller than most.

Pressed against his side, Felicity forgot about the duke and curled her arm around his waist as well.

She remembered seeing other couples do the same last year when Westerley had hosted a party similar to this one. She remembered the feeling that she was missing out. She remembered thinking that the two of them were not like the other couples.

Axel leaned down, the heat of his mouth on her neck causing her heart to skip a beat. "I missed you."

His whispered words exhilarated her.

MAGIC AND MISCHIEF

First, Mantis would dance with her.

Then he would take her walking on one of the shadowed paths.

The worry that had lurked in his mind had fled when, moments before, Blackheart informed him that nothing out of the ordinary had been brought to his attention.

Mantis' lessening of worries had nothing to do with the champagne that had flown freely amongst them over the past hour.

The idea that someone wanted to harm him was a paranoid one. Mantis had no enemies and as far as he knew, had been fair in all of his business dealings. What reason could anyone possibly have? Perhaps he'd only felt suspicious because, for the first time in his adult life, he was actually looking forward to the future.

With Felicity at his side with her arm around him, their life together a certainty, he'd never felt taller, stronger, or more capable of conquering the world than he did in that moment.

Miraculously, she seemed as happy with their circumstances as he did.

The crowd carried them to the dancing area, lights zigzagging overhead, where behind it, an orchestra added to the raucousness of it all.

Mantis turned and bowed over her hand. "May I have this dance, my lady?"

He had known Felicity since even before she'd made her come out and, in all that time, had admired her refined but cool beauty. But in addition to those things, in addition to her status and popularity, she was always kind and compassionate.

But she had been off-limits. She might as well have been royalty.

"I would be honored to, my lord." Delicate pink lips tilted up as she glanced at him, looking demure and shy. As she nodded and grasped his shoulder, their differences in height brought them closer together. He settled his hand around her back, resisting the urge to draw her even closer, and ignored the inappropriate urges that sprang to life.

He'd been unable to forget her quietly spoken confession that had been unfortunately interrupted. *I pretended that I didn't have a choice... in my mind. And if I didn't have a choice, then... I could...*

If I were to drive you into the woods, bend you over a fallen tree, and lift your skirts to take you from behind..."

His suggestion had been most inappropriate, but she'd not admonished him for making it.

How long had these desires simmered inside of her? It wasn't that she wasn't proper. She most definitely was.

But she was also a woman of passion.

If not for that blasted shot in the park, he would have

driven them somewhere private where he could bring one of her delightfully scandalous fantasies to life.

Music struck up, a lively waltz, and Mantis stepped forward, guiding them around the perimeter of the dance floor. With each turn, the steps became easier, almost as though they had done this thousands of times before. He only moved his gaze from hers when necessary, to avoid another couple or to assure he had room to send her on a twirl.

Of which she seemed to enjoy immensely. She laughed whenever he raised his hand, and he couldn't help but laugh along with her.

The dance ended and as they stood together, catching their breath, another began. This one slower, romantic, intimate.

Mantis pulled Felicity closer.

"I've never danced like this before." Her voice sounded thin and breathy, and his groin tightened. She'd sounded the same when he'd made love to her that night.

"You expected me to smash your toes?" Because of his size, most people assumed he lacked agility. At school, he'd used the mistaken assumption to dispense with more than one bully.

That agility, most conveniently, carried over to dancing—a benefit he'd never appreciated fully until tonight.

"I might have," she answered with a wince. "However, do extend my compliments to your dancing master."

Mantis raised their clasped hands to his heart. "You don't believe I was born gifted?" Their hands rested on his chest between the two of them. It wasn't a proper manner for dancing, but they were not dancing at a proper ball.

They were at Vauxhall, where society's invisible lines between titles, position, and power faded. If only for a song.

Mantis would be certain to pass her words along to Masaki.

"It felt like flying, didn't it?"

"It did." He grew serious. "What does this feel like?"

She held his gaze.

Dancing with her, like this, felt like a prelude to making love.

"I don't have a dance instructor, only Masaki, my sensei. But fighting is much like dancing, isn't it?"

"Masaki. Does he work with the children by the docks as well?" Mantis had forgotten he'd told her about that. It wasn't information he shared with many. Not even Cordelia knew about it.

"He's visited a few times."

Felicity asked more insightful questions, and as they swayed together, Mantis found himself telling her about a few of the boys themselves, about Cornell's involvement, and that he felt guilty for having missed a class this past week.

"You were ill. I'm sure they understand."

He didn't expect them to have to understand. "It's not fair to them."

"Are you opposed to hiring a new valet? That way, Cornell can keep up regular classes when you have other responsibilities." It wasn't something Mantis had wanted to consider, but then again, he'd not planned on starting a family so soon.

He pressed a kiss to her forehead. "When did you become so wise?"

She laughed, and Mantis couldn't help but send her on a slow twirl.

"You mentioned that you box," Back in his embrace, Felicity picked up their conversation. "And that you enjoy fencing? Is this Jiu-Jitsu much different than those?"

"It is different, but also so much more."

She leaned back and tilted her head. "How?"

"I've always been large for my age, but I wasn't so large that I could fight off a gang of bullies." He laughed at himself, not wanting her to think he'd appreciate her pity. "My... intellectual deficiencies made me something of a target. I took it up to learn to defend myself, not realizing the greater value I'd take from practicing--not realizing that it would help me grow to be... " Mantis swallowed hard. "A better person."

Rather than comment or question him, Felicity simply held his gaze.

"My father told yours that I was simple. The servants at Stonegate Manor would likely agree with him. Whenever it came to reading or solving mathematical equations..." he shook his head. "None of that came easily for me. I spent an hour on something others could complete in five minutes."

He watched her. Was this the thing that would turn her away from him? But gazing down, he failed to see even a smidgeon of disdain in her eyes.

"My last governess did not limit my lessons to only English history. I remember reading about meditation. But it was in relations to religion—a form of prayer."

"It's similar, but the mind turns inward."

"Yes." Felicity understood. "It's in the breathing, from what I remember. This helped you with your studies?"

"Not that I will ever be much of a scholar, but yes." But he was tired of talking about himself.

In fact, all of his focus had moved to her mouth—her pink, plump, inviting mouth. "I want to kiss you properly."

She touched the tip of her tongue to her top lip. And those lips weren't only plump and inviting; they glistened now.

"I want you in my bed, spread out beneath me." Mantis

would summon one of those erotic fantasies she'd confessed to. "Naked."

A tremor ran through her.

"And then what?" she asked. God help him, that breathy tone laced her voice again.

"I'll give into my wicked, wicked desires, and if you fight me, I will punish you."

"Oh." She stared up at him with eyes dark with desire. Pink spots flushed her cheeks, and he could feel her breasts rise and fall against him.

Oh, indeed.

Halting only so he could adjust her hand in his, Mantis all but dragged her off the floor. One more minute of imagining what other fantasies burned in her mind, and he couldn't account for who he embarrassed.

"This way."

His hand slid down her wrist and she entwined her fingers with his. If memory served him correctly, he'd find one of those dangerous paths just around the next... Yes.

This trail hadn't been recently tended, forcing him to slow so she could pick her way carefully behind him. The noises of the music and the dancers and revelers dissipated, and gradually his eyes adjusted to the dimmer light provided by the moon and the stars.

Highly motivated to have her alone, his libido raced as he searched for somewhere discreet, somewhere private. And when he caught sight of an even more overgrown path, he led them into it.

Ten steps in, and he had her pressed against a tree, devouring her lips, one of her legs hitched up around his waist.

"Say the word and I'll stop," he managed.

~

THIS.

This was what she'd been waiting for all evening.

The surrender of herself. By allowing him to breach her defenses, she could lay her desires bare. Propriety was nonexistent. All that mattered was the sensation of his cock pressing against her center, of his mouth laving at one breast and then the other.

All that mattered was the piercing anticipation of knowing she was going to be thoroughly, fantastically ravished by this magnificent man.

"Is this what you want?"

"Yes." Was that her voice? Deep, guttural. It didn't matter. The rules that once defined her life lay in a million pieces on the dance floor behind them. "I want you in me."

"Fucking you?" The harsh sounds of his voice filled a void she had never wanted to admit existed. This man… wanted her… violently.

"Yes."

He released her hands, dropping his own to unfasten his trousers. Yes. This was what she wanted.

Desperately.

Violently.

Moonlight caught his face, revealing the jagged edge of his scar. His brows were furrowed, his gaze intent. Everything about this should be terrifying, but it wasn't. Axel could be like this, growling, looking as though he was out of control, but she knew beyond a shadow of a doubt that she was safe with him.

Her back pressing against the tree, his hands gripping her thighs, she welcomed him into her body, relishing the exquisite invasion. So large-, thrusting deeper, filling her. She raised her hips, wanting to feel him everywhere and not caring that her hair was caught in the branches behind her, or that the sounds coming out of her resembled something a wild animal would make.

"Felicity," he chanted her name against her lips and then her skin, wherever he could taste her. "So beautiful."

He owned her. She was his. She'd locked this part of herself away for too long, hiding her deepest emotions, her fears, her anger. No more. No more!

"Axel." And then… "Fuck me. Harder."

These wants were like simmering lava, and she, the rumbling volcano. White heat poured through her, seizing her muscles and nerves, heating her blood to a boil. Her soul went up in flames. Axel. Axel. Consume me. Own me. *Become me.*

Felicity thought it was over when he withdrew, but then he turned her around impatiently. "Brace yourself like this." He placed her palms against the trunk of the tree, pushing her so she was bent over. Keeping one hand around her middle, he shoved her feet apart with his boots.

Dazed and startled, she found herself staring down at the ground. He must have sensed her hesitation, for he paused.

"Too much?" He had one hand on her hip, the other looped beneath her skirts, reaching down and fondling her from the front.

She shook her head. "No."

"You like this?"

Very much. "I do."

She ought to feel weak and satiated, but already she was on fire, needing him to fill her again. "Yes."

He wasted no time, moving his hand to her hair, tugging

on it so that her back arched as he entered her again. He moved faster this time. And oh, dear God, even harder.

Rules? What were rules? Her weight lifted off her feet as he clutched her, seeking his pleasure inside her body. The vortex from before grew more turbulent, and as he stiffened inside, releasing his seed, Felicity surrendered her soul a second time.

Clinging to the tree, she tried catching her breath while Axel rearranged her skirts and then fastened his trousers. Even after he'd wrapped his jacket around her and lowered them both onto the ground, her weak limbs had her feeling more like a string puppet than a live person.

"Are you all right?" He stroked his hand down her arm. "*How are you?*"

"Good." She was too satisfied to be embarrassed. "Wonderful—exhausted." She doubted she could ever be embarrassed with this man again.

"Mmm…" He kissed the top of her head. "You drive me mad, do you know that? Not sure I'm going to survive fifty or so years pleasing you."

"You'll manage." More than that. Good lord, he seemed to understand the workings of her depraved mind.

And then she turned, touching her palm to his cheek. "*How are you?*"

"Good. Wonderful." He kissed her again. "Now."

It was a perfect moment.

Or rather, it ought to have been the perfect moment.

Her first indication something wasn't quite right was the sensation of Axel bracing himself beside her—just as he'd done when the errant bullet had shot past them in the park.

The menace moved beyond a mere threat when multiple dark figures broke through the nearby brush. She saw several flashes of light, of moonlight on metal, and then screamed in horror.

Those shiny metal objects were knives!

"Felicity—Run!" Axel pushed her behind him, but her knees were weak, and she tumbled backward. Where had they come from? What did they want?

With these questions spinning in her head, she made her best attempt to scoot away, pushing with her feet and hands but finding herself trapped by her skirts.

Furthermore, she couldn't tear her gaze away from Axel.

In the dark, it was difficult to count how many assailants attacked. Outfitted in all black and wearing masks over their eyes, there might have been as many as a dozen or as few as four or five. Axel landed his shoulder into one man's midsection, causing him to grunt, then a snapping sound had the villain sprawled on the ground. When a second man jumped on Axel's back, Felicity's urge to help warred with a certainty that she'd only get in the way.

Axel managed to get a hold of the second assailant's arms at the same time he kicked out at a third. When two more drove toward him, Axel bent forward, tossing them both and allowing their momentum to carry them into the brush.

One landed at Felicity's feet, and peering up at her with a snarl, the menace reached his knife toward her. All but frozen at her predicament, she didn't move swiftly enough to prevent him from slicing his blade along her ankle. "Get off me!"

Axel must have thought she'd already made her escape. He whipped around in surprise, and looking rather fierce, dragged the attacker by the legs. "Go! Now, Felicity!"

She nodded, even as another one of the men seemed to have recovered. "Behind you!" she shouted. She needed to get away before her presence got Axel killed.

Not caring about the warm blood trickling down her foot, or ripping her skirts, or that she'd lost both her shoes, Felicity shot to her feet. She needed to find help!

Following the distant sound of the revelers, Felicity pushed her way through branches and leaves, breathing a sigh of relief when she discovered the path.

Fearful that Axel would be killed before she could bring help, she ran faster than she'd ever run, startling as she slammed into something—someone—another fellow dressed in black. She twisted, attempting to get away, but just before she reached up to claw at him, a booming sound, and then fireworks lit up the sky, effectively illuminating the face of the man she'd run into.

It was Blackheart, and he wasn't alone. A handful of men stood behind him.

"They're going to kill him!" Felicity pointed behind her, sending Blackheart's companions sprinting in that direction.

Blackheart removed his coat and dropped it onto her shoulders. "Don't worry about Mantis. I have every confidence he'll emerge alive."

Felicity burst into tears.

THE AFTERMATH

"*I* don't know who the hell they were." Mantis was disgusted with himself. The villainous cretins had all been wearing masks, similar to the one Blackheart wore that night.

Greystone, along with Chaswick, Blackheart, and a handful of the duke's men, had appeared relatively quickly following Felicity's sprint into the darkness. Thank God she'd escaped. He'd never forgive himself if she hadn't.

"Footpads?" Greys asked.

"No."

Common thieves possessed an unmistakable odor that had been noticeably absent on these attackers.

Mantis had been lost in a fog of sensual gratification, and by the time he'd heard the branches breaking he'd been mostly concerned that he and Felicity would be discovered.

Separating themselves from the other guests so he could be alone with her had been the height of idiocy, and thanks to him, she'd been injured. Good God, she could have been killed

Once she'd fled from the danger, Mantis' skills had taken

over. He was certain he'd broken one of their arms, possibly unmanned another, and nearly strangled one to death.

But he wasn't a killer. When Blackheart's men swooped in, he'd loosened his grip, and the man had fled in the same direction as the others.

"You're certain you hadn't seen any of them before?" Greys asked.

Blackheart's arms were folded across his chest. The duke's disgusted expression matched his own.

Mantis bent over and spat out blood that had pooled in his mouth.

Felicity had insisted on waiting to see for herself that he'd not been killed but then been quickly ushered away to Chaswick's carriage, Lady Bethany's arm around her for comfort and Chaswick following.

Her hair had been hanging down her back, her lovely gown wrinkled, with dirt and leaves clinging to it.

"She cannot show up at Brightley's looking like that." Mantis said. The earl would never forgive him.

Damn his selfish cock. He should not have risked her safety to appease his inconvenient lust.

"Lady Chaswick mentioned taking her to Byrd House first." Greys rubbed the back of his neck.

Mantis had thwarted more than one knife from plunging into his chest.

He'd not been paranoid. Someone was trying to kill him.

He shuddered to think what the blackguards would have done to Felicity if given the chance.

"I'm an ass. I put her in harm's way."

"I'm the ass. I should have seen it coming." A highly unusual statement on Blackheart's part.

"No doubt Chaswick is kicking himself for not catching

any of the bastards," Greys added, sounding slightly more like his normal, unflappable self.

"One of them will be nursing a broken arm." Mantis wasn't sure who had been more surprised by the snapping sound—the victim, his partners, or himself. "Took off like a scared rabbit after that."

Mantis had wanted to chase after the assailant but needed to see for himself that Felicity had made it to safety. He'd sent her off alone in the woods. He'd placed her in danger enough for one night.

"All of this, it makes no sense whatsoever." That bullet wasn't a coincidence, then. And the illness? Had he been poisoned? "If someone wants revenge on my father, they've chosen the wrong victim to use to take it."

"We'll get to the bottom of this." Greys brushed at his coat. "I need to attend to my other guests. They'll wonder at your early departure."

"Tell them—" Mantis couldn't stop the turning in his mind, which was already searching for any reason for the attacks. "Tell them—"

"Lady Chaswick took ill," Blackheart supplied. "And Lady Felicity is comforting her friend."

"Yes." But it was the other way around. And Felicity wasn't ill—she was carrying a child. He needed...

A deep breath.

"Meet me at Knight house," Blackheart said. "I'll have a rug rolled out in the ballroom. We'll figure this out after a few matches."

Wanting to do more but also realizing this was for the best, Mantis nodded.

∼

I MUST BE IN SHOCK. That must be what this numb feeling was.

But this could not be good for the baby.

And her father. What would he think if he saw her like this? Felicity couldn't stop shivering.

"I'll have a hot bath made up, and we'll send word to your parents that you are staying with me tonight, that we wanted to catch up." Bethany squeezed her hand. "Chase will send for a doctor."

"I'm f-fine. It's only a scratch." She fought to keep her teeth from chattering. It could have been so much worse for both of them!

"You must have been terrified!"

Felicity met Bethany's concerned gazed. "T-t-tea will help." Tea fixed everything.

"Of course."

"Th-th-those men." Felicity was shaking. "They t-tried to k-kill Axel." If not for Axel's strength and agility, one or more of those knives could all too easily have pierced his heart.

But of course. "The gunshot in the park! That wasn't an accident at all."

Felicity met Lord Chaswick's gaze across the dark carriage.

"I'm afraid that would have been too great of a coincidence for it not to have been," he agreed.

The driver drew the vehicle to a halt, and Felicity wasn't sure if the carriage or her own thoughts caused the tremor that shook her.

"Here we are," Bethany said. When Felicity hesitated, she added, "Our servants are discreet. I promise. You needn't worry about them gossiping."

The baron was out of the carriage, and in no time at all, Felicity found herself sitting in a hot tub, a cup of tea in her hand, and flames flickering in the hearth across the room. After draping a white night rail and a few towels near the fire, Bethany's maid disappeared, reminding her mistress to use the bell-pull to summon her when needed.

Leaning forward and sitting on the small stool placed beside the tub, Bethany's eyes twinkled. "You are engaged!"

"I am. And you are married!"

"I am!" Bethany squealed. "To Chase!" This felt more normal. This was what Felicity needed. "And you are going to marry Lord Manningham-Tissinton? I would never have guessed. I might think you accepted him only because of Westerley's betrayal if I hadn't seen you and Mantis together. This doesn't have anything to do with Westerley, does it?"

"No." Felicity needed this. Susan was a wonderful and loyal maid, but she was also her father's employee. Bethany was simply a dear, dear friend. "He comforted me the night of your mother's ball at Westerley Crossings."

"That was the night Westerley announced his engagement to Miss Jackson."

"I was… disappointed."

Bethany frowned. "I didn't realize… you never said a word. I should have known."

"Westerley is your brother." Felicity pointed out. "And his wife is your sister now. Anyway, I'm quite over him. In fact, looking back on all of that, I am grateful that Miss Jackson came along."

"Just so long as you are happy."

Was she? She might be if they knew who was behind these attacks on Axel. The memory of him fighting off all those men terrified her but also summoned that fiery sensation that was becoming all too familiar.

"I am quite taken with my viscount," Felicity admitted. "He

fought off all those men with nothing but his bare hands. He saved both of our lives tonight!"

"Do you…" Bethany leaned forward to rest her chin on her fist. "Do you love Mantis?"

Did she? She had been pretending to love him for her parents' benefit. And she'd allowed him unmentionable intimacies. He was to be the father of her child! But did she love him? Was she *in love* with him?

"I care for him deeply." Very deeply. And because she had known Bethany for most of her life and knew she would never reveal her secret, she added, "I'm with child, Bethany. I'm going to have Axel's baby." Moisture welled in her eyes.

Bethany's eyes flicked to where Felicity's belly was submerged in the water and then back up again. "Felicity!" She was blinking rapidly. "Oh, Felicity!"

"It came as quite a surprise."

"I can only imagine." Bethany smothered a giggled. "I'll have to revisit the meaning of the word comforting." But then she reached out and squeezed Felicity's hand. "So long as you are happy. That's all that matters," she repeated.

"I am." How could Felicity not be happy to marry Axel? How could she not be thrilled at the prospect of having such an honorable man for a husband—one who she respected, one who could make her laugh, and who also possessed extraordinary lovemaking skills?

Which reminded her of what they had done earlier that night.

Which, in turn, reminded her that he'd nearly been killed.

"Who would want to kill him?"

"Chase insists Mantis is more than capable of defending himself. Apparently, he and Blackheart have learned to fight from an eastern teacher."

Felicity nodded. "But that is no help against a gun, or..." Another horrifying realization. "Someone poisoned him." She told Bethany about his recent sudden illness, and the gunshot.

"But Mantis knows to be careful now." Bethany seemed quite sure. "And now that Chase and Westerley are back—and Mr. Spencer. Between all of them, I have no doubt that whoever is behind this will find himself on a ship for the America's before the week's end."

"I hope so." Felicity wished she had half the confidence her friend had.

But then Bethany's eyes widened. "I forgot to tell you the most spectacular news! I've been sworn to secrecy until after they've made an official announcement, but you don't count. Tabetha is getting married as well. The two of you ought to have a double wedding..."

"So she landed her duke then?" Knowing Tabetha, Felicity doubted very seriously that Bethany's sister would be willing to share her wedding day with another bride.

"Not a duke..." Bethany smirked. "It really is a most amusing story..."

The bathwater was almost tepid by the time Bethany fell silent, and when her maid returned, she reprimanded both of them for not sending for her sooner.

"You'll catch your death, my lady." She wrapped the warm towel around Felicity. "But at least you're no longer shivering."

"Do you have need of anything else? More tea?" Bethany asked as she moved toward the door.

"No. Just sleep." She did, in fact, feel somewhat better for having spent time in the company of a friend.

"Felicity?" Bethany turned back, her fingers tapping away at her thumb. "I was terrified I was going to lose you after

Westerley. Anyway, I'm so happy that I didn't. And I am so happy for—everything. You mustn't worry about Mantis. He's more than capable of protecting himself. He did tonight, didn't he?"

He had, but would he be so lucky next time? "Yes," Felicity answered. "And... thank you, for everything."

Bethany blushed and then slipped quietly into the hall, closing the door behind her.

Feeling almost lost in the giant bed provided for her, Felicity burrowed deeper, hugging one of the pillows.

What was Axel doing now? Was he drinking scotch with Greystone and Blackheart? Or was he in bed, where he ought to be, resting so that he could recover completely?

She grimaced to herself. Her plans for a quiet, early night were a distant memory.

Not quiet at all.

And if the things he'd done when he'd had her pressed against that tree were any indication of what they would share in their marriage... Oh. My.

She wiggled, and the tenderness between her thighs assured her she had not imagined any of it.

THE THORNS

unctioning on less than four hours of sleep, Mantis lifted the knocker and shuffled his feet while he waited for Mr. Michaels to open the door. After a very, very late night spent in Greystone's billiard room with Westerley, Chaswick, Spencer, and of course Greys and Blackheart, although they had a few theories, the six of them weren't any closer to determining the identity of who might be behind the recent attacks.

Felicity's mother was hosting an "at home" to which he'd been invited and that allowed Mantis the perfect opportunity to spend time with his fiancé.

He knew from Chaswick, who'd surprisingly joined them for a few hours, that Felicity had spent the night safely tucked away in the guest chambers at Byrd House.

But Mantis needed to see her.

He needed to apologize. He needed to reassure himself, and her as well. He just... needed... her.

So by the time he'd been escorted up the staircase and into

the large drawing room to find her sitting with his very own sister, his relief was almost dizzying.

And although she might appear mysterious to anyone else, he saw right through it. She might be holding her teacup just so, and making proper conversation with those seated around her, but she was a woman with secrets. Secrets he was extremely grateful to be in on.

"Do sit down, Manningham," Felicity's mother interrupted his thoughts.

He had not expected to find Louisa in attendance, seated beside Lady Brightley. Apparently, all was forgiven.

"Ladies," he bowed. "Louisa."

His father's wife indicated the space beside her. "I understand you had quite the harrowing experience at Vauxhall last night."

What the devil?

Felicity would not have told anyone about the attack. In fact, they'd all decided to keep it under wraps. So who…?

Mantis lowered himself onto the settee. "It was nothing," he answered cautiously, his gaze shifting to Felicity.

"It was harrowing, but I imagine Vauxhall is a favorite spot for thieves and pickpockets." Felicity shrugged.

Beautiful, sexy, sweet, and on top of all that, clever. Despite being targeted by some unknown murderer, he'd not change places with another man in all the world.

"It is coming to be something of a common occurrence. Odds were that it was bound to happen to one of us at some point," Bethany chirped. She then brushed at some lint on her skirt and turned to address his stepmother, specifically. "Who was that handsome child you were walking with this morning?"

"My son, Conner Lupton, the fourth. Saturday morning is

our day to walk in the park. As long as he completes his studies, of course. And he is even smarter than he is handsome. His tutors say he'll enter university at least two years earlier than his contemporaries."

"The younger boy is named after the earl?" Lady Brightley's brows furrowed. This was not the first time someone would show confusion at their names.

It wasn't at all normal, and Mantis usually kept silent rather than explain that his father had refused to give his name to an infant who was sure to die.

"Speaking of walking," Felicity turned to him, "Will you stroll with me in the garden? I'd like your opinion on which flowers we ought to use as centerpieces."

"Centerpieces?" Mantis rubbed his palms along the tops of his legs. "But of course."

"Young love. Isn't it the most wonderful thing?" Lady Brightley had already moved on to what he was beginning to believe might be her favorite subject—her daughter's pending nuptials.

Mantis only hoped she didn't mention the babe in front of her other guests today.

But he refused to worry about that. Mantis rose and offered Felicity his arm.

"How are you?" He waited until after they'd stepped into the sunlight.

"I am well," she answered. *"How are you?"*

He laughed. "Much better now. I'm always better when I am in your company. Did you really want my opinion on the decorations? Because I must warn you, I know next to nothing about flowers."

She giggled, and in that moment, he realized he'd forgotten something vital in his urgent quest to protect her.

The courtship.

"What is your favorite flower?" he asked.

"It is quite unoriginal, I'm afraid." And then she sighed. "Red roses. Did you know they signify romantic love? My mother says this is because they are not only beautiful and silky, but because the thorns can be merciless. There isn't anything more beautiful, nonetheless, than a red rose in bloom."

She brushed some hair away from her face as they strolled along the well-tended flagstone path. "A complicated flower," Mantis commented.

"Indeed."

She had been caught in a rosebush the night he'd first made love to her. Had that been fate, or just an ironic coincidence?

"But also, one might say, universally appreciated," he said.

"What do you mean?"

He searched his brain to figure out exactly what he'd meant.

"Although its beauty is rivaled by other blossoms, it is never mistaken for anything other than a rose. It is always identifiable, always recognized, and always valued."

She dropped his arm and stepped off the path to examine a shrub covered in small pink roses. "Like a sunset," she said.

"Or a beautiful woman." His eyes held hers. "Do the different colors have different meanings?" Mantis flicked his gaze to the miniature blossoms she'd been admiring.

"Oh, yes. In fact, the meanings even change depending on the stage of the blossom, the shade, and whether or not it has thorns."

She picked a cluster of the pinks. "These buds represent an innocent heart." She moved to point out the more mature blossoms. "These are a bright color, so... happiness. If I were to offer them to you as a gift, I'd be saying that I appreciate your gentle nature and grace."

She held them out, and feeling self-conscious, Mantis accepted the small cluster.

"Careful of the thorns," she warned.

He examined them and then followed her between other clusters of blossoms.

"Red roses with ivy," he announced his decision.

"For the centerpieces?" She sounded surprised.

"Unless you prefer something else. Perhaps..." He waved his hands in the air as he tried to remember the name of any other flower than roses. "Geraniums."

She laughed. "Red roses will be fine."

"What's wrong with geraniums?"

"Aside from the fact they will not be blooming? They signify folly."

"I see." He clasped his hands behind his back, still holding the pink flowers but with the fingers of his free hand wound around his opposite wrist.

"Hyacinths?"

"Acting rashly." She grinned. "And those will have already blossomed."

She was walking backward, watching him, while he followed her slowly. Holding her gaze, he reconciled this flirtatious lady with the one he'd danced with at Vauxhall.

Red roses were the perfect flower for her. Classic. Stunning. But with all the passion of life's sustaining force.

Even determined to properly court her this afternoon, he couldn't stop imagining... remembering.

And the look in her eyes revealed that she was remembering as well.

"Did you feel guilty? After?" He lowered his voice.

Before, she might have blushed and told him ladies didn't speak of such things. Before, he hadn't even begun to learn what she liked... and what drove her to the edge.

"Should I have?" she teased.

"Not at all. Should I?"

"Not at all." She'd backed herself into a cluster of lilac bushes.

Voices sounded in the distance as some of her mother's other guests made their way outside. It really was a beautiful afternoon.

But the presence of the other guests prevented him from stealing even a single kiss. He ought to have taken advantage of having her alone earlier, but that would have been risky since he tended to lose all sense of time and place when she was in his arms.

Her gaze flicked toward the door, aware as well that they were no longer alone.

She straightened her spine and took on that proper look she wore most of the time.

She took his arm, and the two of them promenaded quite properly back to the formal path. "Are you frightened?" She asked, lowering her voice.

"Should I be?"

"I MIGHT EXPECT that anyone with someone trying to kill them might be afraid." Felicity couldn't joke about this.

Although today, Axel seemed sturdy, healthy, and hale once again. It was almost possible to dismiss the bumbling attacks.

But even a bumbler got lucky every once in a while.

Axel tugged at the back of his neck. "I'm not afraid for myself. But two of those attacks have put you in jeopardy. And I have no idea—" He shook his head.

"None at all?"

"My only thoughts are that someone wants revenge on my family—for something my father may have done. But if that's the case, they're going about this all wrong."

Felicity hated that. She hated that his own father didn't value Axel enough that he would be harmed if something were to happen to him.

"What else did you eat the night you took ill? Do you remember?"

"Aside from what I ate for dinner here," he shook his head. "Nothing."

Her father's servants had worked for her family for as long as she could remember. They were nothing if not utterly loyal.

"You had nothing else to drink?"

He paused and rubbed his chin. "A few drinks from my private stash of whiskey, gifted to me by Westerley and..." He glanced down at her with a wince.

"Miss Jackson?" She squeezed his arm. "I am quite past my resentment of the new countess, so you needn't worry."

He cocked a brow. "Are you past the reason for that resentment?"

"I am past that as well." The feelings she'd had for Westerley seemed anemic compared to the emotions Axel evoked. Merely holding his arm and walking together stirred up all sorts of inappropriate thoughts.

She had wanted Westerley's kiss because it would have

signified his commitment to their betrothal. She wanted Axel's kiss because she would wither away without it.

Axel nodded and then turned so they could continue their stroll. Perhaps, he too, felt the vibrating desire humming inside her.

Before knowing Axel, she'd been fine—but that was all. Since then, she'd experienced a spectrum of emotions she hadn't even known existed. She felt more alive than ever before.

But was this love? Or merely a heady effect of mining her passions?

"If it was the whiskey that made me ill, then that would mean someone would have had to have broken into my father's house while we were here for dinner."

"Or it could have been a disgruntled servant."

"The servants are well aware of my father's ill regard for me. If they wanted to harm him, they'd know I was not the person to attack."

"Who would they attack then? Your stepmother?"

"Or my brother, Conner. And Conner may be spoiled and far too arrogant for his britches, but if anything were to happen to him, I would track them down, and they would pay dearly."

His tone was uncompromising. But, of course, Axel would protect and defend his younger brother.

"Is he a happy child?" Felicity had wondered this. Was Axel's father's cruelty strictly reserved for his older son?

"Louisa dotes on Conner, so he has that. But my father is mostly apathetic. I want to teach him Jiu-Jitsu. But one of his tutors has deemed the practice wicked, and Conner refused our lessons the last two times I've offered." Axel sent her a wry grimace. "I had myself convinced that my presence at

Crest House mattered to him but… He no longer seems interested. I fear he's going to have difficulties once he goes off to school."

"You think he'll be bullied?"

"It's possible. He has an air about him…"

Even when they didn't want him to, Axel protected those he considered to be his own.

"He'll come around," Felicity offered.

"I hope so."

She didn't understand the dynamics of his family. Was it possible that his father blamed him for his first wife's death? But then why not blame his sister?

And it was odd that he would be apathetic toward his second son. Something niggled at her brain.

"If something happens to you, Conner inherits the title," she said.

"Yes." But then he caught her eye, having guessed the conclusion that could be drawn from that fact. "My father hates me, but not to that extent." He seemed almost hurt at the suggestion.

"Of course. I'm sorry." Felicity stared down at the blades of grass peaking between the stones as she carefully chose her steps. "I hate that someone is out there… I hate that you are in danger."

Felicity inhaled a steadying breath through her nostrils. A very ugly possibility was forming in her mind. If she and Axel were prevented from marrying, not only would she give birth out of wedlock, but their child would be born a bastard.

Meaning Axel's younger brother would inherit their father's title. It wasn't an unheard-of motivation—she'd read of at least a dozen instances where family members had killed in order to gain power.

"Perhaps we ought to marry by special license." She felt dizzy at the thought. Would he be safe after they'd married? Perhaps... if her suspicions were correct.

Foregoing a church wedding meant nothing compared to ensuring Axel's safety. As she'd found herself doing more and more often, she flattened her hand against her belly, which wasn't as flat as it had been even one week before.

Likely, they ought to have married already anyway.

As much as she wanted to, she couldn't let go of the terrible possibility that Axel's own father was the one who'd initiated these attempts on his life. That night after dinner, she'd witnessed pure hatred in the man's eyes. Her future father-in-law was a cruel and heartless man.

"I promised both your mother and your father that you would have your wedding at St. Georges."

"Axel, please listen to me." She felt sick to her stomach. "If you are—" She couldn't even say the word. "If something were to happen to you before our wedding, your father's title would go to your brother."

Her most gentle fiancé's face darkened, and for the first time in the course of their attachment, he stared at her with disapproval and annoyance. But she could not keep this to herself.

"Stop. My father is an ass, and... I make no excuses for his despicable treatment of you, but you are speaking of my flesh and blood. I value your opinion, but I must ask you to keep such accusations to yourself in the future."

The tone in his voice sent a chill sweeping through her. Felicity hated that he'd taken offense at her words. She hated, even more, the pain she saw in his eyes.

But this affected both of them. Any person who would be willing to kill his own son might be equally willing to harm his son's child.

"If I'm wrong, then there is no harm done. But if I'm right—"

"You're wrong—" He dropped his gaze to the ground, clenching his jaw, the muscles beneath her hand tense.

She would drop the idea.

For now.

Nonetheless... "Catching this villain must be top priority —regardless of who he is." Axel had told her he was mostly frightened for her. "Because you are forbidden to leave me to raise our child alone." On this point, she refused to compromise.

"I won't allow that to happen." He squeezed her hand, but his smile was tight. "As for the other—I'll look into it. And if there's any merit, I'll discuss it with Greys and Blackheart. Until then—"

"Please be careful, Axel." She turned and buried her face against his arm. "I can't lose you."

SUSPICIONS

*M*antis took his leave from Bright Place with his heart in a vice and a black cloud where his soul ought to be.

She was wrong.

She had to be wrong.

Did she think so little of him that she imagined his own father wanted to kill him? He marched along the street, knowing that she hadn't intended to hurt him, but unable to dismiss that she had.

She was scared. He understood that. And even now, guilt was setting in for the abrupt manner in which he'd taken his leave. They had been having a lovely afternoon. For once, their courtship had felt normal.

No, not normal. There was nothing normal where his feelings for her were concerned.

Mantis squared his shoulders, suddenly faced with the discreet façade of his father's Mayfair townhouse.

Ivy climbed its way up the subdued white brick of the four-story structure. He remembered when the vines barely reached the second floor. The only reason they didn't wind over the roof now was because they were diligently tended to.

Home.

Somehow, despite making no conscious decision, his feet had carried him here. He glanced down at his timepiece—a quarter past six. Most likely, Crestwood would have just returned from his clubs.

Clasping the cool metal lever, he paused. Although far and few between, his time spent here was not without fond memories; time spent with Cordelia, and even Conner, who could not be blamed for the sour attitude that had been instilled in him. Nonetheless, Crest House had always been his home. The idea that his own father wanted his demise... it was unthinkable.

So why had he come here now?

Inside, the air was cool and familiar, and the tall foyer ceiling loomed majestically overhead. Crest House wasn't as grand as some mansions in Mayfair, definitely not Black-hearts, the Ravendales, or even Greystones, but it rivaled almost everything else.

A sound from behind made him jump, and he felt foolish to realize it was only Mr. Mortimer, standing patiently to serve him.

This residence had never been the welcoming refuge many of his friends knew growing up, but it was his home.

"I didn't hear you enter, my lord. My apologies for not getting the door."

Mantis handed over the hat that he carried more than he wore, along with his gloves, and then rolled his shoulders.

She'd made him unnecessarily paranoid. He had nothing to fear here.

"My father?"

"Is in his study, my lord."

This, Mantis realized, was the only way he could dispense with the suspicions she had planted.

Forcing a bravado he didn't feel, Mantis climbed the stairs two at a time and, once reaching his father's study, pushed the heavy door open without bothering to knock first.

He was tired of apologizing for his existence. He belonged as much as anyone. He was the heir. He was his father's son.

Eyes nearly identical to his own peered up at him over a pair of spectacles.

"I'm working." His father kept his head down, revealing what was still an uncommonly thick head of greying hair, effectively dismissing Mantis in order to attend to something more important than his son.

"Someone is trying to kill me." Undeterred, Mantis stepped inside and closed the door behind him.

With hands that seemed to shake more than usual, the earl turned the page of his incredibly important document and then exhaled a long breath to signify his annoyance.

"What the hell did you do to provoke him?"

"I haven't done anything." Of course, his father would assume that. "Have you? Do you know who's behind it? *Is it you?*" If Mantis had thought his heart was in a vice before, no doubt it had abandoned his body completely while he awaited his father's response.

Because Felicity's suspicions wouldn't have bothered him if there wasn't some buried part of himself that thought she could be right.

"Why the devil would you think that?"

"Motive."

His father burst out laughing. "If I didn't think you were

simple before, by God, your accusation today would give me cause to do so."

"Conner has the intelligence that I lack. Why wouldn't you want me out of the way?" Mantis stood ready, alert, almost as though to fend off an attack. At the same time, his feet and legs felt numb. He'd had confrontations with his father in the past, but nothing like this. And always, Mantis had entered into them thinking that at some time he'd be granted his father's...

Fucking approval.

Acceptance. Respect. *Damn my eyes.* For far too long, all he'd wanted was some indication of his father's regard.

The older man shrugged. "That, dear Manningham, would hardly serve my best interest. God knows it's always best to have a spare."

Mantis' heart swooped back in his chest and began beating again. At the same time, his lungs filled with air.

Felicity was wrong. Not because his father cared, but because his father stood to lose something he valued in the likelihood of his eldest son's death.

Mantis swallowed hard and then nodded.

"Do you have any opinions as to who might benefit from my demise?" It was a fair question and one of which a man's father might consider delving into.

"You took ill—too much spirits? And you were shot at. Unpleasant, no doubt, but these two events are nothing more than a coincidence. Louisa says you met up with a gang of pickpockets. People don't murder benign gentlemen of the ton. And you, Manningham, are as benign as they come."

Mantis had become numb to his father's criticisms, but this particular jibe cut deeper than most. It was nothing new, nor ought it to have been unexpected, but...

It was enough.

His father didn't care—most likely never would—and Mantis couldn't do a damn thing to change that.

He could, however, get a good night's sleep.

His recent illness that might have come from drinking from his private stash of whiskey had him coming to a decision. "I'll be staying at Knight House until after my nuptials." Mantis had initially declined Greystone's invitation, but this would be for the best. Meanwhile, he would find a residence for he and Felicity to lease until the season's end.

Unless the culprit was not apprehended by then, in which case they would cut the season short and travel to Tissinton Towers.

"Good riddance, then." Crestwood went back to reading the papers on his desk.

Making yet another attempt to harden his heart against this man, Mantis stepped into the foyer. He and Cornell would gather their belongings and leave. It was for the best.

"Hello, Manningham." A small voice stopped him just as he turned to ascend the staircase.

His younger brother stood across the foyer, straight as a board, his dark hair parted in the center and combed perfectly away from his face. The poor boy really did need to spend more time out of doors. He needed friends. He needed to be allowed to be a child.

"Why, hello, Connor. Have you made any friends in London yet this year?" Mantis flexed his hands and shelved his worries to take a few minutes with his only brother.

"No time for that." Conner's high-pitched voice had dropped. Axel remembered when his own voice had changed. No doubt, in less than a year, Conner would sound like a full-grown gentleman.

"No time for friends? That's blasphemy."

Conner shrugged. "I'm not interested in the sports those boys enjoy. What's the use in hitting a ball with a stick? And then running? Mr. Rudolph says it's far more important for a future lord to fill out before testing himself physically. He has scheduled England's finest fencing master to begin instructing me in September. Although I far prefer studying history."

Mantis grazed his fingertips along the raised ridges along his cheek. At least a professional instructor would refrain from leaving scars on his pupil.

"I've a new throw I could teach you. What are you doing presently?"

"Not today, Manningham," Conner shifted his gaze to the stairs. "I'm to meet with my father now. Mother likes me to keep him appraised of all the things I am learning."

How had his father sired two boys so unalike one another?

Mantis wouldn't give up on Conner. If practicing the ancient arts had helped him, as a damn-near simpleton, there was no telling the advantages someone like Conner could gain.

Mantis doubted he'd have survived if not for the discipline.

"Are you excited to go to Eton at the end of summer?" At school, Mantis had discovered precisely how important hitting balls around actually was. Physical prowess, arguably, made a man more powerful than any title—at that age anyhow. "You'll want to make friends there."

Conner merely lifted his chin. "They will like me. They will have to like me."

If Conner entered the all-boys school with that attitude, the lessons he learned might be both humiliating and painful.

Mantis reached out, and despite Conner's attempt to avoid

his hand, scrubbed the ridiculous part out of his hair. "Much better," he laughed. His brother was also going to have to find a new hairstyle because adolescent boys could be merciless indeed.

"Not well done of you, Manningham. Mr. Rudolph shall have to repair it now." The tightly wound child turned all starch and vinegar as he backed away, scowling.

"Not so fast," Mantis stopped him. "I won't be living here any longer."

"You're leaving?" Conner's scowl, Mantis knew, was his way of showing some disappointment.

"I'm not going far." For now. "I'll be staying at Knight House. After I marry, I'll provide my wife with her own home."

"Are you taking Cornell? To your new house in Mayfair?"

"Yes to both." Regardless of where Mantis lived, he'd make arrangements to spend time with this boy. "You aren't going to miss me, are you?"

Conner twisted his mouth into a grimace. "Not at all." But then he added. "You will visit, won't you?" Even after Mantis resided elsewhere, he'd make time for this boy.

"I'll do even better than that. You can stay with me any time you wish."

Conner mulled this information over and then shrugged. "Very well." He dashed down the stairs but then stopped and turned, "Don't forget to tell mother where you live."

Much later that night, seated around a felt-covered table in Greystone's study with Westerley, Chaswick, Stone, Greys, and even Blackheart making an occasional appearance, Mantis felt the importance of good friends even more acutely. These men had all come into his life around the same time— when he was only slightly older than Conner was now.

And even though half of them were either married or on the cusp of being married, much like himself, he would lay down his life for any of them.

Or he would have before...

Because—

Felicity.

"Are you in or out?" Stone Spencer, due to marry only one week following Mantis and Felicity's nuptials, met his gaze from across the table, cocking one brow.

In answer, Mantis tossed three coins into the pile.

These men were like brothers to him, but the nature of that brotherhood was shifting.

Westerley had already announced he would be bowing out before the hour grew too late. He had no desire to keep his countess... his wife, waiting. And Chaswick, married to one of Westerley's sisters now, was no different.

Although, Mantis glanced at his timepiece. It was nearly two in the morning already.

Hopefully, their respective wives would be forgiving. Once the whiskey had begun dulling their faculties, sense of time dulled as well.

"Any leads on the blighter who jumped you in the park last night?" Chaswick leaned back, chewing on a cigar.

"He wasn't a member of any of the gangs." Blackheart leaned casually against the wall. "Not according to my sources. Just as Mantis suspected, the man wasn't after blunt."

"Which gives one cause to consider... closer threats." Greys, of whom he'd told Felicity's suspicions earlier, tossed in his bet and met Mantis' stare from across the table.

"You can cross my father off that list," Mantis insisted and then grudgingly explained to the others that the woman he was going to marry suspected his own father of trying to kill him.

And how was it that he could be angry with her and miss her at the same time?

He could marry her by special license, but once married, would she and their child be in danger as well then? If this was about his father's title… it might.

Best all-around to simply catch whoever was behind this.

"Why the rush? Why not postpone the wedding until after you resolve this situation?" Westerley asked.

Of course, that would be Westerley's inclination. He was an expert at postponing Felicity Brightley's needs—he had put them off for years, in fact.

For which Mantis was eternally grateful.

"We are not in the position to postpone it," he said.

Westerley stared over his cards with narrowed eyes.

"Did you—"

"No. She considered herself betrothed to you. She fully intended to fulfill her obligations."

Felicity's former betrothed lay his cards face down and cracked the joints in one of his fingers. After cracking a second knuckle, he shook his head.

"I realize it's none of my business, but do you love her?"

Hell and damnation. Lying to his and Felicity's parents about it was one thing… to his friends, quite another.

The image of her sweet face floated through his mind, along with the memory of whispered secret passions. Of walking in the garden with her, driving in the park, and even sitting beside her in her mother's drawing room.

Damn his eyes. He'd likely been at least a little in love with her for years but hadn't allowed himself to acknowledge it.

"I do."

Another cracking sound. "I had hoped your countess would have put an end to such a deplorable habit." Greys never failed to take Westerley to task for this.

"She loves me just the way I am." Westerley winked but then grew serious again. "Lady Felicity feels the same?" Westerley seemed stunned by the possibility—the cocky jackanapes.

"Did you think she'd pine for you forever?" Westerley had made quite certain that Felicity was no business of his. Mantis leaned forward. One more word and he would—

"We need to set a trap." Chaswick, always the peacekeeper, changed the topic of conversation. Disputes amongst them were generally limited to bets and wagers. They'd never had cause to fight over a woman before.

"Mantis is safe residing here." It was Spencer who began outlining a plan. "But don't go out without one of us, or one of Blackheart's men. Your assailant will make another move, and we'll nab him."

Mantis nodded. He was more than capable of defending himself, and he hated that he would be depending on others.

But there wasn't much he could do to stave off a bullet.

Mantis nodded. Yes. The plan wasn't all that original, but it was better than to wait around like a sitting duck.

Because if he wasn't alive, he couldn't protect Felicity.

RED ROSES AND CHOCOLATES

"This came for you."

Two days following Felicity's unfortunate disagreement with Axel in the garden, Susan entered her chamber carrying a single red rose and a small package wrapped in pink tissue. It was only one rose, but it was exquisite.

It was, perhaps, the most perfect rose she'd ever seen.

"The thorns have been removed." Susan handed over the small package. "There's a note attached. Should I put the rose in water?"

Such deep reds, almost in full bloom. Felicity held it to her nose and inhaled the sensual scent. It wouldn't last much longer. "Thank you."

Turning to the package, she slid the tiny note from beneath the bow. Carefully printed, it only consisted of four words.

Forgive me?

Yours, Axel

But there was nothing to forgive.

She turned it over, looking for something else. But no. That was all he'd written.

No invitation to go driving or offer to take her to Gunter's. As her mother wasn't hosting an at-home for another week, and the next ball was four days away, she wondered when she would see him again.

Inside the tissue, she found a single piece of chocolate. Sweet, rich... She set it aside for later that night.

And even though she knew it wasn't proper, Felicity located her small writing desk and penned a response.

Dearest Axel,

I'll only forgive you if you forgive me first. The rose is beautiful. And thank you for the chocolate.

She tapped the blunt end of the quill on her lips. She wanted to say more. Are you being careful? Have you discovered who is trying to kill you?

Do you miss me?

When are you going to kiss me again?... and do... other things?

She would not bring up the subject of his father again without more definitive proof.

Leaving all those questions off, she dipped the quill into the ink.

Yours,

Felicity

After dabbing a drop of her perfume onto the parchment, she sealed it and asked Susan to ensure it be delivered into no one's hands but his.

The following day, a second red rose arrived - with a second chocolate and another note.

You are forgiven.

Yours, Axel

Practically a week passed, a flower and chocolate arriving each day, a tender message attached, and yet not a single visit or invitation. Furthermore, he'd absented himself from the Middlebrook ball. Was he purposely avoiding her?

He had responsibilities other than her: his Jiu-Jitsu students, his clubs, tracking down would-be murderers.

And yet, doubt niggled at her. If he was avoiding her, that didn't bode well for their marriage. Especially considering their wedding ball was little over one week away.

And the day after that—their wedding.

The very day she determined to track him down herself, Susan peeked inside her chamber with excited eyes.

"Another flower?" Felicity asked.

"No. The viscount himself is here—in the front drawing room."

Felicity's mother had gone shopping, and her father was at his clubs. She ought to send him away until her mother returned, or at least make him cool his heels while she decided whether or not she would entertain his visit.

Such thoughts lasted less than ten seconds. Dabbing at the hair around her face, she turned to her maid. "Do I look presentable?"

"Always." Susan held the door. "But try not to look quite so eager."

Felicity schooled her features. Susan was right.

But she had missed him.

"Would you like me to act as chaperone?" Susan's voice stopped her.

"No. No. I doubt the visit will last very long, and... I'll leave the door cracked."

Susan of course, wouldn't insist, but she looked torn.

Felicity didn't take the time to reassure her but once she

was in the corridor, forced herself to walk at a sedate pace on her way to the drawing room.

She was as angry with him as she was excited to see his dear face. Apparently, the saying that absence made the heart grow fonder had some truth to it.

Even if it also made one's heart grow annoyed.

He was on his feet the instant she appeared and rushed across the room to take her hands in his.

"Felicity." A lock of his chestnut hair curved along his jaw as he pressed his lips to the back of her hand. *"How are you?"*

For once, seeing that he hadn't been ill, injured, or maimed in any way, Felicity didn't answer the question immediately. She couldn't allow herself to be softened so easily, but...

She tamped down the rush of affection from a single glance at his broad shoulders and tapered waist and his capable hands. Not to mention what she was coming to believe must surely be the most handsome face in all of England.

"I am fine." She forced displeasure into her voice. Six days had passed since he'd made any effort to see her. The flowers had been lovely, but...

"I wanted to come to you." He closed the door behind her and with one hand on the small of her back, led her to the settee in the middle of the room. "But I need to be careful. Twice now, I've put you in danger."

He lowered her onto the cushions to sit beside him.

"So...you haven't stayed away because of our argument?" Oh, but she sounded petty and clingy. "Did you catch the villain yet?"

Rather than answering either of her questions, he swept her into his arms and quite effectively erased all the supposed slights she had imagined. His mouth on hers, she smoothed her hands up his torso so her hands could play with the hairs at the back of his neck.

"Does it feel like I wanted to stay away from you?" He growled into her neck several minutes later.

"No." She wanted… Oh, she wanted more than just a kiss.

In just as swift of a move, he drew back. "Fetch a cloak or one of those floppy bonnets or whatever it is you ladies wear these days. A large one that might hide your identity. I have something to show you."

"Because of the danger?" But Felicity was already pushing herself to her feet. If she wished to go out alone with him, they'd best leave before either of her parents returned. "What is it? Tell me."

"A townhouse, for after the wedding. For us." His eyes danced in excitement. "But I want for you to see it before I sign the lease."

So… they wouldn't have to live with his father and step-mother for even a single day. More than pleased, she nodded and moved toward the door. They were going to look at a home that would belong to just the two of them!

Not five minutes later, she sat beneath the hood of a covered gig, not at all on display as they had been in his curricle.

One hand on her knee, Axel signaled the horses back onto the road. "The location isn't as exclusive as Brightley Place or Crest House, but it's more modern and has plenty of space to entertain. A mature garden, and a nursery…"

"Why?" She couldn't help asking. She wanted to know if he suspected his father now.

Her question silenced the stream of details he had been listing.

"Why?" He stretched his shoulders forward and then sat

back. "My father isn't trying to kill me." He sent her a warning glance. "But I'm done with his criticisms, and I won't give him the opportunity to insult you again."

She nodded. "You confronted him," she guessed. He drew his shoulders forward again, obviously uncomfortable with this train of conversation. But she persisted. "I'm going to be your wife, Axel. Don't shut me out."

This was an altogether different sort of intimacy than either of them had shared. She watched his throat move as though swallowing an unwanted emotion.

"The reason I'm not suspicious of him isn't that I have some misguided belief he's been harboring affection for me. It's because having two male offspring is something that's important to him."

Which made sense—with any other person. And yet, she found it difficult to dismiss her suspicions.

"I've been staying at Knight house," he said as he steered the carriage to the side of the street. "I doubt there's anywhere safer in London." They hadn't driven far, and the street was not an exclusive one, but it was inside the boundaries of Mayfair, and the house appeared to have been well maintained.

Axel was no longer residing in his family home. She would leave it be for now.

"That one." Mantis pointed to the house adjacent to where they stopped, and her breath caught. Not because there was anything extraordinary about it, but because it could be her future home.

The three-story house, set back from the street, was made up of red and maroon brick and was surrounded by an ornate iron fence. "It's lovely," Felicity breathed. "Can we go inside?"

"Of course." He assisted her out of the gig and opened the gate. "The back should have been left open for us."

Felicity pushed the cloak away from her face now that they were off the street and allowed the breeze to cool her skin. Well into the season now, summer wasn't long-off.

"How did you find it?"

Axel grinned. He seemed as excited about this as she was. He told her that Chaswick's father had kept the house for his mistress and her three daughters, who had been his daughters as well. Chase had taken responsibility for them after the old baron's death, but he no longer wished to keep them hidden. Bethany and her husband had decided to give his half-sisters the opportunity to participate in society.

With their mother having moved to the country with the youngest of them, the two older girls were now settled at Byrde House.

"That's rather daring of them." Felicity would help her friend, however. Presented properly, with backing from a few powerful members of the aristocracy, the illegitimate girls stood to be accepted by most members of the ton.

Not all—there would always be sticklers unwilling to forgive the circumstances surrounding their birth.

"Chaswick made updates upon his father's death." Mantis pushed the door open, and they stepped into a gleaming kitchen. "We'll hire servants, of course."

Felicity drug her fingertips along the edge of a countertop.

Her own home.

Their own home.

By the time he'd taken her upstairs to the main part of the house, she was quite enamored with the idea.

"And the master chamber." He gestured for her to enter. "We'll order new furniture, and I'm sure you'll wish to change out the wallcoverings. And there's an adjoining chamber for you..."

Felicity did not need to see it.

"I love it."

He hesitated with a frown. "You're not just telling me what you think I want to hear? I wasn't sure since it belonged to the old baron's mistress..." He searched her gaze anxiously. "It isn't nearly as—"

She threw herself into his arms. And in case he'd not heard her properly before, "I love it."

His arms clamped around her. She didn't care who had previously lived in the house. It was going to be theirs!

After a rather dizzying kiss, he lowered her onto her feet and then bent his forehead to rest it against hers.

"So." His breath fanned her lips. *"How are you?"*

"Perfect." Felicity trailed a finger down the side of his face, tenderly tracing the raised skin of his white scar.

He covered her hand with his.

"My father did this," he whispered. "I never meant to shut you out."

She held her breath, shocked at what he was telling her and... given her suspicions... that he was telling her at all. She needed to be worthy of his trust.

"He refused to use foils when he sparred with me. Said I needed to comprehend what real danger felt like."

Felicity flicked her gaze away from the hazel depths of his in order to examine the scar closely. About three inches long, it was mostly straight except for one section where it widened. He'd told her once that it had gone deep.

At the hand of his own father.

"Our child—boy, girl, sickly or strong—will never doubt my love," Axel vowed.

Felicity moved her fingertips to his lips. She hadn't doubted this for an instant. "I know."

But beware of your own father. She wanted to beg.

"I'm just trying to protect you." His voice sounded gruff.

Of course, he was. Felicity nodded, a swell of emotion threatening to dissolve her into tears. Blinking hard, she pushed them down.

"Now tell me what is being done to capture whoever is causing us so much trouble." They didn't have much time. Her parents were likely home already and preparing to reprimand the two of them for going off together alone.

But she also needed to know what was being done to ensure his safety.

He explained that assistance was never far off—that even now, just outside, two of Blackheart's men had followed him and were likely surveying the gardens. Unfortunately, although they'd laid a few traps, they'd failed to lure the assailants into the open again. They couldn't pinpoint the person behind the attacks without capturing one of the hired thugs first.

"I hate the thought that even now, you're in danger. Because of me," Axel said.

She couldn't help but think that the attacks had something to do with their engagement… and the baby. And that the only people who knew about the baby were their respective families.

The incentive to end his life would be diminished after their marriage. Because then, not only would Axel stand in the way of the earldom, but her child as well.

If the child was a boy.

And as long as the culprit wasn't willing to kill all of them.

"Let's wed by special license," the words flew from her

mouth almost frantically. "And then leave for the country." She didn't care about setting up her household in Mayfair. All that mattered was that nothing happened to him or their child.

Sometime between last March and now, those two lives had become more important than her own.

Axel touched his mouth to hers. "Hush now. One more week. I'm going to return you home, and I promise to keep you appraised of our progress. But being with you today, like this, it's selfish on my part. I want you safe."

But they wouldn't find the culprit if they persisted in looking in all the wrong places!

It was his father. It had to be his father.

"You promise you'll tell me when you learn anything new?" She didn't want him to take her home yet.

A bed beckoned just a few feet away. She dropped her gaze. What if it was their last chance?

"Felicity." He commanded her attention. "Look at me. I will handle this. I want... no. I need you to trust me. I—" He turned to look out the window across the room before meeting her stare again. "It isn't my father, but he's being watched anyway. Does that make you feel better?"

It did. She nodded and then tilted her head back, parting her lips because she already craved his kiss again.

"You weren't at the Middlebrook ball."

"My attendance could have put others at risk. I'll be scarce until we draw him out again. But wild horses won't keep me from our prewedding ball."

The prewedding ball—to be held at Crest House.

Felicity shivered. Unless she was wrong, they would be entering the lion's den.

But he'd said his father was being watched. Could Axel be

protected from the man in his own home? From loyal servants?

She was going to have to trust him.

The words *I love you* were on the tip of her tongue, and then she caught herself.

She loved him?

She did.

Good lord.

Felicity buried her face against his chest. She'd truly fallen in love with her fiancé this time, and some unknown person was trying to kill him.

"If you don't show up for our wedding, I'll kill you myself," she grumbled and only held onto him more tightly when she felt his chest shake with silent laughter.

"If I don't show up, I'll deserve it."

THE DAY BEFORE

*F*elicity stared down at the street below her window, the early morning sun casting a delicate light on the grass and flowers bordering the street.

One more day before she and Axel were to take their wedding vows. And one more day—she couldn't help but believe—until their marriage would protect them both.

But if the attacks hadn't originated from Lord Crestwood, then who?

She'd even gone to her father, asking him if he knew of anyone who might want Axel killed.

He'd told her the attacks were likely nothing more than a few pranks gone wrong, but offered to speak with Lord Crestwood about it. Felicity told him that wasn't necessary.

She'd promised Axel that she would trust him. Surely, he knew his father better than she did?

Asking her father to step in was hardly the way to make good on her promise.

Furthermore, she hadn't bothered correcting her father's assumption that the attacks had only been pranks.

Because then she'd have to explain to him that she'd felt the air from the bullet as it whistled past them in the park, and she'd have to explain how she'd seen the glint of knives pointed at them with deadly intentions. She'd have to provide some explanation for why she and Axel had been separated from the others at Vauxhall, to begin with.

She hugged her arms in front of her and shivered at the memory of shedding all her inhibitions and relinquishing control of the most intimate parts of her body.

It felt like a lifetime ago. Had it even been real?

The door pushed open, and Susan appeared in her chamber carrying a tray filled with tea and biscuits and a few other breakfast foods.

And another single rose. So far, she had received fifteen, and she'd carefully pressed all but the one from yesterday in her leather journal.

Not bothering to wait for Susan to set the tray down, Felicity hurried across the room, swiping the flower off the tray and opening the note that was attached to it.

Save me a few dances.

Axel

She all but choked on relief as she dropped onto the chair beside her bed. Not only was he safe, but he was in good humor and had even managed to sound romantic. Just as she'd treasured the flowers, she kept each note hidden away in her jewelry box.

Someday, she would read through them and look back on this time and laugh at the drama of it all... that, or cry.

She prayed she wouldn't be looking back on it alone.

"I'll certainly be happy when all this is over." Susan went to work mixing a cup of tea the way Felicity liked it.

"Me, too, Susan." Which was the understatement of the century.

The last time he'd come to her, his visit had been short, barely allowing him time enough to fill her in on their progress—or lack thereof. She hadn't asked for details because in the moments her mother stepped out, Axel had taken it upon himself to show her in no uncertain terms how much he missed her.

Tomorrow, after the ceremony and the wedding breakfast, she and Axel could begin their lives together without having to please anyone but themselves. They wouldn't have to worry about being stumbled upon or interrupted, and the two of them could do all sorts of delicious things in the privacy of the bed-chamber in their own house on Farm Street.

They could simply *be* together.

"I have your gown pressed and laid out on the bed. A bath will be readied shortly." Susan examined the list she'd been keeping. "And the roses are scheduled to be delivered at five this evening. Can you think of anything I might be missing?" Felicity shook her head. She couldn't ask for a more efficient lady's maid.

The gown she would wear to her wedding tomorrow was made up of mint green and pristine whites. She would wear a crown made up of ivy and tiny white flowers and carry a similar bouquet.

Tonight, however, she'd gone in an entirely different direction.

Her silk gown was a deep scarlet color and would have been considered exceptionally revealing, but for the lace fichu she would tuck into her bodice. And in her hair, Susan was going to weave fifteen tiny red roses.

"Not eating isn't going to help time pass any more quickly," her maid pointed out helpfully.

"Quite right." Felicity buttered a piece of her toast and shivered unexpectedly. One more day. He would be safe in one more day.

~

"OUR UNINVITED GUEST is still out there," Stone Spencer announced. "He disappears behind the large oak and then shows up from the opposite side."

After three failed attempts to trap the weasel, Mantis had kept himself hidden for the past two days. In that time, they'd spied a very unexceptional looking person lurking on the street for no apparent reason. Dark brown coat, grey trousers, dusty boots, and a dulled black cap would have been commonplace anywhere else, but this was Mayfair.

His very blandness was, in fact, what set him apart.

He had to be their man.

Mantis was ready—*more than ready*. He bent forward, tapped the side of his boot where he'd hidden his knife, and then straightened, flexing his hands and summoning his focus for the task on hand. His heartbeat was slow and even, and the air filling his lungs sent power surging through him.

"You remember the route?" Greystone stood beside him, looking even more like a dandy than usual—intentionally.

Mantis and the marquess would appear to be in deep conversation. They would feign disinterest in their surroundings and seem distracted from the possibility of any threats. The ruse would hopefully be invitation enough for the villain to make his move.

Blackheart held the door, and Mantis and Greys stepped

outside, Greys swinging a gleaming walking stick and Mantis clutching his hat in front of him.

Without having to look, Mantis felt the man watching them. As he and Greys made their way toward an unpopulated parcel of the park, he had no doubt they were being followed.

They would be successful this time, and Mantis could put Felicity's worry at ease. The two of them could finally look toward their future.

But he couldn't think about that now.

He leaned toward Greys and nodded, feigning interest in whatever his friend was going on about.

"Do you think Chaswick's sisters will take?" Greys, it would seem, intended to make actual conversation. Chaswick's sisters? Ah, the one's who'd grown up in the house on Farm Street. Would their illegitimacy hold them back despite their titled brother and sister-in-law's acceptance?

"The ton is fickle," Mantis said. "Some will accept them, but not all."

"Delightful gels, very pretty really. Violet says they have excellent manners."

An unusual tone in his friend's voice had Mantis slanting him a sideways glance. "You're not taken with one of them, are you?"

A forced laugh and then, "God no. Far too young for me." Greys tapped his walking stick jauntily. "And unsophisticated."

But then he frowned. Their arrival at the entrance to the park prevented Mantis from probing further. He needed to train all his wits on their surroundings now. This section of the park offered all the seclusion a would-be attacker could dream of.

Mantis and Greys turned onto the dirt trail.

Spying a forested area, Mantis couldn't help but recall Felicity seated on the bench in the woods, her head thrown back while he'd pleasured her intimately. Which then had him remembering how she'd looked with her hands pressed against the tree, her back arched, vulnerable, trusting... the sounds she made leading up to her completion... and the sighs afterward...

Even though he'd taken a few occasions to visit her father's house and sit with her, a concerning distance had wedged itself between them.

She said she trusted him, but he'd seen the doubt in her eyes. And seeing that doubt stirred doubts of his own.

She never would have consented to marry him if circumstances hadn't compelled her. She'd insisted she no longer pined for Westerley, but had she only been saying that because it was what he wanted to hear?

She wanted him. He didn't doubt that. And God knew he wanted her.

They'd pretended to be a love match for her parents, and somehow, he'd found himself believing all of it.

Damn his eyes. He needed time alone with her—time to simply enjoy her without worrying about some blighter waiting around the corner intent upon plunging a knife in his heart.

And he would have that time. Tonight was their prewedding ball and tomorrow the wedding. If somehow they failed today, he would load up a caravan of carriages and whisk his new bride and their unborn child to his country estate the day after.

Along with a handful of outriders.

Armed.

"Up ahead at two o'clock," Greys commented, and Mantis shoved all thoughts of her away. Now was not the time to lose focus.

"Another at five," Mantis spoke between clenched teeth.

He and Greys had other fellows around them as well. Two of Blackheart's men, and of course, Spencer, Chase, and Blackheart himself.

The next turn would place he and Greys in an even more isolated setting. Mantis forced himself to appear relaxed.

But he was ready.

The two of them strolled casually into the darkened section of the path, and less than five seconds after ducking into the shade, heavy footsteps set off a scurry of chaos.

A rope dropped over his head from behind. Mantis caught hold of the rough fibers before they could tighten around his neck, but he couldn't shake the man as easily as he'd have liked.

Mantis was a sizeable man, but the person behind him was even larger. And stronger. Both of which Mantis would use against him.

Crossing his left arm over his right, he bent forward, effectively using the bastard's own momentum to throw him onto the ground at his feet.

Beside him, Greys brandished his cane and sent a second villain fleeing.

Blackheart was scuffling higher up the side of the hill, and in a similar move to the one Mantis had used on his attacker, flipped the criminal, and would have sent him tumbling down the hill alone if only his opponent had been so obliging as to loosen his grip on Blackheart's coat.

The two landed not three feet away. Mantis winced at the cracking sound.

Unfortunately, their sudden appearance was enough of a distraction for the man he'd nearly neutralized to land a fist in his gut, temporarily robbing him of air, and then whip out another weapon.

The second knife hovered, but Mantis grabbed hold of the man's wrist and squeezed.

When a gunshot sounded behind him, Mantis didn't allow himself to be distracted.

Because, by God, he'd promised Felicity she would not be forced to raise their child alone.

A hand wrapped around his neck, but Mantis kicked back, sweeping his attacker's legs out from under him.

And then they were both on the ground.

Dirt flew in his eyes, causing him to momentarily lose sight of the knife at the same time he bent the villain's arms unnaturally. The man grunted, and then spit, and then wrapped his legs around Mantis' waist to unbalance him.

It was precisely what Mantis needed, and in the next second, he was straddling the bastard, pressing his assailant's grubby hands into the ground.

Blackheart retrieved the knife.

"Who sent you?" Mantis demanded. The man turned his head and spat again. There was something familiar about him. Likely he'd fought him off at Vauxhall. "Is someone out to avenge my father? Tell me who sent you."

His question was met with silence. Mantis applied more pressure on the man's wrists, nearly enough to shatter bones. "Answer if you ever want to use your hands again."

"Nothing to do with Lord Crestwood," he grunted.

"Then who?"

More bodies hurled at them from out of the brush, and turning, Mantis loosened his hold when a fist connected with one of his eyes. Seeing the flash of yet another knife, he twisted the man's arm just as one of his cohorts piled onto the two of them.

Mantis smelled the blood, as did the others, who scrambled away as quickly as they appeared. Blackheart's men would take chase. They would catch most of them.

But when Mantis sat back on his knees, he swore. The weight of the second fellow had plunged his attacker's knife into the man's own chest. The unfocussed gaze staring up at him was unmistakable.

He'd get no more answers out of this one.

He could only hope one of the other men knew who was behind the attacks. Because if they had nothing to do with his father, that meant someone had wanted him, Mantis, dead, for some other reason.

THE PERFECT WALTZ

*M*antis exited onto the front step of Crest House just in time to watch Felicity's father's carriage draw to a halt. They had been invited to arrive early so as to join Mantis, Crestwood, and his stepmother in the reception line.

By tomorrow at this time, Mantis would be a married man.

He curled his shoulders forward inside the tightly fitted jacket Cornell had ordered for the occasion, and then fidgeted with the embroidery edging his scarlet waistcoat. He might as well have pilfered the garments from Greystone's wardrobe.

This particular ensemble was only slightly less elaborate than the apparel laid out for him to wear tomorrow morning. His wedding day.

Standing before a church full of people was not something he'd normally be willing to do. Returning to his father's house for the prewedding ball wasn't something he'd been keen on either.

But for Felicity.

He would do anything.

A footman had hopped off the back of the carriage and was pulling down the step. Mantis, however, beat him to open the door.

Brightley exited first, glanced curiously when he caught sight of Mantis' eye, which was swollen and purple, and then assisted Lady Brightley behind him. Mantis shuffled his feet impatiently.

He'd managed to visit her only twice since they'd inspected the townhouse together, and her mother, most unfortunately, had been present for most of both occasions. But for all of about seven minutes, he'd not been allowed to be alone with her.

But it had paid off. She was safe.

Lady Brightley moved away from the step, finally allowing Mantis to lean into the carriage to take her hand.

Air whooshed out of his lungs for the second time that afternoon.

Only this time...

It was due to the astonishing revelation that this woman... was going to be his wife.

Her scarlet gown, which accentuated her pale, swan-like neck and delicate face, hinted at the passionate nature she hid from the rest of the world.

Red roses threaded through the golden silk of her hair.

"Felicity." He reached inside. None of the compliments he summoned were good enough.

She's too good for me. She placed her gloved hand in his, allowing him to draw her out of the carriage and into the warm evening air.

Precious indeed, the lavender scent he loved mingled with the heady perfume of the roses.

"What happened to you?" She reached up to touch her fingertips to the corner of his eye. How many times had she done the same with his scar?

"Nothing." He'd tell her everything later. Although there wasn't much to tell. "But it's over."

As luck would have it, the man who'd died at the hand of his own knife had been the ring-leader—the intermediary—between the person who'd wanted Mantis killed and the people being paid to accomplish that.

Trouble was, without the dead man to pay them, the various thugs were no longer eager to complete the job they'd set out to accomplish.

For now, anyhow, Mantis could breathe a sigh of relief.

"Did you find out who it was?" Felicity whispered while her parents preceded them into the drawing room, where they would partake of drinks with his father and Louisa.

"The man who jumped us at Vauxhall is dead, and his helpers are no longer interested in killing me."

"But... who? Why?"

Mantis wished he had more answers. "Unless the culprit hires others to do the job, he'll remain a mystery. And with word on the street that payment was withheld, it's all but impossible he'll be able to hire someone else." He twisted his mouth into a wry smile. "Apparently, murder isn't cheap."

"But he is still out there."

"Possibly. But we are safe for now."

One hand at her back, he led his betrothed into his former home and, he supposed, his future home, to celebrate the eve of their wedding.

"I am more than happy to forget about knives and guns and poisons for the rest of my life, if possible." Felicity relaxed and grinned up at him. Halting, she turned and drew one hand down the front of his waistcoat. "We match."

Mantis pinched back a grin of his own. "A serendipitous coincidence."

"Knowing my maid, I've no doubt she consulted with your valet."

In no hurry to join their parents, the two of them continued slowly inside, exchanging entertaining anecdotes about her maid and his valet.

And it felt good. Very good.

"Sherry, Lady Felicity?" Louisa greeted them with a wide smile. "Don't the two of you look simply charming this evening?"

"I wasn't sure about the scarlet," Lady Brightley began. "But it's truly the most stunning I've ever seen. Our children are going to be all the rage."

Axel's father peered at his fob watch. "When does the blasted festivity commence?" He placed himself at the window where a few carriages were pulling to a halt below. "I'll be happy for some peace and quiet when all of this is over."

"Nice shiner there, Mantis," Lord Brightley commented.

"I occasionally spar with Mr. Stone Spencer. Failed to dodge his left hook."

The Earl narrowed his eyes but then nodded. "Broke my nose a few times myself when I was your age."

Mantis chatted with Lord Brightley while his own father added to the conversation with an occasional grunt. Felicity conversed with Cordelia, but their mothers were far too concerned with final wedding details to engage in casual chit-chat.

"Now would be an excellent time to form the reception line," Mr. Mortimer announced from the door.

Which would bring him one step closer to having Felicity in his arms again. Because, of course, he and his bride were expected to lead off the dancing—a waltz.

And given half a chance, he would whisk her into the shadows of the garden later on.

But first, he'd need to make his bow to damn near every breathing resident in all of Mayfair.

Nearly an hour later, Felicity grasped his arm, leaning into him. "I don't remember having to curtsy this much at my come-out."

Mantis wound an arm around her, remembering how pale she'd looked when she first arrived in London. She had wanted a proper wedding, but he hadn't considered how it might affect her health.

Louisa sent him a warning look—because, of course, holding his future wife in public like this wasn't at all proper.

Propriety be damned. "Do you need to sit down?"

"No. No. I'm fine," Felicity assured him. But he kept his hand at her back.

"Just a little longer." He glanced toward the door, grateful to see the end in sight. Any latecomers could say hello to him some other time, and if they didn't like that, they could go to the devil. An appreciation for promptness was one of the rare things he had in common with his father.

With most guests already in the ballroom, Mantis endured the pomp and circumstance of being announced and promptly found a place for Felicity to sit.

"You do look pale, Felicity." Louisa hovered nearby. "I'll fetch you a lemonade."

"I'm fine, really."

He knew that those present would want to mingle with the guests of honor, but for a few moments, he wanted Felicity to himself.

Mantis lowered himself beside her. Turning his back to their guests, he effectively blocked anyone who might take it upon themselves to approach.

"Have you eaten anything?"

"Some meat and fruit before we came." She squeezed his hands. "Really, I am fine. But... thank you."

He grimaced. "Are you sure? I've not much experience with this sort of thing, but I do know that a single evening isn't worth compromising your condition. Did you approve of the midwife?"

"I did. And I have an appointment scheduled for next week. Now," Felicity tilted her head. "I'm fine. I promise to tell you the second I feel otherwise. Trust me?"

The same request he had made of her.

"Yes."

Her gaze flicked to his eye, and she reached up to dab at the corner. "Does it hurt?"

"Only if you poke your finger in it," he grinned and she rolled her eyes at him.

Would he ever not worry about her?

Felicity glanced around the room and then lowered her voice. "I'm glad it wasn't your father. I only wish we knew who..."

Mantis placed his finger over her lips. "We aren't talking about this tonight, remember?"

"I forgot."

"I forgive you."

She laughed. "I'm glad to have such an excellent partner to

lead me. I had no idea our mothers would invite so many people."

He'd not once seen Lady Felicity Brightley nervous in any social situation. "It won't be the same as it was at Vauxhall," he sighed.

And at the mention of the pleasure gardens, her eyes darkened.

~

"I DON'T SUPPOSE it will be." Tingling awareness flowed from Felicity's fingertips to her core. "But, perhaps we could walk in the garden after."

His brows rose. "Perhaps we could."

"You could show me some of your fighting moves," she teased. She could hardly wait for the two of them to do normal things together.

"So you want to grapple with me?"

"Is that what you call that?"

Axel didn't answer out loud, but his eyes sparkled with promise.

But not until later. How was it they were so different than one another but wanted the same things?

"I'm so glad it was you." The instant she said the words, she realized they didn't make sense. "Before… all of this happened. I always admired you—your strength, and loyalty toward your friends." Despite his size, he'd never seemed threatening. And although she hadn't allowed herself to think about men other than Westerley, his looks had not gone unnoticed by her. "You are the most handsome of all of them."

He shook his head. "My father says I am benign."

It wasn't a description she would have expected his father to use. It meant gentle, kindly, non-threatening.

She remembered how he'd held her hands against the tree, how she'd trusted him unreservedly. In some ways, the word was wholly accurate. If he'd been any other way, she never could have surrendered herself the way she had.

But she had also watched him fight off a gang of knife-wielding villains using nothing but his bare hands. And he'd not hesitated to stand up to her father.

Her gaze landed on his mouth. No. He was so much more than kind. He was... potent.

"He does not know you then," Felicity said. Because her giant of a viscount was so much more than the amiable man most took him for.

His eyes darkened.

"I'm going to make you happy," he said. "Keep you satisfied."

Felicity held her breath.

"I know we've been pretending—"

"You cannot live in one another's pockets all evening." Felicity's future mother-in-law appeared just behind Mantis, peering down on them. "You'll have plenty of time for that later."

Mantis had clamped his mouth shut.

"Even after you're married, it's considered rude for a gentleman not to make himself available to at least a few of the wallflowers." Lady Crestwood clucked her tongue.

Felicity's big-hearted, obliging viscount was on his feet. "Of course. But I'll return shortly."

"Something cool and refreshing for you." The countess pressed a cold glass into Felicity's hand even as Mantis backed away.

"Thank you, my lady," she murmured.

"You must call me Louisa," her future mother-in-law smiled warmly.

"Thank you, then, Louisa." Felicity set her glass on a small table and stood. "And you are right. What will our guests think if I sit here alone all evening?" As if on cue, her dearest friend appeared with a stunning redheaded lady at her side. Lady Westerley.

"You look positively stunning! You are glowing!" Bethany said.

Lady Crestwood slid a meaningful glance to Felicity and over to the untouched refreshment. "Don't forget to drink up, dear." She waved at someone across the ballroom and then slipped away.

Felicity turned her attention to her friend. Bethany had changed since her marriage to Lord Chaswick. She seemed more confident and happy, and if anyone glowed, it was her. "I only hope marriage suits me as well as it obviously suits you."

Bethany smiled secretly. "Seeing as Mantis can hardly keep his eyes off you, I have no doubt that it will."

Knowing it was time, Felicity turned to greet the other woman. "You are looking lovely this evening, Miss Jack—my lady."

Felicity never stumbled on names, but the last time she'd spoken with Westerley's bride felt like a lifetime ago.

"Thank you, my lady. And, of course, you look absolutely stunning." Westerley's countess bit her lip. "I know you must hold me in contempt for everything, and I am so terribly so—"

"No," Felicity stopped her. "I am happy. And I am glad you are happy. Everything has turned out for the best."

And she meant it with all her heart. Because she *loved* Axel.

And she wished she could tell the world, but first, she ought to tell him.

Tomorrow. After the ceremony... when they could be alone.

"I have felt horrible about all of it." The lovely American, indeed, looked pained.

"Please, don't. In fact, I want to thank you," she added in case the other woman was left with any doubt. "Westerley and I didn't suit."

"I just..."

"Honestly. Everything has turned out for the better."

After a pause, the love of Westerley's life exhaled with a nervous laugh.

Before her former betrothal had been called off, Felicity had liked the American heiress. She'd wanted to be friends, and now, as it turned out, it was possible again.

Miss Rachel Somerset, another girl who'd made her come-out with Bethany and Felicity, stepped into their circle and leaned in conspiratorially.

"Does not Lord Manningham-Tissinton look even more handsome with his eye swollen and purple?"

Felicity wasn't sure how she was supposed to answer something like that. Because, of course, he did. But that didn't mean she appreciated other ladies, especially Rachel Somerset, ogling him.

Bethany eyed the other woman and scowled, but Lady Westerley shook her head. "It isn't fair! If it were you or I with a blackened eye like that, we'd need to wear a mask to cover it, or more likely, go into hiding until it faded and hope our servants didn't make up stories as to how we got it."

"My mother's maid would no doubt spread all kinds of stories," Miss Somerset offered.

"Chaswick's servants are wonderfully discreet—quite unlike my mother's," Bethany said. "Which reminds me…" She twisted around, "Chaswick's sisters are here tonight. He's making the rounds with them, and I promised I wouldn't be gone long. Last week, at the Middleton ball, I found Collette hiding behind one of the plants while Diana accosted a duke."

"They'll take. Let me know if I can help in any way." Before Bethany could disappear, Felicity reached out and squeezed her friend's hand. "I'm so glad you are here." And to Lady Westerley, of whom Bethany looked about to drag away with her. "Thank you."

Just then, the conductor of the small orchestra took his place, and a moment later, Mantis appeared at her side.

"Ready?" he asked.

"Absolutely." And she realized that she had looked forward to this moment for days now.

Not being the center of attention, not dancing, nor showing off her beautiful new gown. But being in his arms.

Dancing with him.

Touching him.

And as he led her onto the shining wooden floor, warmth blossomed in her chest.

She'd been foolish not to have noticed him before Westerley broke off their engagement. She had been blind.

Because Viscount Manningham-Tissinton—her fiancé, her friend, but also her lover—was by far the most handsome and elegant man in attendance that evening.

And he was hers.

He settled his arm around her back, clasping her hand with his other.

Proud. Aristocratic. Masculine. But so much more!

She could barely suppress a shiver of awareness.

The music began, and he whisked her around the floor, making her feel like a princess... light and airy, almost as though she was flying.

Like an angel.

Even with all eyes watching them, he leaned closer and whispered, "I'd hold you closer if I thought I could get away with it."

"I might allow it even if you couldn't."

To which he growled—growled!—near her ear. He spun her effortlessly, and Felicity didn't bother stifling her laugh.

Because she was happy.

"When are you free to walk in the garden?" Axel's question was a good one, and she glanced at the card her mother tied onto her wrist earlier that evening.

"You did save another set for me, didn't you?"

She moved her hand to check again, but... "I'm going to kill my mother." Even the Supper set had been promised—to a distant uncle no less.

"In that case—" Axel pulled her closer, almost as scandalously close as he'd held her when they danced at Vauxhall. "I'll have to make the most of this one. But tomorrow night, you are all mine."

NIGGLING DOUBTS

Felicity had hoped she would get a good night's sleep when she climbed into bed. The last thing she wanted was to look haggard and tired when promenaded toward her groom at the altar.

Her body, however, refused to cooperate.

Or rather, her mind refused.

Because as she lay in her bed, she couldn't stop reimagining the events of the night, remembering conversations, and reliving the most romantic dance of her life...

Axel had been as preoccupied as she had been. Not on the dance floor, although he danced some lively sets with both Lord Greystone's cousins and Lord Chaswick's sisters, but mostly with other gentlemen. He all but disappeared for the second half of the night, and almost as though by habit, she'd found herself worrying for his safety. Even after her mother had reassured her that he was heartily engaged with the gentlemen in the card room.

She would have felt better if she'd been able to find him to say goodbye.

"A bridegroom mustn't see his bride on their wedding day," Lady Crestwood had insisted while sending her mother an indulgent smirk. "And since midnight has come and gone, I refuse to send for him. I'll have no part in inviting bad luck."

Felicity rolled to her other side and punched her pillow.

There was no such thing as bad luck.

He'd told her he didn't believe himself to be in any danger. That man that died had told him his father wasn't involved.

Was it wise to believe the words of a criminal?

Was it possible to love Axel and not trust his judgment?

Felicity threw an arm over her eyes. This was ridiculous. She had no reason whatsoever not to trust him.

The next morning, when she stared into the looking glass over her vanity, the first thing she noticed were dark circles etched beneath her eyes.

"Whoever decided weddings should be held in the morning deserves to be shot," she grumbled.

"Cold feet?" Susan teased.

It wasn't cold feet. Felicity inhaled a deep breath. Not at all.

Because she loved, and she trusted, her fiancé. The thought calmed her. Axel knew his father. Furthermore, he wasn't one to fool himself.

"Just nerves."

"You'll feel better after a hot bath and some tea. And before you know it, you'll be happily married to your handsome viscount."

Felicity hoped so.

She forced a smile and did her best to appreciate that this was a day she'd waited for all her life.

For as long as she could remember, she'd thought her

bridegroom would be a very different man. Now, she could not imagine marrying Westerley.

Westerley was a good person, an honorable gentleman. But he'd never made her feel the way that Axel did. His kisses had been pleasant, but they hadn't heated her blood, filled her heart with so much affection, nor her body with so many wicked urges.

She smiled and lowered herself into the scented water Susan had prepared for her. "The rose petals are a delightful touch. Thank you, Susan."

Her maid handed her the soap. "I'll wash your hair, and then you can sit back and soak."

Felicity tilted her head back allowing the hot water to run down her neck and over her shoulders.

"You are acquainted with Polly, Lady Bethany's maid, are you not?" Very often, whenever Bethany and Felicity ventured out together, their maids followed behind them.

"She is one of my closest friends," Susan confirmed.

"Tell me, and I promise your answer stays between the two of us—is she a gossip? Has she ever revealed anything private about Lady Chaswick, or the household in general?" Last night Bethany had maintained that her servants never gossiped. This was one of the thoughts that had been bothering Felicity.

"Never. In fact, she has told me that she'd never lived in a household where their family's privacy took such high priority. Likely has something to do with the baron's history."

"And what history is that?"

"You'll not be catching me gossiping so easily, my lady." Tsking, Susan poured another pitcher of warm water to finish rinsing her hair and then used a soft washcloth to soap Felicity's shoulders and back. "To be honest, all I know about that is from the papers. Is it true the Baron presented his half-sisters to society?"

"With Lady Chaswick's sponsorship. And they are lovely girls." Felicity leaned forward, allowing Susan's hands to massage her back and neck. Why was this important?

Somebody had said something which had made her think Bethany's servants gossiped. Why would that matter?

MANTIS PACED across the unfamiliar chamber where he'd been told to wait. On one wall, a crucifix suspended between two dark but religious paintings. On the other, richly covered garments draped on hooks beside the bishop's headdress. It reminded him of the costumes hanging in the dressing rooms backstage at the theatre on Drury Lane.

Mantis had woken at sunrise, despite not retiring until the early morning hours. Blackheart, along with Westerley, Greys, Chase, and Spencer, had toasted he and Felicity's future with some of the finest whisky ever made.

Hell, they'd lifted their glasses even before the ball concluded.

Several times.

Of which his head wasn't shy in reminding him.

After bathing, having a shave, and then dressing in his finery with Cornell's help, he had walked to the church early. Nothing. Absolutely nothing could keep him from standing at that altar, watching Felicity walk toward him on her father's arm.

He glanced at his watch. Only half past the hour. Doubtful she'd even left Bright Place yet.

Aside from the first set of the night, their waltz, both he

and Felicity had been busy with well-wishing guests for the remainder of the night. When he'd stolen a moment to himself, she, inevitably, was being led in a dance by some relative or another. And the few times he'd spied her, hopefully looking around for him, he'd been unable to extract himself in time to claim her.

At the end of the night, when he'd emerged from the card room to find her, Louisa had informed him that her parents had already escorted her home.

He'd felt... bereft.

Likely that was why he was sitting in this vestibule with far too much time on his hands. Because he missed her and thought that waiting here would bring him closer to the moment he'd become her husband.

Her most devoted, ridiculously besotted husband.

The door opened, and a face he hadn't expected to see appeared.

Wearing his butler garb, one arm in a black sling, Blackheart stepped into the priestly place of solitude.

"Grey's household will have to run without your services over the next few weeks." Mantis grimaced at the Duke's injured arm. "I hope this doesn't mean Chaswick and I are going to have to bare our arses for all to see at the end of the season."

He sincerely hoped not. If he lost the bet, he'd have to make other arrangements. Because he was seriously contemplating taking Felicity to Tissinton Towers before the season's end.

Blackheart closed the door behind him. "Not at all, Mantis." And then he tapped the side of his head with his good hand. "Butlering isn't much different than running a dukedom—simply requires efficiency and management."

"So I'm safe then?"

In answer, his friend smiled enigmatically.

"I'm sorry to have missed our morning session," he said. "Thought I'd see how you're holding up." Even while making an apology, wearing a sling, Blackheart appeared imposing.

"Meditating only goes so far," Mantis replied.

Blackheart nodded. Of course, he understood. "But regrets?"

On this, Mantis was quite confident. "None at all. I do wish, however, that we could have fleshed out who was behind—"

"The attacks originated from inside your father's household—not your father."

"A servant?" Mantis mentally ran through the roster of individuals working at Crest House.

"I have a man on it, and I'll know more this afternoon. But I wanted you updated."

Mantis nodded, glad nothing had happened during the ball last night. And seeing as he had no intention of returning there anytime soon… he exhaled. "Thank you."

He'd be happy to begin his life with Felicity, minus that unfortunate cloud hanging over them. With the matter concluded, he and Felicity could remain in London for the rest of the season, which would allow for the repairs and renovations to be completed at Tissinton Towers before taking her there.

"Another reason I've come," Blackheart slipped a hand in his pocket and withdrew a familiar drawstring velvet bag. "His Lordship left these sitting on his bureau."

"Greys forgot the rings?" Mantis laughed as he shoved the small purse into his own pocket, thinking it might come in handy sometime in the future. "My thanks."

Blackheart landed his good hand to Mantis' shoulder. "You've made an excellent choice for your bride—regardless how it came about. I wish you happy."

At the unexpected glimpse of emotion in his friend's eyes, Mantis' throat thickened.

He cleared it.

"My thanks, again. For everything."

"It's what I'm here for."

And as quickly as he arrived, Blackheart disappeared.

Shrugging off the uncomfortable sentimentality, Mantis rubbed the back of his neck.

Someone in his father's household? But who? And why? Something Conner told him flashed in his mind. Something about his tutor...

"Mr. Rudolph says it's far more important for a future lord to fill out before testing himself physically."

A future lord? Assuming Mantis lived to be an old man, assuming he and Felicity produced a son... Conner's claim to the title of lord was almost non-existent. Why would his tutor tell him that...?

"Knock knock?" This time, it was Louisa who peered around the half-open door. "I brought you tea and some biscuits and jam... We miss seeing you at Crest House and I thought you might appreciate some sustenance while you're waiting."

"That wasn't necessary." The sight of his stepmother, in an elegant gown and ornate feathered hat, standing in this very masculine abode was a jarring one.

Taken aback by her presence, he watched as she lowered a tray to one of the only uncluttered tables and then poured hot brown liquid into an irritatingly fragile teacup.

"One sugar, no cream?" She asked.

He nodded. "Yes."

Louisa had always been cordial enough to him, but it was odd that she would suddenly decide he would want her maternal affection.

Had she decided to make amends for the past?

"Thank you." He accepted the cup. As Felicity had told him more than once, tea was always a good idea.

THE WEDDING DAY

"Is it true the Viscount and those other lords captured the person trying to murder his lordship?" Susan finished pinning the elaborate knot on the crown of Felicity's head and began winding the ivy around it. Several small white flowers lay out on parchment, waiting to be attached to the coiffure as well.

Felicity frowned. "He did. But where did you hear about that?" Despite their attempts to keep the attacks mostly private, news of it had apparently spread like wildfire.

Susan paused and tapped a finger to her chin. "I believe one of the delivery men told cook about it."

Felicity rolled her eyes in dismay. Not a day had passed after the Vauxhall incident before the news had been made public. They might just as well have sent details to the Gazette.

Apparently, the servants at Byrd House weren't as discreet as Bethany believed them to be.

But...

Felicity closed her eyes, a troubling memory teasing her.

"I understand you had quite the harrowing experience at Vaux-hall last night."

Lady Crestwood had known... How had she known?

Felicity supposed word could have traveled from Chaswick's household to Crestwood's household, but...

Lady Crestwood's son was Axel's father's spare. But if her and Axel's child was born a son, and legitimate, their child would usurp the younger brother.

And when Lord Crestwood died, Axel would take over the earldom, leaving Conner a mere mister.

Felicity stared at herself in the mirror, a horrific possibility striking her.

Was ensuring her own son his father's title reason enough to murder his older brother?

A tingling sensation crawled along her shoulders.

Lady Crestwood would have known about the attack if she'd been the person behind it.

She could have added the poison to Axel's whiskey with no one being the wiser.

"I need to get to the church." Felicity bolted off of the chair, and it would have toppled over if Susan hadn't caught it.

"You have plenty of time."

"But... I need to talk to Axel—" This morning would be Lady Crestwood's last opportunity to ensure their child wasn't born legitimately. "I need—"

Felicity's chest tightened.

"But you don't have any shoes on yet!" Susan held up a hand.

Shoes. And it was her wedding day. And what if she was wrong?

But what if she was right?

Susan scrambled about until locating the beautiful satin slippers that had been dyed to match her gown and was nudging Felicity back into the chair.

"He might be in danger. Lady Crestwood—"

"Very well. But you cannot leave for the church without shoes. And let me pin this last flower in your hair. When we arrive, I'll send one of your groom's handsome friends to check on him. No doubt one is with him now. Isn't that what those lords who stand up for one another do before the ceremony? Drink whiskey and joke about taking on a ball and chain?"

Felicity knew Susan was only trying to help, but rather than wait for her maid to tie both laces, she leaned over and did the second one herself. "We need to go now!"

The following minutes proved even more frustrating as her mother wasn't quite ready and insisted on driving over with Felicity and her father.

And every time Felicity thought to voice her suspicions, an irritating voice reminded her that she might very well be wrong.

"Ah, the carriage is out front." Her father, at least, seemed to appreciate her desire to make a timely arrival.

"One moment," her mother held out a hand.

"Mother!" After wasting far too much time when her mother realized she didn't quite like her hat, Felicity all but danced in her seat on the drive over. One more delay, and she might burst into tears.

"You look beautiful."

"We're so proud of you."

Normally Felicity would have basked in her parents' compliments, but as the carriage painstakingly drove them through Mayfair, all she could think about was Axel's safety.

What if Lady Crestwood tried poisoning him again?

What if she'd hired another shooter?

Indeed, if something had happened already, somebody would have sent word to her?

Felicity clung to that. As his bride, if he'd been murdered this morning, she most definitely would have been informed.

"So many are here to celebrate today, Felicity!" Her mother commented, peering out of the carriage as it pulled up outside of St. Georges' Cathedral. Crowds of onlookers milled around the church, there to enjoy the spectacle but also hoping to catch some of the coin traditionally tossed by a lordly groom.

If her father hadn't prevented her, Felicity would have thrown the carriage door open herself. But he caught her wrist and stared into her eyes.

"Breathe, daughter. There is nothing to worry about. See there? At the top of the stairs? Your future husband's groomsman is smiling. If something had happened to your viscount, I do not think this would be the case."

Felicity nodded, holding onto her father's words while the door was opened, and he ever so slowly exited first.

And then, her mother... who seemed to be doing everything in her power to draw out the pomp of this morning's ceremony.

By the time Felicity took her father's arm and was being led to the entrance, perspiration had soaked the inside of her gloves, and she felt dizzy because surely, she wasn't breathing.

"You're early," Lord Greystone greeted them as they stepped inside. "As is your groom. An excellent sign, would you not agree?"

"Indeed, it is," her father answered.

But Felicity could hardly keep from swooning. "Is he alone?" she asked.

"Blackheart was with him last I checked."

The duke.

He would be safe with the duke—his sparring partner.

"Wait in here, darling." Her mother drew Felicity out of sight and into a small room set off from the entrance. "We don't want the guests seeing you before the ceremony. You wait here while I allow Lord Greystone to escort me to my seat. Your father will collect you when it's time."

Felicity inhaled and then appreciated her mother's embrace. "Thank you, Mama." She hadn't called her mother that in years and she suddenly struggled to keep a storm of tears at bay.

Stop, Felicity. She blinked and then dabbed her fingers beneath her eyes.

She'd been in a panic for nothing. He was fine. He was here. He was waiting with Blackheart.

A moment after her mother disappeared, leaving Felicity alone in a space little larger than a closet, Bethany opened the door and slipped inside.

"You're supposed to carry this." Bethany presented a bouquet made up of ivy and roses.

"I thought I ordered a much smaller one made up of mostly white daisies and anemones.

Bethany's blue eyes danced. "Your groom insisted you have roses."

"Oh…!"

Nothing could halt her tears this time. "They are perfect!" She held them beneath her nostrils.

Her dearest friend, however, while laughing and also uttering sympathetic words, had fished a handkerchief out of her reticule and was dabbing Felicity's cheeks. "I hardly had a minute to get nervous before my wedding. I didn't appreciate it at the time, but watching you fall apart like this is giving me cause to rethink my hasty ceremony."

And then, gripping Felicity's shoulders, Bethany pulled back to meet her gaze… looking rather stern, really.

"No crying allowed; do you understand me? Because I am this close," Bethany released her just long enough to hold her fingers up with nary an inch between them, "to coming to pieces myself, and if that happens, there won't be hope for either of us."

Felicity nodded and managed a laugh of her own. "Do you know that I love you, Beth? That I don't know what I would have done without you all these years? You are like a sister to me."

"I was sorely disappointed when I realized you and West-erley weren't marrying, but I see that you do love Mantis far more than you ever did my brother. You were far too composed where Jules was concerned. And we are sisters. We will always be sisters in spirit."

"Yes." Felicity nodded again and then glanced down at the beautiful roses Mantis had thought of. More tears threatened —happy tears, which she was better able to blink away.

She felt utterly ridiculous but also full of hope and joy.

"Very well. I'm leaving you now to sit beside my handsome husband and my obnoxious younger sister to watch you take your vows."

"Thank you, Bethany. For everything."

And then, Felicity was alone again.

She dabbed the handkerchief beneath her eyes and then pinched her cheeks and bit her lips. Any moment, she would be standing beside him, promising to love and keep him in sickness and in health.

Her father would be here any moment.

She hugged her arms in front of herself and paced as much as was possible in the confines of the room.

What was taking so long?

She paced back and forth again.

Something was wrong. With no real reason to keep herself hidden any longer, she opened the door and peaked outside.

Her father met her gaze, frowning.

"Is it time?" she asked. But the expression on her father's face conveyed that time wasn't the issue.

"He hasn't come out yet." Her father forced a smile. "Greys has gone to check on him."

But this time, her father's reassurances weren't good enough.

Felicity turned to face the sanctuary, every pew filled, people standing along the wall and some in the back.

"Felicity, wait!"

She ignored her father's voice as well as the gasps as she sprinted toward the altar. None of these people's opinions mattered. Nothing mattered if something happened to Axel.

He would be waiting in the room behind the altar... from where the bishop normally entered. Still clutching her bouquet of roses, she dashed around the side and pinned her gaze on the only door in sight.

HIS FATHER'S WIFE

"*J*need to go out." Mantis rose, beginning to feel uneasy. "I'm sure my bride has arrived by now."

Louisa's demeanor, which had initially seemed conciliatory, had turned somewhat brittle.

"You have plenty of time. Brides are always late anyway. Why stand at the front of a church full of strangers when you can be comfortable back here with me? Now, tell me, are you thrilled at the prospect of becoming a father?"

He tugged at his jacket and stepped forward. "Excuse me." Louisa shot to her feet and was moving toward the door as well.

"But you haven't finished your tea."

As Mantis stepped aside to circumvent her, she scurried to the table. Just as he reached to open the door, her voice halted him.

"I'm sorry, Manningham, but your bride is going to have to be disappointed."

Mantis turned to see Louisa, *his father's wife*, holding a pistol pointed at his chest.

The person behind the attempts on his life had not been his father at all—nor any of the servants.

It was his brother's mother—his stepmother!

You are forbidden to leave me to raise our child alone. As he stared down the gleaming barrel pointed at his heart, Felicity's words ought to have taunted him.

Instead, they strengthened him.

He wasn't about to allow a lifetime with the woman he loved to be stolen out from under him.

"Put the gun down, Louisa." Mantis went to move forward but halted when he noticed her finger tightening on the trigger. "It's not too late. No one need know. Just put the gun down."

But she was shaking her head. A brassy curl escaped her updo to hang in front of one of her eyes, succeeding in adding to the irrational look on her face.

Brandishing a weapon at one's stepson imparted one with a hint of madness, after all.

"Drink the tea." She jerked the gun back to where he'd been sitting. Her hand shook. She didn't want to shoot. She simply wanted him dead.

Mantis would take the pistol from her. She was nervous, possibly even frightened to be holding it. He could not think of Conner, or how he would feel when his mother was sent off to an asylum. He couldn't stop to wonder how his father would react when he learned of his wife's duplicity.

Louisa's eyes flicked to the tea a second time, but before he could make a move, the door behind him flew open, and he froze.

Because that gun was now pointed at Felicity.

"You!" Felicity shook her bouquet of roses at Louisa. "It was you all along." She didn't seem at all surprised to find him holed up at gunpoint. She looked terrified but also enraged. "Axel, are you alright?" Her eyes flicked to the tea at Louisa's side. "You didn't drink it. Tell me you didn't drink it."

"Just a sip."

Louisa exhaled a harsh laugh. "You should have waited at the back of the church, Felicity." Something about Felicity's arrival, if anything, had had a calming effect on Louisa. "You, and your child, are safe so long as Manningham expires before your wedding."

"You poisoned his whiskey."

"If it had been me, he wouldn't be alive today. Unfortunately, if I want something done properly, I need to do it myself." And then she pinned her gaze on Mantis again. "Drink the tea, Manningham, and I will spare your fiancée and unborn child."

Again the door opened to interrupt them.

"What the hell is taking so long in here?" His father's voice echoed around the chamber, and Mantis' heart dropped. Had his father come to help his wife finish him off?

"Louisa. Explain yourself."

His father didn't know!

Crestwood closed the door, locking it behind him, and then stepped around Felicity to approach his wife. "Put that thing away. The guests are in something of an uproar, having watched the bride tear through the sanctuary as this one did." He shifted a disgruntled gaze in Felicity's direction.

"But we discussed this." Louisa's voice sounded uncertain for the first time that morning. "You said Conner would be a better earl. You told me you couldn't abide handing the title over to Manningham."

"Good God, woman. And you think the answer is to shoot him?"

"Then how? Do you imagine Lord Brightley's daughter is going to allow this mongrel to hand over an earldom once her own son is born?"

"No guarantee it's a boy. Nor that she'll deliver a live child." Mantis' father ran a hand through his hair.

"Put down the gun, Louisa," Mantis overcame his shock to speak again, edging in front of Felicity at the same time. Because if, by chance, Louisa squeezed that trigger, he'd be damned if he'd allow anything to happen to the woman he loved.

Or his child.

But his father, it seemed, had other concerns.

"What the hell am I supposed to do now, Louisa? What will people think if they discover your scheme? Because rest assured, I refuse to be taken down with you." Rather than be shocked that his wife was holding a gun pointed at his own son and future grandchild, his father worried about appearances.

And likely, a few legalities.

"It's over, my lady." Felicity's voice rang out from behind Mantis, unfortunately drawing Louisa's attention back to where he was trying to block her with his much larger frame. "Lord Greystone will be here any minute, and if you shoot that gun, or if anyone is harmed, you'll be locked up for the rest of your life, and you'll never see your son again."

"But Conner will be the earl."

"What kind of earl would he be, knowing his mother killed his brother in order to secure the title for him?" Felicity persisted. "He is a good boy. He can never be happy knowing you would sacrifice Axel's life for him."

"Shut up." Louisa squeezed her eyes closed and then just as quickly opened them. His father, looking troubled but not nearly so troubled as one might expect, dropped into the chair Mantis had vacated and groaned.

"Help me, Crestwood. What should I do?" Louisa cried. But when Mantis' father didn't answer, her face darkened. In a panic now, she shot her stare around the room.

And then his father spoke, confirming once and for all that everything Mantis had done to try to win his approval all these years meant nothing.

"I don't care. Do what you must."

I.

Don't.

Care.

"You--! You--!" Felicity sounded as though she would kill his father herself.

Careful to keep himself between Felicity and his deranged stepmother, Mantis pinned his gaze on the weapon and, bending forward, barreled across the room.

He was almost quick enough.

An explosion echoed in his head... She'd gotten off a single shot. By his ear. Had she shot his ear off? A piercing sound sent spikes of agony shooting through his brain, but he would worry about that later.

Her willingness for violence eradicated the aversion he normally had to harm any woman. They were fragile, break-able—the weaker sex. Mantis pried the gun from her surpris-ingly strong fingers and then clamped one hand around both of her wrists, effectively restraining her on the floor beneath him.

The gunshot ringing in his ear subsiding, Mantis sat back on his knees and turned to his father. What was wrong with him? Why wasn't Crestwood moving?

Mantis' gaze met Felicity's, where she now stood over his father, her face almost as ashen as the lace on her dress.

"He drank the tea," she said. The bouquet of roses tumbled from her grasp, a riot of blood-red on the wooden floor.

"Felicity," Mantis said.

He wanted to cross the room and take her into his arms but the banshee in his grasp and the pounding on the door prevented him from comforting her the way he wanted to...

The way he *needed to.*

Because holding her would comfort him as well—possibly even more.

"Felicity, sweetheart," Mantis addressed her, sounding much calmer than he felt. Was she in shock? "Greystone and Spencer are outside. Can you unlock the door for them?" *His father had locked them inside*—with the woman trying to kill them.

Felicity nodded and then, moving as though she was in a trance, crossed to the door. Another glance at his father and Mantis turned his head away and gagged.

Had Crestwood known the tea would kill him?

The poison in the hot beverage had been far stronger than what had been used to lace the whiskey. Furthermore, the whiskey's flavor had hidden it.

But the tea—it hadn't tasted like tea at all, but of almonds... Bitter almonds.

He'd stopped after that one small sip, despite Louisa urging him to drink more.

Spencer, Greystone, Westerley, and Chaswick, as well as a few faces he recognized as Blackheart's loyal men, filed into the room like a second wave of soldiers arriving at the end of a battle.

Mantis welcomed a return to reality.

"I've got her." Spencer had locked his hands around Louisa's wrists and was dragging her to her feet. "Your head is bleeding."

Westerley was draping one of the priest's garbs over his father's body while Chaswick examined the tea. "I'll send for Blackheart," Chase said to no one in particular. "Might need this for evidence."

Mantis dabbed at the side of his head, relieved at not finding a hole where his ear was supposed to be, and then stared at the blood covering his fingers.

"She shot you!" Felicity was at his side now, roused to life by the appearance of the other gentlemen—gentlemen who were more than friends, men who were his family.

"No." Mantis held out one hand, checked by her beauty and the pristine gown she was wearing.

She was a vision in her wedding gown…

"I don't want my blood on your dress. It's… beautiful… You are," he stumbled as his thoughts caught up with him. She was too good for him. "We've kept our guests waiting too long already."

She was shaking but hugged her arms across her chest and studied him.

"You need to see a doctor first."

Mantis held a handkerchief against his ear. "Not until after I've made you my wife."

PRIORITIES

*F*elicity choked on a sob at the conviction in his voice. "Oh, Axel." *This man.* "I don't care about my dress." She lowered herself to where he knelt on the floor and, ignoring his ridiculous protests about ruining her gown, wrapped her arms around his sturdy, dependable, *precious* shoulders.

No one had protected him from his father's words, but she would do her best to heal the resulting wounds... in every way that she could.

Beginning with this—holding him—and being held.

"I'm so sorry, Axel, my love. I'm so very sorry." She felt his tremor all along her body and tightened her arms around him.

"Sorry to intrude upon such a tender moment," Lord Greystone interrupted, "but allow me a moment to look at that ear."

Felicity drew back. "Please." The handkerchief was more red than white. "And he drank some of the poison—" She met Mantis' tired gaze. "A sip." He nodded.

"Barely that." But Axel did not sound relieved.

He sounded...

Defeated.

"What did it taste like?" Greys asked.

"Almonds. But I only had a drop."

"Laurel water." More than one masculine voice announced.

"Brandy helps dilute its effects." Westerley removed a flask from his jacket. "I only have whiskey, but I imagine it's the alcohol and not the vintage that matters." He handed it to Mantis, who took a quick swallow, and then a second, longer one.

He is in pain. Felicity pinched her lips together to keep from coddling him. His pain, both physical and emotional, felt tangible to her.

The marquess peeled away the bloodied cloth. "Took off a piece at the top, but looks like it only grazed you. By god, you're going to be even better looking than before, missing part of your ear."

Mantis lifted one corner of his mouth in a weak attempt at a grin. "I think my wife is going to have to be the judge of that."

Only... They were not married yet.

And with Lord Crestwood dead, his son would be expected to observe a mourning period.

"Is everything all right in here?" An elderly man peered into the room—the bishop. "I'll announce that the ceremony has been canceled."

"No," Mantis answered, his gaze not wavering from hers. "Unless you've changed your—"

"No." If anything, she was more eager than before to

pledge her love to this man. In fact, she wanted to shout her feelings to the world.

Something highly improper, and she didn't care in the least.

"Greys, any ideas for a makeshift bandage that would hide my ear? Tie something around my head, perhaps? I'd prefer to not bleed all over my bride while we take our vows ."

"This will do." Lord Greystone was already loosening his cravat. He flicked a reassuring look toward Felicity. "My lady, we'll have your groom at the alter in less than five minutes."

"And not to worry, I'll handle this... her." Mr. Spencer had tied Lady Crestwood's wrists and was moving both of them toward the open door. "I certainly hope my wedding is not as eventful as this one."

The bishop raised his brows.

Mantis ignored all of them in favor of watching Felicity closely, studying her.

"You are quite certain?" he asked.

Felicity realized that there would not be a more perfect time to tell him. No, this moment, *this very second*, was the perfect time.

"I've never been more certain of anything in my entire life. I love you, Axel, and of course, I want to marry you. Not because of the baby. And not because it's expected of us. But because sometime between that night in the orangery and now, you captured my heart. You've brought feelings to life inside of me that I didn't even know existed. For so many reasons." So many that she suddenly felt tongue-tied. "I just... I love you."

She faltered, and the room fell silent. If Axel didn't feel the same, then she was going to be pitied by all of these gentlemen—for the second time that year.

But she didn't care.

She just *loved him.*

"Can we have a moment?" He spoke to those present but kept his gaze fixed on her.

She didn't quite know what to think while she waited for the room to empty, but when the door closed behind them, Mantis cradled her face in his hands.

"I love you. I don't deserve you—you deserve so much better. You deserve someone—"

"I want *you.* I want you, Axel. And only you." The emotional wounds inflicted by his father went far deeper than the cut on his face had gone. "I don't care how long it takes me to convince you of this, but I have never known a better man than you. You are the perfect husband for me, Axel."

He blinked and turned his head to the side.

Felicity held her breath while she watched a single tear escape and roll down to his jaw.

"Marry me? Please?" She added.

When he turned back to face her, his eyes were shining with tears but also something else.

Hope. "I'd be a foolish man indeed to deny you that." He helped her to her feet, drawing her into his arms and burying his face in the curve of her neck. "I'm going to make you happy."

"You already have."

"Again," Greys was peering around the door. "Hate to interrupt, but…"

"Yes. We're coming," Felicity assured him.

Westerley entered and picked the roses up off the floor. When he met her gaze, he smiled encouragingly and… with a brotherly affection.

"Mantis, do I have your permission to escort your bride to her father now?"

"Absolutely."

Felicity stood on her toes and pressed her mouth against Axel's before being rushed to the back of the church. Her father merely raised his brows but then gestured toward the sanctuary. "Shall we?"

"Absolutely."

EPILOGUE

SUMMER AT STONEGATE MANOR

"Umm..." Felicity leaned into the familiar arms that wrapped around her from behind.

"I pay people to do this, you know." Axel's voice growled where he nuzzled near her ear.

"I know." In fact, more than one groundskeeper tended the gardens. "But I enjoy it." It was one of the first things she'd noticed when her new husband had shown her around Stonegate Manor. "And you know I love the roses."

After taking their vows, in what the London Gazette had written up as a most unusual ceremony, Axel and Felicity had been immediately faced with far more challenging concerns than most couples tackled in a lifetime.

The most pressing which had included what to do with the now Dowager Countess of Crestwood, and what would be best for Axel's younger brother.

Rather than take up residence in the house on Farm Street, or travel to Tissinton Towers, Felicity and Axel, with input from Cordelia, had agreed it would be best to withdraw from London to Stonegate Manor. A new tutor had been hired, however, and Axel had begun teaching Conner some of his fighting techniques.

Rather than turn Louisa over to the local magistrate, Axel had made arrangements for her to be kept securely at an asylum. The institution was located less than a day's drive from Stonegate, and that had been important in case she showed improvement. She was Conner's mother, after all.

And one of the least pleasant of all, they'd had his father's body packed in ice so that his eternal resting place would be the Stonegate family mausoleum.

"How did the lessons go this morning?" Felicity slowly turned in her husband's arms, thrilling inside at the sensation of her belly pressed between both of their bodies.

"He's coming along." Axel's mouth trailed around her ear. "You smell delicious."

Felicity realized that even with the man dead, wounds left on her husband by his father were going to take a long time to heal, but she couldn't help but believe that spending time training and helping Conner had done wonders.

What the two men had failed to ever get from their father, they seemed able to provide for one another—connection, brotherhood.

She tilted her head back and relished the sensation of Axel's kisses down her neck to her shoulder.

"You are certain he's ready to enter school this fall?" The family was officially in mourning. And although Axel had said Felicity need not wear black, she and Cordelia had dyed several of their gowns in order to do so for a minimum of six months. Axel, Conner, and the menservants wore black armbands over their jackets.

They did not, however, cover the windows with crepe paper and intended to go about estate business normally.

Which meant that Axel had taken his new wife around to meet all of their tenants, and she, in turn, had invited some of the local landowners' wives for tea.

Not one of them had questioned their decision. In fact, several had applauded it.

"He needs to meet other boys his age." Axel answered. "He still might struggle at first, but that's normal enough. I'm no longer as concerned that he'll be bullied." Axel's hands moved up her sides and around to cradle her breasts. "Enough talk of my brother."

"You wish to talk about the new irrigation system?" Even as she teased, her breath hitched, and that now familiar ache settled between her legs.

In answer, Axel swooped her into his arms and began marching toward the house.

Even with his wife some five months along, Axel carried her as though she weighed no more than a butterfly. Climbing the stairs, he sent her a heated glance, but his breathing remained even and steady.

She loved everything about this man—his heart, his humor, his character and mind, his good looks, but there were times when her favorite amongst them all was his body—his size—his sheer maleness.

Not only did the strength and dexterity he exhibited elicit the sensation of being cherished and protected, but they also resulted in lovemaking that was more creative and exciting in manners she'd only ever imagined, and then some!

Which was especially useful lately, in that her pregnant belly was already becoming quite pronounced.

So pronounced, in fact, that at her regular appointment a few hours earlier, her midwife had offered up the startling possibility that Felicity might very well be carrying twins.

Immediately upon arriving at Stonegate Manor, eager to erase any reminders of the previous occupants, Axel and Felicity had sat down together and ordered all new furnishings and décor for the master and mistress bedchambers, of which had only recently been completed.

Felicity had also asked to have one of the adjacent guest chambers repurposed to be a nursery. The completed space was almost as opulent as their own chambers, with a playroom, a fantastic, canopied crib, and an attached room for a nurse. Which reminded her...

"We might need to make some changes to the nursery."

Axel lowered her onto their massive, incredibly comfortable new bed and raised his brows.

"Do you think the babe needs more room for toys?"

She bit back a grin. She'd wanted to wait until the midwife was more certain but couldn't keep such a huge possibility to herself.

Not from Axel. Because he was her everything.

"We may need a second crib."

He tilted his head, perplexed.

"And a second rocker. And we might also require a second nurse."

By now, realization donned, and the gold flecks sparkled in excitement from his hazel eyes. But he also showed concern.

"Two babes?"

"Alice says it's possible. My womb measures larger than mothers carrying only one. Since you are a twin..." She trailed off. She hadn't meant to worry him.

"Two?" And then he lowered himself on the bed beside her. "How do you feel about this? *How are you?*"

"Excited. Thrilled. And a little terrified." She lay back on the pillow, relaxing to the hypnotic feel of his fingers removing the pins from her hair. "That feels good."

"What does Alice say about a woman in your condition gardening?" He kissed her temple.

"She says that so long as I don't experience any twinges of discomfort, it ought to be safe for now. In fact, she believes it's best for me to take regular exercise."

"I'll show you how to meditate if you'd like." They'd discussed this before but had been too busy to follow through with it. "You were already a little scared. It could help."

"I'd like that." His fingers were stroking the lengths of her hair now, and she amazed at how this man could be both extraordinarily passionate but also as gentle as a fawn.

"And what about…" He claimed her mouth with a soulful kiss. Only a few seconds passed before his arousal became apparent, and she was lifting her hips and assisting him in sliding her gown up around her waist.

Rather than move between her legs, however, her magnificent husband leaned back to rest on his heels in order to untie her bodice, which conveniently laced at the front. "I need to touch all of you," he provided a most excellent explanation.

Felicity rose as well to begin unfastening the buttons of his waistcoat. She loved the way the curling hairs on his chest and legs felt against her skin.

One of the buttons had been skipped. "We really need to hire you a new valet," she smiled. Cornell, a rather interesting gentleman's gentleman, had remained in London to ensure the Jiu-Jitsu instruction on the docks continued uninterrupted. And in a surprising twist, Axel's former instructor, Masaki, had agreed to run the school alongside the former valet.

"Perhaps," Axel grinned. "But for now, I like it better when you undress me."

She dragged her fingertips along his jaw, which, sported two more cuts from where he'd shaved himself. "You know how I feel about your scar, but many more, and I don't think I'll be able to look at you without swooning." She lovingly pressed her lips to his ear.

"I'll write to an agency tomorrow," he laughed. But after he drew her gown over her head, he inhaled sharply, his eyes darkening.

She only wore half stays, of which, Felicity realized, most effectively pushed her bosom up as though on display. "I like this look on you." Gripping her shoulders, he claimed one upturned nipple.

"Ah… I like that," Felicity said as he drew her deeper into his mouth, his teeth grazing her sensitive skin. "Very much."

At the same time, he'd reached one hand between her legs. He could be quite efficient that way.

Felicity unfastened his falls, and between the two of them, they managed to shove them down his muscled thighs. She was too impatient to even think of removing his boots and shirt, and he seemed perfectly happy with her partially clothed state.

Grasping her waist, Axel fell back on the bed, flipping her so she sat straddling his hips. "Ride me, love." His hands covered her breasts now, kneading them, his gaze flicking back and forth from her face to where his hands worked.

Felicity pushed the tails out of her way. She was wet and she was ready. Preparing herself for his size, she inhaled and lowered herself onto him.

"So good," she said, and they both sighed at the same time.

Axel paused and held her gaze. "You're sure this won't hurt the—?"

Not allowing him to finish the question, Felicity rotated her hips, something she'd learned he particularly enjoyed.

"Good then." His hands gripped her hips, helping her along now.

"So good," she repeated, holding his shoulders. She held his gaze, her hair hanging down so as to keep out everything in the world but the two of them. "I love you, Axel," she whispered.

"I love you, love." He thrust his hips off the bed, deepening their connection. This, she thought, was what was meant by the words: *the two shall become one.* Because every single time they made love, their bond became stronger—so much so that she experienced moments where she became a part of him, and he became a part of her.

Without having to think or guess, she matched her rhythm to his. Or perhaps he was matching to hers. It was simply, theirs.

Her husband never failed to bring her to completion, and in what might only have been a few minutes, she welcomed the primitive sensation that also felt as though it came from the heavens.

Axel paused, trailing his hands down her arms. "Ready?" He whispered, and at her nod, he began moving again.

"So beautiful," Axel growled. Sometimes, all she required were a few words, and she would tense and shatter again. He stroked her skin with his hands, and at the same time, he stroked her from within. Felicity had tasted him a hundred times but would never get enough.

"My wife." He clutched her closer. "Mine."

"And you're mine, husband," she whispered. "Forever."

A sharp slap on her behind, and the storm of her final release rained down. "Oh, hell," Axel stiffened inside of her, and shaking and shuttering, she warmed at their shared pleasure.

A few minutes later, too tired to move, she snuggled into his chest, his body acting as her mattress.

"Do you know what?" She asked, feeling drowsy and content.

"What?" Axel roused enough to ask.

"I'm the luckiest lady in all of England."

"And I," he smoothed his hand down her back, "am the luckiest lord."

BONUS EPILOGUE

CHRISTMAS EVE, 1829

"*I* hope at least one of them turns out to be a boy."

Mantis barely registered his brother's words as he paced from the window to the hearth. The snow swirled and piled up outside, and he was more than grateful the midwife had arrived before the storm moved in.

"What's that?" Mantis halted his steps. "Did you say something?"

Conner had returned from Eton for the Holidays, having grown no less than six inches. In addition to that, his voice no longer cracked, and if Mantis wasn't mistaken, there were the beginnings of what would someday become a beard dappling Conner's chin.

His brother laughed. "I said I hope at least one of them turns out to be a boy."

"Why is that?" He asked.

"I want to sail ships," Conner announced. "I want to travel the world."

This young man could hardly be much different from the broken child he'd comforted last spring.

"That would be difficult to do while running an Earldom," Mantis agreed.

"Not that being Crestwood isn't impressive, mind you," Conner continued. "But it does tend to tie a man down."

Mantis managed to bite back a grin, wondering what Louisa would think if she heard her son's opinion on all of this. Although, Mantis doubted it would affect her one way or another. The last time he'd visited, she'd sounded like a little girl, having seemed to have lost all sense of reality. He was glad he hadn't had her transported or imprisoned.

Despite the fact she'd tried to kill him, he only felt pity for her now. She had lost everything, while he was likely one of the happiest men in all of England.

Or he would be, that was, as soon as he knew Felicity emerged from childbirth safely.

"Do you miss him?" Conner asked, surprising him again. Mantis knew exactly who his brother was referring to.

Mantis inhaled deeply and then exhaled. In the time since his father passed, he'd gone from denying he felt anything, to anger, to a peaceful sort of acceptance.

"I miss the hope I felt while he was alive," Mantis admitted.

"What do you mean?" Conner persisted.

"As long as our father was alive, I believed it was possible that he would change—that he could one day be a better person, a better father."

"I think I felt the same." Conner lowered himself to the small table and chairs where a board and chess pieces were set up.

"It's always sad when someone dies, Conner," Axel said. "But just as in grappling, how we can use our opponent's momentum for our own advantage, we can turn unfortunate events to better ourselves.

"Is that what you did after father's death?"

"Yes. Take the good you learned from Crestwood and keep it in here." Axel touched his chest. "And the bad stuff? Learn from it, but then let it go."

"Father was good with numbers," Conner said.

"He was."

"Not so good at fathering," Conner added.

"And ultimately, he lost for that," Mantis agreed.

"Care for a game to help the time pass?" Conner, his mind already seeking other stimulation, gestured for Mantis to join him. "I'm determined to beat you before I return to school."

Mantis didn't feel like playing but supposed it couldn't hurt. How was Felicity doing now? He'd always heard that ladies screamed throughout childbirth, but so far, he'd not heard so much as a whimper escape from their chambers.

"Do you think one of them will be a boy?" Conner opened by drawing one of his pawns two spaces to the center of the board.

Mantis countered without really contemplating his strategy. Likely, Conner wouldn't have to wait until the end of his holiday to get his win.

"I'll be happy with either," he answered.

Ultimately, of course, every man wanted a son, but mostly all he cared about in that moment was that the babes be delivered safely—and that his wife suffer as little as possible for it.

He closed his eyes and counted as he drew in a calming breath. She was so small, so delicate and fragile. How could she not suffer for delivering two of his children? He opened his eyes and stared down at his hands which were shaking—giant hands, like the rest of him.

It wasn't fair, what women had to endure. He glanced at

the clock on the mantel for the ten-thousandth time that afternoon.

Her pains had begun early the day before, and his exasperating wife had gone walking around the manor with their housekeeper. Felicity had told him she needed to ensure Mrs. Blicker knew precisely where to hang the garlands and mistletoe in the event that she herself was not able to supervise. Mantis had followed behind, terrified the babes would decide to come the moment he turned his back, all the while Felicity went about sounding perfectly reasonable and maddeningly calm.

When a particularly strong pain struck, he had carried her upstairs and plunked her onto one of the settees in their private sitting room. On the off chance she got any more ideas about meandering around the estate, he'd firmly ordered her to stay put.

The midwife had arrived ten minutes after that, along with another woman to assist. Mantis, aside from being allowed a few brief visits, had thusly been barred from the mistress' bedchamber ever since.

The last time he'd been allowed to enter had been five hours ago.

"Manningham," Cordelia stood at the door. "Or should I call you Papa?" She looked unusually frazzled, but the smile on her face sent relief flooding through him.

He jumped up so quickly, he sent half the game pieces tumbling to the carpet on the floor.

"She's... They're all right?"

Cordelia was nodding, and Mantis thought he heard an infant's cry from the direction of their bed-chambers.

"Felicity is magnificent. She's already feeding one of them

and is anxious for you to join her. A boy and a girl! Can you imagine? They're perfect."

Mantis required no further inducement to sprint out the door, through the chamber they shared together, and followed encouraging cries through to the room where she'd given birth.

The sight that met his eyes ensured that once and for all, even if only for that instant, he was indeed the happiest man in all of London.

One babe suckling at her breast, Felicity reached out her hand for him to join her. "Axel." She met his gaze, her eyes shining almost turquoise from unshed happy tears. "Meet your son."

"And this is your daughter." Susan had carried a noisy swaddled bundle to the opposite side of the bed.

"They are healthy?"

"And then some," the midwife offered with a chuckle as she moved efficiently around the room, gathering linens and bloodied rags.

Mantis approached almost tentatively.

"Can I have a moment alone with my husband?" Felicity asked most graciously, and in less than a minute, his daughter in his arms, the door closed behind him.

"*How are you?*" He asked.

"I am very sore." She smiled. But then laughed. "And tired. But surprisingly well. And relieved. *How are you?*" She tilted her head.

Mantis swallowed hard. Because the emotions he experienced in that moment were indescribable. And then he answered with the one word that was tearing circles around not only his head, but his heart as well.

"Happy," he said. "So damn happy."

***

Thank you so much for reading Axel and Felicity's happily ever after. Be sure to preorder Lord Greystone's story **COCKY MARQUESS** next!

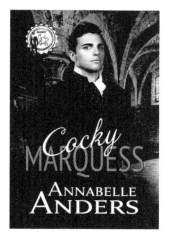

Miss Diana Jones, illegitimate sister to the Baron Chaswick is determined to make the most of her season. Trouble is, even with her brother's support, no titled gentleman is willing to take her seriously.

Lord Greystone has a problem and he doesn't even know it. But Diana does. She also knows exactly how to help him solve it. Until that is, the solution to their problems creates the biggest problem of all!

COCKY MARQUESS
Available now!

REGENCY COCKY GENTS

A NEW ANNABELLE ANDERS SERIES

Cocky Earl

Jules and Charley

Cocky Baron

Chase and Bethany

Cocky Mister

Stone and Tabetha

Cocky Brother

Peter Spencer's Story

(Formerly Mayfair Maiden)

Cocky Viscount

Mantis and Felicity

Cocky Marquess

July 6, 2021

Greystone's Story

Cocky Butler

September 14, 2021

Blackheart's Story

ABOUT THE AUTHOR

Married to the same man for over 25 years, I am a mother to three children and two Miniature Wiener dogs.

After owning a business and experiencing considerable success, my husband and I got caught in the financial crisis and lost everything in 2008; our business, our home, even our car.

At this point, I put my B.A. in Poly Sci to use and took work as a waitress and bartender (Insert irony). Unwilling to give up on a professional life, I simultaneously went back to college and obtained a degree in EnergyManagement.

And then the energy market dropped off.

And then my dog died.

I can only be grateful for this series of unfortunate events, for, with nothing to lose and completely demoralized, I sat down and began to write the romance novels which had until then, existed only my imagination. After publishing over thirty novels now, with one having been nominated for RWA's Distinguished ™RITA Award in 2019, I am happy to tell you that I have finally found my place in life.

Thank you so much for being a part of my journey!

To find out more about my books, and also to download a free book, get all the info at my website!

www.annabelleanders.com

Made in the USA
Las Vegas, NV
30 October 2021